Aug 2023

GUARDING DANGER

SINCLAIR & RAVEN SERIES

WENDY VELLA

This is a work of fiction. Any resemblance to actual persons, living or dead, business establishments, events or locales is entirely coincidental. All rights reserved. Except for use in a review, the reproduction or use of this work in any part is forbidden without the express written permission of the author.

Guarding Danger is published by Wendy Vella

Copyright © 2020 Wendy Vella

OTHER BOOKS BY WENDY

Regency Rakes Series
Duchess By Chance
Rescued By A Viscount
Tempting Miss Allender

The Langley Sisters Series
Lady In Disguise
Lady In Demand
Lady In Distress
The Lady Plays Her Ace
The Lady Seals Her Fate
The Lady's Dangerous Love
The Lady's Forbidden Love

The Deville Brothers Series
Seduced By A Devil
Rescued By A Devil
Protected By A Devil
Surrender To A Devil
Unmasked By A Devil

The Raven & Sinclair Series
Sensing Danger
Seeing Danger
Touched By Danger
Scent Of Danger
Vision Of Danger
Tempting Danger
Seductive Danger
Guarding Danger
Courting Danger
Defending Danger
Detecting Danger

The Lords Of Night Street Series
Lord Gallant
Lord Valiant
Lord Valorous
Lord Noble

Stand-Alone Titles
The Reluctant Countess
Christmas Wishes
The Earl's Encounter
Mistletoe And The Marquess

*This book is for us, every single one of us,
because not in our wildest imaginations
could we believe we'd face what we are today.*

*"You're braver than you believe,
Stronger than you seem
and smarter than you think."
-Christopher Robin*

*"A little consideration,
A little thought for others,
Makes all the difference."*

-Eeyore

PROLOGUE

It is said that when lowly Baron Sinclair saved the powerful Duke of Raven from certain death in 1335 by single-handedly killing the three men who attacked his carriage, King Edward III was grateful. Raven was a wise and sage counsel he had no wish to lose, therefore, he rewarded Sinclair with the land that sat at the base of Raven Mountain. Having shown himself capable of the duty, Baron Sinclair was now, in the eye of the King, to be the official protector of the Ravens.

Over the years the tale has changed and grown as many do. There were rumors of strange occurrences when a Sinclair saved a Raven in the years that followed. Unexplained occurrences that caused many to wonder what it was that the Sinclairs were hiding, but one thing that never changed was their unwavering duty in the task King Edward III had bestowed upon them.

To honor and protect the Raven family was the Sinclair family creed.

CHAPTER 1

Harry Sinclair watched the woman walk along the deck of his ship. In her arms she held a little girl. Soon she would disappear into the London streets and he'd never see her again, and that should not be a problem. Strangely, it was.

The first time he'd seen her was in Calais. Harry had been watching his cargo being loaded, letting his eyes wander occasionally to see if he knew anyone below, when suddenly unease had gripped him. With eyes that saw more than any other human he'd met, he'd searched and found her seated on a crate, the child in her arms. Her shoulders were back, her posture rigid. But it had been the expression on her face that caught and held his attention. Fierce. Daring anyone to approach. She'd protected the child with a hand on the small head, the other around her body.

She wore a faded gray dress but no bonnet, and her hair hung in a braid over the swell of a breast. She was beautiful, but not in the soft, cosseted way Harry usually admired. Slender, whether by nature or circumstance he couldn't be sure, and her brows arched over golden eyes that were framed with dark lashes. When she looked his way, he'd seen the desperation she fought to hide.

Desperation that had sliced through Harry, forcing him back from the railing. He'd then found Barney, his bosun, and asked him to approach the woman to see if she needed assistance.

He'd watched the encounter, wondering what he'd been thinking to do such a thing. Harry never got involved in the lives of people he did not know or trust. He was certainly never spontaneous.

The child had woken, weeping as Barney approached, and the pain in Harry's chest had grown into an inferno.

Barney returned to the ship minutes later, telling Harry the woman was seeking passage to England. He'd provided it, much to his bosun's shock. Harry was not known as an accommodating man, and he was definitely not known for random acts of kindness.

She'd seated herself in the corner of the deck and never moved in the hours it took to cross the channel. He'd sent her food via Barney. The woman had been suspicious, but took the offerings for her child, who played around her with the resilience of youth, happy now her belly was full—but she had not left her mother's side. With only a shawl to ward off the cold, the woman's expression never changed, but as the distance between them and France grew, the other emotion he'd seen, fear, eased from her eyes.

The only time he'd seen her face change was when the child patted her cheek, and she'd smiled with so much love it had literally rooted him to the spot.

Her beauty moved into exquisite in that moment.

"The men will begin unloading then, sir?"

"Yes, thank you, Deacon," he said to the ship's captain, who jolted him back to the present.

London lay before Harry. A place he loathed and yet

visited for business purposes. France was his home and where he belonged. London was a place from his past that held nothing but bitterness.

His eyes swung back to the woman. She was walking carefully down the gangway, the child clinging to her, a large bag in one hand. He'd acknowledged her once, when their eyes caught, and then she'd looked away after responding to his nod with a small smile.

Reaching the bottom, she skirted ropes and men, then lowered her bag to the ground. The hand she rested at her side clenched into a fist. He felt it again, that pain, but this time it was followed by another deep sense of unease. Looking skyward, he saw the day was still clear and blue; she was not in imminent danger of a drenching, so why was he still worried about her?

Harry wasn't a man to worry about things outside his control. He'd raised an empire that way, ruthless and determined. There were not many who would cross Harry Sinclair.

Looking left, then right, Harry searched for something… anything to explain what he was feeling. The panic that was suddenly slithering down his spine.

"Christ!" He started running. The woman and child were standing at the base of a small incline, and the barrels that had rolled off the back of a cart were now heading their way.

"Move!" he bellowed as he sprinted down the gangway at speed. "Move!" he roared again.

She didn't hear him, couldn't with the cacophony of noise around them. Heart pounding, Harry leaped off the bottom.

People were now fleeing as the barrels picked up speed, but she still hadn't seen them. Her eyes were focused on the child in her arms.

"Run, woman!" She turned at his words but still did not move. *He was too late, she'd be hit.* Harry took two huge steps then dived at the woman and child. Lifting them into his arms, he carried them with him and onto a pile of rope, landing on his back, his arms holding them close.

No one moved for several seconds, and then everyone seemed to at once. Harry struggled to draw air into his abused lungs, the woman fired off a volley of French, and the child screamed.

"Sir! Wh-what are you doing?" She pushed at his arms with her free hand. Harry released her. She scrambled off him.

Harry felt the blessed relief of air filling his lungs and was able to regain his feet.

"How dare you touch us that way!"

"If you'll look about you, madam, you'll realize that in fact I just saved the lives of both you and your child."

She turned, her eyes taking in the barrels. One bobbed in the water, the other had crashed into a crate and splintered into pieces. The pungent aroma of alcohol now filled the air.

"You were directly in the path of those barrels," Harry said.

The top of her head came up to his nose. Her eyes were tawny, not gold, and he had never in his lifetime seen a pair like them. The beauty was there in the line of her cheek and soft curve of her jaw. Her mouth, however, now that was made for sin, and as sin was a specialty of Harry's, he was drawn to it.

"I-I don't know what to say." She searched his face as he did hers. "Sssh now, darling." She tried to quiet the child, but clearly she was still terrified over what just happened.

Harry cupped the child's head, touched her soft brown curls.

"Don't touch her!" The fear was that of a mother protecting her young.

"Quiet, please, madam. I will not hurt her." He continued

to stroke the small head that almost fit into his palm. The child's cries eased to sniffles. "There now, lovely, no need to cry." He ran a finger down a damp cheek, and she grabbed it, gripping it tight.

He then looked at her mother, who appeared stunned.

"My daughter does not usually take easily to people."

"She knows I mean her no harm."

"I don't know what to say to you." The words tumbled from her lips in French.

"Thank you is a good place to start." Harry replied in the same tongue. He then smiled down at the little girl who was looking up at him with solemn eyes. She still held his fingers.

"Of course, forgive me. Thank you for saving us."

"You're welcome. My name is Harry Sinclair, and it was my ship you sailed on from Calais."

"You own that ship?"

"I do."

"I saw you but had not realized."

"As I saw you."

She looked away from him, and Harry studied the curve of her jaw. Something about this woman intrigued him, but he couldn't work out what. She was in no way alluring or flaunting her beauty; in fact her dress suggested the exact opposite.

"Then now I have more to thank you for, Mr. Sinclair." She spoke in a solemn voice. "I knew that the fare I paid was low, as others had tried to charge more, but I needed to get to London—"

"And it was more than enough, madam." Actually, it had been half what he would normally charge, but he wouldn't be telling her that.

"Thank you again for your kindness. There are not many who would do as you have for us. I'll say good day to you, as we must go."

"Are you wanting a hackney? Perhaps I could secure one for you?"

Her eyes were really rather stunning. They reminded him of a lion he'd got far too close to once.

"Thank you, I have no wish to detain you further, Mr. Sinclair. I will find one."

"Your child is weary, madam. Perhaps it would be better if you stayed here and I located one for you?"

"I have no wish to further inconvenience you, Mr. Sinclair. I am more than capable of securing a hackney. Good day." She bent to pick up the bag, and jiggled the child into a more comfortable position on her hip. She spoke gently in French to the girl, asking her to let Harry's fingers go. He felt strangely bereft when the little fingers released his.

"Good day, Mr. Sinclair." She walked away. So small and vulnerable, Harry thought. All around her was noise and movement; at any moment she could be knocked over. Where was her husband? Family? Why was she alone in this crowded city?

Looking in the direction she was going, he saw no hackneys nearby. He followed and reached her side in seconds.

"I'm sure you are more than capable of finding a hackney, madam, but as I have offered, please allow me to assist you."

Her chin rose. "There is no need."

Harry ignored her and headed down the street. Minutes later, he raised a hand and waved a hackney to his side. Pulling some money out of his jacket pocket, he handed over enough to take her wherever she wished to go to the driver. "I will return shortly with your fare. Please wait here."

"Right you are."

Harry walked back to where the woman stood, still wondering why he was going to all this trouble for a woman he did not know and would likely not see again. A woman who was exhausted clearly, and her child fretful.

"Come, I have secured you a hackney." He took her bag and urged her before him. She said nothing, just allowed him to nudge her in the right direction.

Harry opened the door and placed her bag inside, then turned to help her in, but she was talking to the driver. He missed the address she gave, and that was a good thing. He didn't want to know where he could find her.

Women did not disturb him or occupy too much of his time. He never allowed it. The course of his life was set; there was no time for messy things such as emotion.

"I cannot thank you enough for your kindness to us, Mr. Sinclair." Her smile was small but genuine.

"There is no need. Everyone needs the help of a stranger at least once in their life."

Her child was nearing sleep again, eyes slits as she struggled to stay awake. Her head now rested on her mother's shoulder. Harry touched the soft cheek once more, and the child gave him a sleepy smile.

"It's my hope that when you need help, sir, someone will be there for you also."

Their eyes locked, and in that moment for Harry the world stood still. Every noise and sound faded; there was just him and this woman.

"I-I must go."

"Of course." What the hell was the matter with him?

Before he could stop her, she'd risen to her toes and kissed his cheek. It was brief and over in seconds. It felt like she'd branded him.

"You are my *ange gardien*."

He helped her into the carriage, and she settled on the seat. *Don't let her go.*

"Vivre une vie longue et heureuse." Harry shut the door and the voice inside his head out after wishing her a long and happy life and nodded to the driver. Standing back, he watched the woman and child roll away from him and wondered if he was ailing for something. No other explanation was possible for what he had just felt or done. It was as if something monumental had just happened in his life and it was rolling away from him, never to be seen again.

Only when the carriage turned the corner at the end of the street did he return to the ship.

"It's this place," he muttered. Coming to England always made him wary and on edge. Somewhere out there he had family, and he laid the entire blame for what had just occurred on the doorstep of anyone who carried his blood. It wasn't logical, but in that moment it helped him push aside the madness of what had just happened.

Never trust a Sinclair. Remembering his father's words, he turned and walked back to the familiar. His ship, his livelihood. Little else mattered.

CHAPTER 2

Shaking off his momentary madness, Harry, at a much more sedate pace, walked back up the gangway and onto the *Charlotte Anne*. He'd named her after his mother, who he only had a distant memory of, as she'd died when he was a child. She was the first ship he'd owned, and the one Harry loved most.

"You saved that woman and babe, Harry. They would have been crushed or drowned had you not. 'Tis a brave thing you did."

"Thank you." Faris was his assistant and friend. He understood his business almost as well as he did. Like Harry, he had moved to France as a babe. His mother was from India and his father French, so his was not always an easy path to tread.

"Will you be leaving the ship?"

"I have business meetings, as you know."

"Business, yes, but what of your family?"

"I have Grandmère to care for—"

"You know I did not mean her," Faris interrupted.

"We have already discussed this many times, and I have

no wish to do so again. I have no other family but Grand-mère. Of course I will leave the ship to see her. She has insisted on staying in the finest hotel in London, of course."

Faris laughed.

"With her ancient maid, who was once a friend, and her other ancient friend who is now her companion."

"She is happy and enjoying your wealth and status; there is no harm in that, surely," Faris said.

"I don't begrudge her what she now has, Faris, I just find it amusing that she has all the appearance of someone born in a French chateau when in fact it was in a bed with her six siblings in a one-room cottage."

"While I love your grandmère very much, Harry, she need not be the only family you have, surely."

Once, when he and Faris had been at sea steadily working their way down a bottle of spirits, he'd made the mistake of telling his friend that his father had brothers in England. It had been a mistake, because unlike him, Faris believed in happily ever afters. Family was vital to him, as he had a large one, and he failed to understand Harry did not wish for the same.

"I believe I have told you this subject is closed." There were not many willing to cross swords with Harry; unfortunately, Faris was one of them.

"You will be a lonely old man, as even your grandmother cannot will herself to live forever."

"I'm sure I'll find someone to keep me company when that day comes."

"Family are different to the women that you bed, Harry. Even you will lose your legendary powers of seduction one day."

"Jealous, Faris?" Harry knew the words were beneath him, but he was feeling raw and off balance after his encounter with that woman.

"I am engaged, as you very well know."

"Just checking you had no regrets." And yet he knew Faris loved his fiancée deeply, as she loved him. Harry would admit, but only to himself and very occasionally, that he was jealous of such a love.

"My only regret is that you refuse to find those of your blood. Your stubbornness will make a lonely companion. There are Sinclairs in shipping; perhaps they are related to you?"

"I'm sure it is a common name, and I don't wish to find if they are related," he said with a calm he was not feeling. "My mother was not good enough for them, therefore they are not good enough for me. Now we have chewed this particular morsel to death, and I wish to discuss it no further, Faris."

"I could—"

"Go and do some work. It's what I pay you for." Harry walked away, ignoring his friend's mutterings, although he knew they would not be complimentary.

Faris was the only man he allowed to speak to him that way, and he still had no idea why.

Harry ran a shipping business from France, and extremely well if his bank accounts were telling the truth—which of course they were. His ships carted goods around the world and most often with him on board. He had other business interests and owned property and enjoyed challenging himself by always seeking new ventures to interest him.

He walked the upper deck, looking at the bustle below. Sailors, travelers, dock workers; there were people of every variety milling below him. Now the woman had gone, some of the tension inside him had eased… but strangely, not all.

London had never appealed to Harry. Yes, he'd been born here, but France was his love. He watched one of his crew carrying two large valises down the gangway. There would be more to follow, all belonging to his elderly relative and her companions. She would not leave the cabin until all was ready for her departure.

Walking along the railing, he searched for what else was bothering him. Was it just residue leftover from the encounter with that woman?

Boats to the left and right were of varying and similar sizes to the *Charlotte Anne*. It was the one to his immediate right, the *Lilliana*, that caught and held his attention. On the deck stood three men. All large, all dark, and the frisson of awareness that ran through him told him they were familiar to him. Focusing, he realized why. They looked like him... well, two of them anyway.

The two biggest of the men were staring at him as he was them, green eyes vibrant, also like his sometimes were. He stepped back, turning away and breaking the contact.

His chest felt tight as he struggled to haul in a deep breath. Maybe he really was ailing for something.

Harry knew of Lord Sinclair. The man owned ships as he did, but he'd dismissed him as someone he was unlikely to meet nor want to. Could one of these men be he?

Was he a relative?

It seemed likely, considering their appearance.

Seeking the sanctuary of his cabin until they'd left and he'd calmed down, Harry headed across the deck. Once there, he shut the door and rested a hand on it. What the hell had just happened? Had he imagined what he'd just seen? Had those eyes looking back at him been the same as his?

Harry had never told anyone about what he saw.

He poured himself a shot of whisky and threw it back. First the woman and child had disturbed him, and now those men.

The tap on his door minutes later had Harry stiffening.

"Yes!"

"There are three men here wishing to speak with you, Harry," Faris said through the wood.

He wanted to yell back that he was busy and couldn't see anyone. Anything to stop from meeting those men. It was them of course; it had to be.

But Harry had not been raised a coward. He'd faced down far more dangerous foes than three English gentlemen. He stalked to the door and wrenched it open to see the smiling face of Faris.

"They have the look of you, Harry."

"That means nothing to me. Where are they?"

"One could be Lord Sinclair. We've heard of him, Harry, but as yet have not met him."

"I don't care if he's the King, Faris, the name means nothing to me. Now where are they?"

"On the upper deck."

He stalked past his still smiling friend and made his way to where the men waited. Tension rode high on his shoulders; tension, and the feeling that his life was about to change and there was absolutely nothing he could do to stop that happening.

They waited, arms at their sides, feet braced, eyes focused and intent on him as he approached. A frisson of awareness travelled through him as he encountered the green eyes.

Never trust a Sinclair. His father's words filled his head. He'd repeated them many times to his son over the years.

"How can I help you gentlemen?" He would be calm and businesslike; it was, after all, what he did best.

"We saw you from our ship." The one who spoke was the eldest. His black hair had gray at the temples, and there was an air of authority about him. "Are you the owner of this vessel?"

"I am."

"Are you Harry Sinclair?"

The question had been spoken by the smaller of the three men. Still big, but his build was slighter. His eyes weren't as intense either. Harry watched as he sniffed the air. *Odd.*

"Can I ask what business you have on the *Charlotte Anne*?" he said instead of giving them his name.

"Are you Harry Sinclair?" The eldest stepped closer.

"Tell me who you are first." Harry wasn't sure why he didn't want to tell them who he was, but the urge was strong.

"I am Devonshire, Lord Sinclair. This is my brother, Cambridge Sinclair, and this is Captain Christian Sinclair, but we call him Wolf."

The tension between them was so thick it cloaked the air. *Dear God, it can't be.*

"I am Harry Sinclair."

Lord Sinclair's smile was slow to bloom, but when it did, it filled his face and lit his eyes. Harry kept his features composed.

"We've heard your name, of course; your reputation is well known here."

Harry knew what he was. He was ruthless yet fair in business but was sure some saw it differently.

"What do you wish to discuss with me?"

"The black sheep's son." Cambridge Sinclair smiled. "How wonderful! We wondered when this day would arrive."

"My father was a good man," Harry said calmly, which was not easy, as he felt anything but. "It is your family who treated him so badly he was forced to leave England with the woman he loved and a babe that was only a few weeks old."

"Forgive my brother; his mouth often engages before his brain." Lord Sinclair glared at Cambridge Sinclair. "We are not here to judge your father."

"Then why are you here?"

"As I have said, we've heard your name before and had

wondered if you were the son of Byron Sinclair, our uncle, who left London when I was a child," Lord Sinclair said. "Now we know you are, we would like to get to know you better and introduce you to the rest of your family."

"I have a grandmother, and that is all I need. I see no reason to change that at this late stage in my life."

"Your father still lives?" the man called Wolf asked.

"He does not."

"You have our condolences," Lord Sinclair said.

Harry nodded.

"Grandson!"

The four men all turned as one and watched Harry's grandmother stomp across the deck. He didn't sigh precisely, but the sentiment was there. This day was not about to improve, it seemed.

"Grandmère, I told you I would help you to the carriage once it had arrived. You should have stayed in your cabin." Harry moved to intercept her. Short and round, she wore mustard today, with a green bonnet that made him wince. Fashion, his grandmother said, was a statement, and she was certainly that.

"I wished for air."

Heloise Paquet had been born the daughter of a baker, and when Harry turned his fortunes around and soon had more money than he knew what to do with—her words— she'd decided the simple life was no longer to her liking. She now lived in an expensive townhouse with staff and had the airs and graces of someone born into a title and money. It amused Harry just how well she'd taken to a life of luxury, even if sometimes he found her in the kitchen baking bread.

"You have visitors." She stomped her cane on the deck as she spoke. He wasn't entirely sure why she used it, as she could walk perfectly without, however it gave her a weapon should it be required to quell any insubordination.

"Business, Grandmère," Harry said, hoping the men didn't hear.

"They have the look of you. Tell me their names." Heloise Paquet never asked, she demanded. Her staff were terrified of her, and she loved it that way. In fact, the only person who ever spoke their mind to her was Harry, and that was because he adored her.

"Good day," Cambridge Sinclair said.

Short of ordering them from his ship, Harry could do nothing to stop the Sinclairs drawing closer. The meeting was inevitable.

"Who are you?" his grandmother demanded, peering up at the large men.

"This is my brother, Lord Sinclair, and cousin Mr. Christian Sinclair, and I am Cambridge Sinclair."

Harry watched the men bow and his grandmother's lips twitch. She loved it when people bowed to her.

"Introduce me." One of her pointy elbows jabbed him in the ribs.

"Mrs. Heloise Paquet," Harry said reluctantly, as he knew what would be coming next. His grandmother was exceedingly sharp on all fronts.

"They are Sinclairs, grandson."

"Grandmère—"

"Indeed, we are Harry's cousins."

"Cousins!" She fired off a volley of French, then jabbed him in the ribs once more. "But that is wonderful, grandson!"

"Grandmère—"

"Indeed it is, Mrs. Paquet," Lord Sinclair said. "Our family lost track of Harry's father when he left England."

"My daughter and her husband moved to France to be near me," she said. Which was a whopping untruth. They'd moved back to France as Harry's mother was an unwed maid with a baby, and the father the son of a peer who wanted a life with her. The Sinclair family had disowned him; the Paquet family had not.

"France. You were so close all this time," Cambridge Sinclair said.

They were speaking French in deference to his grand-mère, which he appreciated from a respect standpoint, however it also meant she could understand the conversation, which was not always to his advantage.

She fired off a volley of French as her luggage was carried past and a piece dropped. Stomping away, she went to tell the hapless crewman what she thought of him.

"Will you come with us and meet the rest of your family?" Lord Sinclair said.

"I have no wish to do so or make family connections. I am here to deliver my cargo, conduct business, and then leave."

"And yet you will," Captain Sinclair said in a voice he'd no doubt used on his troops.

"I won't." Harry didn't like anyone telling him what to do. He went where he wanted and did as he wished for the most part and had since his father passed.

"You will like our family. Bring your grandmother. She will enjoy her time with us, I promise," Lord Sinclair said. "But there is another matter we wish to discuss with you."

"What matter?"

"It is a delicate one." Lord Sinclair shot his grandmother a look, but she was still busy blistering the ears of his crew.

"I fail to see what delicate matter you need to discuss with a man you have never met before."

"You're not terribly accommodating, considering you've just reunited with your long-lost family," Cambridge said.

"I believe I have explained that my family was ill-treated by Sinclairs, and you cannot lose what you have never had." There was a definite edge to Harry's tone now.

Never trust a Sinclair.

"But not by us. Our fathers were the ones who did your family an injustice," Lord Sinclair added.

"It matters not. I want nothing to do with anyone bearing that name."

"Seems harsh to rule out all Sinclairs. What if you met one that did not have our blood but—"

"Cam!" Lord Sinclair snapped.

"Right, sorry."

"Just be honest with him. He'll leave if we don't." Wolf Sinclair's eyes were locked on Harry's.

"I'm sure by now you've realized you're different, Harry."

"Perhaps he's not?" Cam said.

"Those eyes suggest otherwise."

Had Lord Sinclair's words been accompanied by a fist, the impact would have been no greater.

"What do you mean?" *You've always known you're different.*

"Do you see better than most, Harry?"

"I have no idea what you mean." But he did.

"Yes, you do. You're the eldest son, as are I and Wolf. We share something, Harry, and not just appearances, because even you cannot dispute the three of us are almost identical."

Suddenly every muscle in his body clenched.

"Come to this address, and we will tell you what that difference is and where it came from."

Harry took the card that was handed him. White with black writing, he noted as he gripped it hard enough so the edges dug into his palm.

You've always known you're different.

He couldn't dispute that. From the first day he'd realized what he was, he'd wondered why him?

"Come, Harry, you will not regret it, I promise. We are good people." Lord Sinclair's hand gripped his shoulder, and a sensation traveled through him like he'd never experienced before.

He stood there as they walked away, stopping briefly to say goodbye to his grandmother. His eyes followed them as they left his ship, then climbed into a carriage. Only when it had rolled away did he draw in a deep breath.

He would not be seeing them again, Harry assured himself, even though inside he wanted desperately to know what Lord Sinclair had meant by his words.

I'm sure by now you've realized you're different, Harry.

CHAPTER 3

"Nearly there, my sweet," Maddie stroked her daughter's soft hair. Fleur had endured much over the last few days, but now she prayed that was over. Her child slept in her arms, the rocking motion of the carriage lulling her back to sleep.

Please let it be over.

The hackney slowed and stopped. Holding her daughter close, Maddie picked up her bag and stepped down.

"How much is the fare, please, sir." She prayed there was enough money left.

"The gentleman paid it, miss."

"He did?"

"More than enough too."

"Oh, well, thank you."

She hadn't lied when she'd called Harry Sinclair her guardian angel. She had known even with her limited knowledge that the fare the seaman who had called himself Barney had quoted her for passage to London was cheap. But desperation had pushed aside her pride, and she'd accepted, eager to leave France behind.

She'd seen the tall, dark, fierce man who'd looked like a warrior standing on the deck of his ship as she'd sat there wondering what her next step would be. He'd looked every inch the gentleman in the clothes he wore, and yet there had been something untamed about him.

He'd saved them from those barrels too. They would have been maimed or worse. He'd taken a risk and carried them to safety in his big, strong arms. Fleur had been distressed, and he'd cupped her head to stop her weeping, and her daughter had settled in seconds. Usually a happy child, this trip had made her grizzly, and yet the man, Harry Sinclair, had been able to calm her when Maddie could not.

"We are safe now, my love." Maddie whispered the words to Fleur and hoped saying them out loud meant they were the truth.

She'd left her cottage in France in the early hours of the morning five days ago, and the memory of the terror that drove her to take the drastic steps was still fresh in her head. She'd packed everything she could as quietly as possible with fear nipping at her heels, then gathered up her sleeping child and slipped from the house.

The trip to Calais had been grueling, but finally they'd arrived, tired and hungry. There, Maddie started enquiries on a fare for them to London.

Her arms had ached, and her eyes were gritty, but desperation had driven her on. Desperation and fear that someone would catch her and lock her away from her child. Luck had been on her side and put her on that ship to England. Luck and Harry Sinclair.

Looking at the house before her, she hoped her brother was inside and her luck continued. Maddie would not contemplate any other option. Rory had to be here. This was the address he'd given her; it was written in the letter she had in her bag. And yet she couldn't read it, so had relied on someone else to give it to her.

Had they got it right?

Well, there is no way of knowing without knocking on that door.

Taking the ten steps, she rapped the brass knocker, then stood back to wait.

Please be here, Rory.

Maddie braced herself as the door opened.

"Good day," the man said. His eyes ran over her and settled on the still slumbering Fleur.

Maddie knew how she looked but had little choice in that. They were rumpled, dirty, and no doubt looked like beggars. Raising her chin, she did not show her desperation. Strength had got her through many ordeals in her life, and it would now.

"May I help you?"

"I wish to speak with Mr. Huntington, please."

"Mr. Maxwell Huntington, or Mr. Rory Huntington?"

"Mr. Rory Huntington."

"And may I have your name, please?"

"Mrs. Madeline Caron."

The butler smiled. "If you will come this way, Mrs. Caron, I will show you to a parlor while I tell Mr. Huntington you have called."

Maddie followed. Her legs suddenly felt wobbly. Now she was here, so close, the fight seemed to have left her.

"Please take a seat."

"I wish to see Mr. Rory Huntington," she clarified.

"Of course, Mrs. Caron. I will return shortly."

Just hearing her eldest brother's name had anger and need battling inside her. It made her want to flee. But Maddie never turned from anything. She'd do this for Fleur if not for herself. Fleur, and the very real possibility that her legs would not hold her were they forced to take many more steps.

Rory had written to her, telling her Max was a good man and that there was much to share as to why he'd left. Maddie wanted to hear none of it. He'd then told her he was to wed and live here in London. That had broken her heart. Maddie had wanted happiness for her brother, but she'd hope it would be in France, near her.

As it turned out, France was now not safe for her and Fleur, so she would need to find another home for them.

Settling Fleur into a soft chair, Maddie covered her with the blanket that had once been cream and was now a grubby brown. Her daughter never moved. She fell into the other seat in the room, resting her head on the back. The weight of fatigue pulled at her eyelids until they closed. Just for a few minutes, just enough to regain her strength.

The sound of running feet woke her. The door burst open, and there stood Max with a huge shaggy gray dog at his side who she knew well. Struggling to her feet, she kept her eyes on the man she'd loved since the day she was born. He looked so different to the angry man who had left her many years ago.

"Maddie." It was a ragged whisper. "Dear God, sister, you are a wonderful sight."

She'd wondered what her reaction to him would be. Would she hate him for leaving her, or would the love she'd always felt for him win over everything else?

In her exhausted state, the latter won.

"M-Max." She took a step toward him, and he to her, and then she was in his arms. Big strong arms, and only then did she let herself fall. Slumping against him, she wept wracking sobs that poured out of her.

"Shhh now, I have you."

He held her close, his hands stroking her back. Maddie

gripped his lapels and burrowed into his chest. *Safe. Was it really the truth?*

She was unsure how long they stood there, but long enough for the tears to flow and ease. As if a dam had burst, she finally let herself let go. Max was here, and for now that was enough.

"Max?"

Maddie heard the voice from behind her brother. Soft and female.

"Can you organize a room, my love? Water for washing, and food also."

"Of course."

She rested, her cheek on his chest, his arms holding her there. For just this brief time, she would allow herself to take strength from another. When the sniffles had stopped, she lifted her head to look at him.

The years had filled out his body. Age had put lines where there had been none, and he looked what she'd heard he now was. A prosperous man with a wife and children.

"What has you here like this, Maddie? Where is your husband?"

She felt the tears build again. Tears for the man she had married. A good man who had provided for his family as best he could. They'd not loved, but respected each other, and for Maddie, who'd never had a home, it had been more than enough.

"He died, Max."

"When?"

"Months ago. He was sick, and got worse, then he passed two weeks later."

"We would have come. I'm sure you could have found someone to write a letter for you. Why did you not notify us?"

Because I opened the door, and the devil walked inside my home, and I was fooled by her again.

"I needed time alone to grieve," she lied.

"What are you not telling me?" His big hands cupped her cheeks, his eyes holding hers. "Those eyes of yours have always hidden more than they should."

"So much, and most cannot be spoken."

"Even to me, the brother who loves you?"

"The brother I now barely know." Maddie eased out of his arms and dropped down to hug the dog she knew so well.

"Hello, Bran, my old friend."

She felt the rough tongue on her cheek.

"He has clearly missed you," Max said.

"And I him."

Her moment of weakness was behind her as she regained her feet. She had always been strong; that would not stop now she was safe.

"We are weary, Max. I would ask for a bed please, so Fleur and I can sleep. I understand the hour is still early, and yet we have not slept well for many nights."

She saw the questions he wanted to ask, but instead he said, "Of course." He moved to where Fleur lay. "She looks so sweet." He bent to kiss her head. "Another niece for an uncle to love."

Maddie swallowed down the lump those words formed. For so long it had been just her watching over her daughter, but now there would be uncles, and for that she would be grateful. Her daughter would be safe should anything happen to her.

"Where is Rory?"

"With his fiancée. I will send word you are here."

"Come, I have a room ready." A woman appeared in the doorway.

"This is my wife, Essie. My love, this is my sister, Maddie."

"I am so very pleased to finally meet you." The woman had dark hair and lovely green eyes, and the smile on her face was gentle. She came forward and wrapped her arms around Maddie. "Your brothers have talked about you constantly, so much that I feel I know you so well already."

Maddie accepted the hug and the comfort it gave. Tomorrow she would once again put distance between herself and others until she could trust them.

"Come now, I can see how weary you are," Essie said. "There will be plenty of time to talk after you have rested."

Maddie turned to pick up Fleur, but Max already had her in his arms.

"I can take her."

"As you look ready to drop where you stand, I will carry her up the stairs for you. Trust that your daughter is safe with me, as are you. Now, follow Essie, Maddie."

She wanted to argue. Fleur was hers to carry, and yet the argument would have been a petty one. Instead she let her sister-in-law place an arm around her shoulders and lead her from the room. Bran followed, the clip of his claws on the tiles a comforting sound as they walked.

She caught fleeting glances of flowers, furniture, and paintings, but her gritty eyes struggled to focus on much. The house was large, grand even, but tomorrow would be soon enough to see more of it.

When they entered the room, all she saw was the bed… a huge, comfortable bed with coverings that would keep Fleur warm. Wide enough to fit a family of four. They would sleep well today.

Max lowered his niece gently onto the mattress. The child did not so much as twitch. Maddie took off her boots and dress, leaving her in a shift. Kissing her daughter's cheek, she whispered her love and then pulled the covers to her chin.

"There is warm water for washing, Maddie," Essie said. "And a tray of food."

"Thank you."

"Will you let me help you get into bed? You must be so tired."

"I can do it, but thank you, Essie." She'd never had help with anything; she wasn't about to start now.

"I thought you would wish to sleep with Fleur."

"I would, thank you, as she will be frightened when she wakes if I am not here."

"Pull the bell if you need anything," Max said. "We will be close." He came to her side. "It is good to see you, sister, and tomorrow is soon enough to discuss what simmers between us. Sleep and regain your strength. The rest will wait."

Maddie nodded, words now beyond her. She felt his lips in her hair, and then he and his wife left her alone, as she'd been for so long. But no longer, Maddie thought, for now she had brothers nearby.

She removed her clothes and boots, and then washed in the warm water. It felt wonderful. Once the travel dirt was rubbed from her body, Maddie pulled on her nightdress and made herself sit in the comfortable chair and eat the food, simply because she needed the strength. This and sleep would set her to rights.

Climbing into the soft bed when she'd finished her tea, she pulled up the covers. Her daughter was safe now, and that alone had her eyes closing. In seconds, the darkness had pulled her under.

CHAPTER 4

*H*arry had told himself in a hundred different ways why he would not be going to the Sinclairs' to find out what they were talking about. He'd run through every reason, several times, not least of all the fact that his father's words were always inside his head.

Never trust a Sinclair.

After delivering his grandmother to her hotel and ensuring everything was perfect, he had spent a day walking the decks of his ship.

Faris had asked him what was wrong, and because for the first time in his life Harry couldn't work out what to do, he'd told him. His friend had said that visiting his family did not present a life sentence of connections in that logical way that made Harry want to punch him. So here he now was, traveling along the street that his cousins lived on at an ungodly early hour, betraying his father.

"But I will not stay," he muttered. It was merely that he needed to know what he was. He would then leave and continue to fulfil his father's wish.

Would the Sinclairs even be awake? He had no idea, as he

rose with the sun, and knew little about the hours a nobleman kept.

He'd come because he needed to know. Damn those Sinclairs; they'd known he would. Known that the differences in him he'd kept hidden all his life would lead him here. But it would change nothing. He would listen to what they said and then leave, no matter that Faris had urged him to make a connection with these people.

Never trust a Sinclair.

The street the carriage stopped in was clearly one of London's better ones. The houses were large and, he was sure, admired by those passing, which was very likely the point. The one he wanted was old and well built. Looking up the imposing façade, he wondered at what and who awaited him inside.

The three men from yesterday? Did they all live here? How many more were there of these Sinclairs?

Paying for the hackney, he stepped down and tried to settle the sudden thud of his heartbeat inside his chest. *Just go in there, find the answers to the questions you've always had, then leave.* It need to be no more difficult than that surely.

"You are a man who spends his days negotiating deals with men equally as ruthless as you," Harry reminded himself. A few noblemen should not disturb him unduly.

He rapped on the front door, and it was opened by— Harry presumed—the butler. Elegantly dressed and with a stately air, he really couldn't be anything else.

"Good day."

"Good day. My name is Mr. Sinclair."

The butler seemed happy about that.

"Harry Sinclair."

"You certainly have that look about you, sir. If you will come this way, I've had instruction to take you to the family when you arrive."

There was a look?

"I only had this day free, and I understand the hour is early, but I have meetings," Harry added, not wanting it to be bandied about that he'd only let a full day pass before hurrying here to talk with them... the Sinclairs. Who were family and yet not anyone he would ever be close with, he reminded himself. Servants, Harry knew, were notorious for gossip.

Never trust a Sinclair.

He followed the butler's straight back, let his eyes settle on the paintings he passed and his feet sink into the rugs he trod. It was possibly what a home felt like; he didn't know and cared even less. Harry and his father had merely slept in their lodgings, they had held little by way of sentiment for either of them. He was a wanderer. He had a bed in many places, but not one of them was a home.

"Watch out below!"

Looking to the top of the stairs, he saw a young lady straddling the banister. Seconds later, she was sliding down it.

"Dear God!" He hurried forward when the butler showed no signs of doing so, but she reached the bottom and slid off, landing neatly on her feet.

"Hurry up, Warwick!"

A young man came next. All legs and arms, minutes later he was standing beside the lady.

He guessed their age to be nearing twenty, and yet he had never been terribly good at gaging such things, especially in women.

"Hello." She smiled at him. Pretty with blue eyes and blonde hair. "I am Samantha, sister to James, Max, Rory, Rose, Emily, and now Maddie. I have as yet not met her but hope to soon."

"There are still more of us," the young man said, which had the girl's lips thinning.

Tall, and still growing into the man he would become, he had dark hair and green eyes and could only be a Sinclair. Harry tried not to stiffen as the young man held out his hand.

"I am Warwickshire Sinclair. I believe you are my cousin Harry?"

Harry bowed before shaking the hand. "Yes, I am Harry. How is it you know that?"

"You've seen my eldest brother, Dev, and cousin Wolf, I believe?"

Harry nodded.

"Well then, the three of you are almost identical." Warwick smiled. "Welcome to the family, Harry."

A simple sentence, and yet one he'd never thought to hear. He absolutely did not feel a warmth in his chest at the thought of belonging. Harry needed no one.

"I will not be staying." His words came out gruff, but the young man simply continued to smile.

"We are hard to resist." He wasn't bragging; it was just a fact as far as Warwick Sinclair was concerned.

"Aren't you a little old for sliding down bannisters?" Harry changed the subject.

"We are far too old to slide down bannisters, and yet still we do it. It's something of a tradition in our families, is that not so, Tatters?" Warwick said to the butler.

"Indeed it is" came the serene reply.

"Yes, and I'm always the best, as I weigh less. Dev set out a mark on the floor, and as yet, no one has reached it but I," Samantha bragged.

"Cam nearly reached it." Warwick's smile slipped. "And I too."

"However, nearly is not close enough is it? It is very nice

to meet you, Harry. We shall join you shortly." She then grabbed Warwick's arm and tugged him with her. Soon they'd disappeared through an open doorway.

"If you'll come this way, Mr. Sinclair." The butler, Tatters, took him up the stairs, and then he was before double doors. Harry had never run from anything in his life before. He had the urge to do so now. *This is a mistake.* The butler opened the doors.

"Mr. Harry Sinclair," he announced, which Harry guessed meant he had to enter the room. He stopped two steps inside. Seated at a huge table were Lord Sinclair and a woman; with them were a boy and two girls.

"Well, now this is a pleasure." He rose and came forward. "But where is your grandmother?"

"She stays at the Grillion Hotel when in London. I did not tell her of this meeting."

"Next time then," he said. "Now, this beautiful woman is my wife, Lilly. This is my cousin Harry, love."

"Hello, Harry, it's wonderful to meet you." She had blond hair styled simply and was dressed as any society lady should be; it was her eyes that drew attention. They appeared to be the color of lilacs.

Harry shook his cousin's hand and bowed before the woman. He could play the gentleman when required, his father had ensured that. Tutors had been a part of his life for many years.

"There are noblemen in every corner of the world, Harry, I will not have my son unable to speak with them as an equal."

And so he'd learned, and in situations like this was grateful for the years he'd studied.

"This is my son, Mathew, and daughters, Hannah and Meredith. Say hello to your cousin."

The boy shook his hand, and the girls giggled their way through curtsies.

"We like cousins," the little girl said with a lisp. "And we shall call you Uncle Harry." She then smiled at him, and he was sure there would be a few broken-hearted men in her future. Harry smiled back because it would be rude not to do so, and he liked children, even if they had the surname Sinclair.

"Now if you three will visit the nursery briefly, we want to have a chat with your new uncle," Lord Sinclair said. He then placed a kiss on the head of each child before his wife shooed them from the room.

I am an uncle.

"You'll forgive the hour of my visit. I have meetings and could fit in no other time, my lord."

"I am Devon, or my family calls me Dev."

"Among other things," his wife added. "And I am Lilly."

"Yes, thank you for that, darling." Harry watched as Devon kissed his wife right there in front of him.

"Stop!"

Harry turned as a woman burst into the room, followed by a man. "This conversation will not begin until we are all present."

"How did you know he was here?" Devon asked. Her reply was to raise a brow.

"Really? You felt him already?"

"It was a strange feeling of anticipation, and I felt I needed to find you. Of course. Essie can't make it, but she saw us hurrying past her door and asked me to tell Harry she will arrive as soon as she can."

"This is my sister Eden, the Duchess of Raven," Lord Sinclair said. "And her husband, James. She is the nosiest among us."

"The Duke of Raven," Lilly added.

It seemed the Sinclairs had married well.

"Your graces." He bowed deeply.

"He has better manners than the rest of you," the duke said, shaking Harry's hand. "I was about to leave for a meeting when my wife told me we were needed here. Of course, her wish is my command, so I followed, obedient to the last."

"Call us James and Eden, Harry." Eden smiled at him. Her eyes weren't green, but gray, unlike the others he'd met of her family.

"God's blood, I have a hunger!" Cambridge Sinclair entered the room next, dragging a woman behind him. "To have been roused from my table without nary a morsel passing my lips, it is amazing I have not fainted."

"You know Cambridge, and this is his wife, Emily," Lord Sinclair drawled. "Besides his family, his main love in life is food."

"Sad but true." Cambridge shook Harry's hand, then wandered back out the door. He was then heard issuing orders about needing more food.

"Hello, Harry, it really is wonderful to meet you." Emily was blonde, slender, and his guess was, a great deal quieter than her husband.

"Right, let's sit before the others arrive and deplete my food stocks." Lord Sinclair waved to the table.

"Others?"

"Many more." Cambridge had returned. Dropping into a seat, he reached for the teapot. "There are plenty of Sinclairs, Harry, but I must add that the Ravens are catching us."

"Ravens?" Harry shot the duke and duchess a look.

"You'll understand once the entire sordid tale is explained to you."

He remembered the conversation between Warwick and Samantha downstairs.

These people were odd, Harry thought. Not like any

nobility he'd met before. There was no pomp or manners. They seemed happy to bandy insults like compliments.

Harry liked to be in control of any situation he stepped into. This was not one of those times. It made him feel uncomfortable when people did not behave as he felt they should, especially families, as he had no prior knowledge of how they worked.

"I really just wanted to talk about—"

"Sit, cousin, we need food for that discussion, and with you standing there I cannot eat, as apparently it is rude to do so," Cambridge said, looking disgruntled.

Harry sat because he wanted to, between Eden and Emily. He would listen and then leave.

"Oh, I did wonder if it was you." Wolf Sinclair arrived. With him was a beautiful woman with red-gold hair. In her arms was a child only a few months old. He was grizzling. She was jiggling him about, trying to soothe him.

His stomach is sore. Harry tried to ignore the infant's wails and the acid swirling in his gut. Rose, who had a surprising Scottish burr, was also attempting to soothe the child by singing to him.

That will not work.

"We were unsure if you would come," Lilly said.

"I would like you to explain to me what you alluded to on my ship, my lord."

"Dev."

"I do not have long, as I am to attend a meeting," Harry lied. "So please tell me what I need to know, as my work cannot wait, my lord."

"Dev."

"He is using your title to put us in our place," Cam added. "He also wants us to know he works, as apparently we don't."

"I never said that, Mr. Sinclair."

"Cam, and you thought it."

"No, I didn't. I know of Lord Sinclair's ships, so clearly he is also a businessman, Mr. Sinclair. I wish only to know what you spoke of on my ship. I will then leave."

"Cam, and we all work actually, but we'll get to that later," he said. "The rest of the family are due to arrive shortly, as we have another member to welcome. A Raven this time."

"How many more of you are there?" he asked Eden

"A great many more."

Wolf got to his feet and took the babe from Rose, but the child's cries got louder.

His stomach is sore! Harry made himself stay seated when everything inside him screamed to get up and see to the child. It was the one thing in his life he couldn't control, this affinity he had with children.

"I will not be staying to make acquaintances. I wish only to discuss the matter we spoke of earlier. I will then be leaving." *Excellent, Harry. Stay on point.*

"We will get to that," Lord Sinclair said.

"Are you hungry? The food should be arriving soon," Lilly asked.

"Of course he is, look at him. He's built like Dev and Wolf," Cam said.

"Uncanny how the eldest sons all look alike." The duke was studying him. "I wonder if the rest will follow as you believe it has, Dev."

Harry felt like he was the only one in the room who wasn't in on the secret. "What is going on?"

"We can explain." Eden rested a hand on Harry's shoulder. The feeling that ran through him was the same sensation he'd experienced when her brother had touched him, or he'd shaken the hand of a Sinclair.

"I really don't think—"

"Good idea, it's not something I've ever perfected," Cam said.

"Amen," Lord Sinclair added.

"It really is not worth tiring yourself out over the matter, especially if your stomach is empty. Now where is the food? It needs replenishing," Cambridge said.

"I came for answers, not a family reunion," Harry protested.

"I think you have to meet someone to have a reunion," Cambridge added. "Don't quote me on that, but I'm fairly sure it's cast in stone somewhere."

Silver-lidded dishes started arriving as servant after servant deposited them on the sideboard and removed the empty ones.

"Can we not just have them on the table, Dev? I have to get up now."

"We have company, Cam. At least give Harry the illusion we have manners for a minute or two."

"It can be a little overwhelming, Harry, but believe me when I say these are good people. In fact, I have yet to find any better," Emily said. "Give them a chance. I promise you will not regret it."

"I just can't stop him crying." Rose looked distressed, and her husband no better. As if on cue, the baby screamed louder, and Harry's stomach clenched, but he fought it.

"I have tried everything." Rose looked near tears.

Pushing back his chair before he could stop himself, Harry regained his feet and approached Rose and Wolf.

It will be all right, little man.

"His stomach is sore."

"How do you know?" Wolf asked him.

"I just do. Give him to me." He held out his hands, and his cousin handed the boy to him. "What's his name?"

"Ruben."

Harry rested the babe facedown along one arm and began to walk about the room, patting his back. It did not take long for the child to stop weeping and let out a large belch.

There now, Ruben, rest easy.

"Christ! So it's children with you?" Wolf was standing with Rose, watching him. It was he who spoke.

"Pardon?" Harry saw everyone had stopped what they were doing and was focused on him.

"It's animals with me," Wolf added.

As if he'd commanded it, the door burst open, and in came a shaggy dog. It made for Wolf Sinclair and settled down on his foot, resting on his leg.

"I don't know what you mean." Harry went to hand Ruben back to his mother, but the boy screamed, so he settled him in the crook of his arm once more and continued to rock from side to side.

"Well, it's not normal behavior, is it?" Cam said. "You the businessman with the ruthless reputation, and someone I don't believe has a wife or child?"

"I do not."

"Well, you just took Ruben, an infant that you've never met before, from a man you don't really know, and began wandering about the room patting his back. I've yet to see anyone else do that."

"He was in pain. His stomach was sore," Harry protested.

"What did you feel when he was crying?" Eden asked him.

"What?"

"Just answer the question, Harry."

"My stomach hurt," he muttered.

James started laughing, as did Devonshire Sinclair.

"I fail to see the humor in this situation."

"Welcome to the family, Harry. You'll fit right in," Rose said, moving to his side. She placed a kiss on his cheek and then another on the cheek of her son before taking her seat at the table with her husband at her side, leaving him standing with her child.

"Sit." Dev waved him back to his place.

With few other options open to him, Harry did as he was told, but only because he wanted to. He settled the babe in the crook of his arm, which Ruben seemed quite happy with, as he waved a chubby fist at him.

"Now, cousin. About these gifts you have," Devonshire said.

CHAPTER 5

Maddie woke to her daughter patting her cheek.

"Hello." She hugged Fleur close, her little body warm as they cuddled together.

"Have we stopped now, Mama?" Her daughter's words brought tears to her eyes. She'd done everything she could to keep Fleur happy and safe during the three years she'd lived. Vowed that she would never know fear like Maddie had. She'd wanted stability for her, and Jacques had offered that until his death.

"Yes, my darling, we have stopped traveling." *For now.*

"Hungry, Mama."

"As am I. Shall we go and find Uncle Rory and get something to eat?"

"Uncle Rory!" Fleur got out of her arms and began bouncing up and down on the bed. "I like Uncle Rory."

"As you've never met him, I don't see how you could." Maddie laughed as Fleur lunged at her.

But she had told her daughter about both her uncles, simply because one day she might have need of their support.

"So big." Fleur climbed off the bed and began to investigate her surroundings with the resilience of a toddler who had something new and exciting presented to her.

For all that the last few days had been traumatic, the child showed no signs they'd affected her, much to Maddie's relief.

Getting out of bed, she went to the windows. Drawing the curtains slightly told her it was daylight, just not what the hour was. She looked down at the road below and a carriage that was traveling along it. This was a different world for them, and not just in what they would see.

"Hungry, Mama."

She found their clothes folded neatly on a chair. Lifting the dress she'd worn to England, she sniffed it, and the scent told her it had been washed. She hadn't stirred when whoever did this came into their room. Maddie was usually a light sleeper, but exhaustion had kept her slumbering for hours, it seemed.

"Pretty colors." Fleur was running her hands over the chair covers.

"It is. Now come here and we will wash and dress."

Getting what they needed out of her bag, Maddie washed both herself and Fleur in the fresh water that had also appeared, and then dressed their hair. Once this was done, she made the bed before leaving the room.

"Did Aimee enjoy her sleep in that lovely big bed?" Her daughter's bundle of rags that she'd fashioned into a doll was rarely far from her side. Fleur had it tucked under her arm now.

"She did, Mama. This is a big house." Fleur's eyes were swinging from left to right as they walked.

She'd been too tired to really see Max's house last night, but now it was very evident her brother was indeed a man of considerable wealth.

High ceilings, chandeliers, cabinets filled with treasures.

"Good morning, Mrs. Caron." The man from last night appeared. "My name is George, and I am Mr. and Mrs. Huntington's butler. If you should need anything at any time, then please do not hesitate to ask my assistance."

"Thank you, George. And thank you for cleaning our clothes."

"I shall pass your kind words on to the staff, Mrs. Caron."

"This is my daughter, Fleur."

He bowed deeply, making the little girl giggle. Like Maddie, Fleur had not had any exposure to the wealthy or their servants. This was all a novelty for her.

"Good morning to you, Miss Fleur."

"Say 'good morning, George,'" she said in French. Fleur understood English, but was more comfortable with her native language.

"Good morning, George."

"Could we go somewhere to have food, George? My daughter has not eaten for some time."

"Of course, Mrs. Caron. If you follow me, I will show you to the parlor where the family are seated eating their morning meal."

"What is the time please, George."

"It is nine o'clock in the morning, Mrs. Caron."

Good Lord, she'd slept for hours.

Holding Fleur's hand, she walked the long hall, following the butler. Soon she would see her brothers; one she wanted to, the other she didn't. Last night, seeing Max in her exhausted state had brought the longing she'd carried inside her since his departure from France to the surface. Today she was stronger. He'd left her, and Rory said his reasons were good, but she still felt the pain and anger of his loss inside her.

George motioned for her to enter a room, and inside she found her brothers along with Essie and a boy. Bran was lying on the floor. The dog rose and woofed as he saw her.

"Maddie!" Rory reached her first. His hug was like Max's. He surrounded her. It was all-encompassing, and she could do nothing but respond.

This was the brother who had not left her. The brother who always kept her safe.

"I have so many questions, but the first is, how do you feel?" He gripped her shoulders, his eyes roaming her face.

Dressed in a deep green jacket, matching waistcoat, and white shirt, he looked a gentleman also. They looked alike, her brothers, with their chestnut hair and tawny eyes. Both big and strong. But Rory had always been the softer of the two. Perhaps that was simply because Maddie knew him better.

"I have never slept for so long, but I feel much better, thank you."

"I can't believe you are actually here and that we are all together again," Rory said. "I'm so sorry Jacques passed away. You should have told us."

"I needed some time, Rory."

"Of course. Will you tell me what brought you to us now?"

She didn't want to lie, but neither did she want to speak of what she'd left.

"This is Fleur, Rory," she said, looking down to the child at her side, who had been watching the adults closely.

He did not question her further, instead kneeling before her daughter.

"Hello, Fleur. I am your uncle Rory. I have dreamed of this day for quite some time. This is Bran. He's big but gentle, and I know he will love you."

"*Bonjour*, Uncle Rory and Bran." Fleur smiled. "Mama told me I would like you."

"Well now, that's handy, as I like you." He touched her cheek. "Am I allowed a hug?"

"Good morning, Maddie," Max said.

Pulling her eyes from Rory and Fleur, she looked at her older brother. He held the hand of a boy, and Essie was at his side.

"This is our son, Luke. We also have a daughter, Claire, who is sleeping. She is three months old."

Claire was Maddie's middle name.

"She is named after you."

Maddie let none of what she felt hearing those words show on her face. She'd not always been strong; in fact, her brothers had called her the gentle member of their family. That too had changed over time. You couldn't stay gentle when you were struggling for survival.

"Good morning, Max and Essie." She leaned closer to her nephew. "Good morning, Luke. It is a pleasure to meet you."

"And you, Aunt Maddie." He had his father's smile.

The jolt hearing herself called aunt was not an unhappy one. Maddie loved children, and this boy was not responsible for any past deeds. He was her blood, and hers to love.

"How do you feel?" Max asked her. "I'm sure the journey was challenging. The property you and your husband lived in was, I believe, some distance from Calais."

"It is, but I am well, thank you, Max."

"Last night, you were exhausted. I thought you would fall asleep while you walked."

"It was a comfortable bed." Unlike last night, today she felt more in control and contained. "Forgive me for appearing as I did."

"As you did?" He raised a brow.

"Travel worn and weepy."

"Because you arrived as you did, it let me hold you. I

cannot fault that. There were no barriers between us as there are now."

"Pardon?" His words surprised her. Once Max would never have spoken so openly.

"Your reaction to me is the same as Rory's was, but perhaps not as angry. But then, you were always the gentler of the three of us."

"I am grateful to be here under your roof, Max, but we are strangers. Surely you understand that?"

"Tell her." Rory now held Fleur in his arms. What surprised her was that her daughter seemed happy there. "Tell her now; then we can begin to heal and be a family. There is much more she will learn today; this should be the first. Don't wait as you did with me, Max."

"Tell me what?" Her eyes followed Fleur as Rory lowered her to the floor. She moved to stand before Luke and smile up at him. Bran trotted over to stand at her side, almost the same height. Fleur hugged him.

"She doesn't usually like strangers."

"We are not strangers, Maddie, we are her family," Rory said. "Mother sold Max to that captain so we could have free passage to France. He was then beaten and tortured at the hands of that man." The words had been spoken so only she, Essie, and Max could hear.

"Sh-she did that to you?" Maddie looked at her brother.

"Rory, here and now is not the time for this."

"When is a good time? Tomorrow, five days, or a month from now? It needs to be spoken. Take her somewhere and make her listen. Only then can we start to heal the wounds that woman inflicted upon us."

"Rory, I need to eat. Fleur is hungry also." His words had shocked her, but Maddie didn't think she was ready to hear the rest. Yet more shock on top of everything she'd already endured.

"You must. I'll look after Fleur. You go." Rory nudged her arm.

"I'm not leaving her!" The words were a low growl and came from the fear that had ridden her for days. Her daughter had kept her strong; she would not turn from her now.

"I understand she has been your sole responsibility, Maddie, but you are not alone anymore. She will be happy and safe with Essie, Luke, and me."

"I will watch her, Aunt Maddie." Luke held out a hand to Fleur, and she took it willingly. "I will read her a story."

"Story, Mama."

"Are you happy to stay with Luke, Fleur?" Maddie wanted her daughter to say no so she didn't have to face whatever awaited her. The little girl nodded, more than happy with the arrangement.

"Very well, if we must do this now, then so be it."

Max had been tortured.

Maddie followed her silent brother from the room. They took the stairs down and walked along another hall. The doors at the end were open, and it was there they stopped.

"Please sit." Max waved her into a chair and took the one beside it. "I would not have chosen to talk to you about this now, considering you have just arrived, but Rory has forced my hand."

The room had a large desk in polished wood and shelves filled with ledgers and books.

"This is my study."

"Rory said you are a wealthy businessman now."

"I am, and was driven to achieve that when I arrived in England. For a while it was all that motivated me, and then I met Essie."

"And... and are you happy, Max?"

"I am. I have a family I love, and you will meet the rest of them later. There is much to tell you, but for now I want you to know I never forgot that I had a sister."

"Is it true that man who gave us passage to France many years ago tortured and beat you, Max? The ship's captain?"

He sighed. "When finally I was able to escape that ship, I came back to you a different person. I was angry, Maddie, and that anger spilled over to you and Rory, so I had to leave or kill her."

She knew who he meant. Their mother had done this to him, as she had done many things to her three children. Maddie had fallen for her mother's lies again after her husband passed away, believing she had changed and wanted to be with Fleur and Maddie during their time of grief. It had not taken her long to realize how wrong she'd been.

"I was wrong to leave you and Rory to her, and for that I am truly sorry. I should have been there to protect you as I had always done. You were never like us; you could be hurt easily."

"You make me sound weak; I am not that. And Rory kept me safe until I wed Jacques."

"And like you, he paid the price."

She looked at the man who had once taken beatings for her, slept beside her while she cried. Soothed her pains. But he was no longer just hers. He had a family of his own now, as did Maddie.

"I want us to be a family again, Maddie."

"I will try" was all she could manage. Too much emotion was surely not good for a person if this was how it made you feel. For so long she'd shut it away, as had all the Huntington siblings.

"Then that is all I can ask. Will you now tell me why you arrived on my doorstep exhausted and scared, sister?"

"I was not scared, I was tired, and it was time to come" was all she managed to get out. She could not tell them the rest. That was behind her now, in France… she hoped. "Fleur needed to meet her uncles."

"Very well, but when you are ready to talk, I am here."

"There is nothing further to say."

"I don't believe that, but for now we will eat, then there are more people I would like you to meet."

"Who?"

"Family. Rory did not want to tell you this news in a letter, but there are more siblings now. Three sisters and a brother, to be precise."

"I don't understand?"

"You will, but for now we will eat and check on Fleur, and while you eat I will attempt to explain about this new family you have gained." Max got to his feet and held out a hand. Maddie looked at it for long seconds before placing hers inside.

Could this really be a new beginning for the Caron women? She hoped with everything inside her it was.

CHAPTER 6

Harry had sat there in silence while they'd talked, and learned that the eldest sons in each of the three Sinclair brothers' families all had the gift of sight. He, Devon, and Wolf could see further and more than any human had a right to.

"But there is a great deal more to this family," Dev said as Harry ate his eggs with a fork in one hand and a child settled in the crook of the other arm. After all, he'd not eaten his morning meal and was hungry, so he may as well eat the food that was before him. Every time he tried to hand Ruben back to a parent, he wailed, therefore Harry kept him. Rose and Wolf did not seem overly concerned that their infant was rejecting them.

They are an odd family.

"I have no wish to hear more, as I wanted only to know about my gift."

"And yet we will tell it, because you are now one of us, and it is not something you can escape," Wolf added. "You will feel more now we have connected."

"I don't understand."

"You're not alone there," James said. "I still don't understand, and I've lived with them the longest."

"Yes, thank you, James, we have no wish to scare Harry any more than we need to," Dev said.

"I am rarely scared."

"How brave of you," Cam drawled. Harry had already come to understand the man was the most annoying member of the family, and he'd not met the others yet.

"Now, Lilly is the only one who can heal with her hands," Dev added. "But it takes a great deal out of her if the injury is serious."

"I beg your pardon. Surely you jest?" Harry looked around the table, but he could see no visible signs of madness. Lilly simply smiled at him.

"She pulled a bullet right out of Dev's chest," Cam said with a mouth full of food, as if he was discussing the weather. "He'd stopped breathing, and she brought him back to life."

Harry rubbed Ruben's back as he grappled with what they were telling him.

"You brought him back from the dead?"

Lilly nodded.

"Were I one to faint, now would certainly be the time," Harry muttered. He couldn't take it all in. Was it possible? And yet hadn't he known he was different, so it was possible others were also.

Dev went on to speak about the rest of the family. Taste, sight, hearing, touch, smell; they had it all, and other things that had manifested themselves as the family grew. The really odd thing about all of this was that he wasn't as shocked as he should be. Well, not exactly true; their words were shocking, and yet Harry had to admit, if only to himself, that he felt comfortable with these people, which in itself was odd.

Harry usually avoided situations like this one. Situations that involved families and their clear love for each other.

Twin Sinclair sisters arrived, Dorset and Somerset, two young ladies who welcomed him with the same enthusiasm as their family. Kate and Alice also arrived, Wolf's sisters. There were more, and they would be here soon.

As a boy, Harry had once dreamed of just such a family. Dreamed he was not alone with a resentful father and no one else in his life but Faris and his grandmother. He didn't need it now but would have relished this once.

"Sinclairs marry Ravens, Harry, so it's likely there will be one in your future," Cam said. "Keep your eyes open."

"Pardon?"

"Need he know this now?" Dev sighed. "Really, Cam, we had hoped to keep him here, not send him fleeing from the house screaming."

"I do not scream," Harry said, offended they would think he could.

"It's like picking a scab, Dev. Get it all off at once."

"Charming though that analogy is, I have no plans to marry, so this conversation need not be added to."

"It's a long-ago legend actually, cousin," Cam added, ignoring him. "We will elaborate further one day."

"Allow me to explain before Cam elaborates and we grow bored," Wolf said. "Sinclairs save Ravens and then often marry them."

The Ravens in the room groaned, Harry noted, as Cam explained you were either of Sinclair or Raven blood in this family.

"I have no plans to marry."

That had them all laughing.

"What is so amusing?" He didn't like to be laughed at, possibly because it rarely happened.

"None of us did," Essie said.

He didn't want to feel comfortable with them. He was betraying his father by sitting among them. Betraying the promise he'd made to never make contact with the family who had broken his father's heart.

Never trust a Sinclair.

"I really must leave." Coming to his senses, he rose and handed the now slumbering infant to his father. "His stomach was sore. You need to put him in the position I did when that happens again."

"We will, and thank you." Wolf gripped Harry's shoulder, and he felt the sensation again.

"Thank you for all you have told me, and I wish you well. I will not see you again, as my ship is to sail soon."

"We are your family, Harry," Dorrie said, stepping into his path as he made for the door. "As such we love you and will always be here for you."

"No!" The word ripped from his chest. "I have no need for that love. The Sinclairs betrayed my father."

"Not these Sinclairs," she said, touching his arm. "These Sinclairs want you to be part of our lives."

"My life is in France."

"With whom? Are you married or promised to someone?"

He looked down at the lovely young woman and thought, *she could be the sister I never had.* He fought against the emotion.

"I am not married nor have a woman in my life." He could not lie to her.

"We are not normal, Harry, but then neither are you. Living as part of our family will mean you can be who you were meant to be."

"I know who I am. The man my father raised me to be. Now, I'm sorry, but I must go." He stepped around her and to the door. His chest felt tight, and he needed to leave and go back to his life. This was not for him.

The door opened as he reached it.

Harry looked at the butler, then lifted his eyes to who stood behind the man, and found her.

No!

She was with two men who could only be brothers, and another dark-haired, green-eyed woman. Essex Sinclair was his guess. The daughter of Madeline Caron was in one of the men's arms.

"This is our sister Essex." Dev came forward to make the introductions. "And these are the Huntington brothers, Max and Rory. Essie is wed to Max, and Rory betrothed to Kate."

He'd heard of Maxwell Huntington; there were not many who hadn't. He was a powerful man with business interests that stretched far and wide.

"And this is their sister, Mrs. Madeline Caron. Hello, Maddie, it is wonderful to finally meet you," Dev said, leaning in to hug the woman Harry had saved yesterday. Harry saw she was uncomfortable with the gesture, body stiff, holding herself away from Dev.

Confusion as to how the Huntingtons fit in with the Sinclairs and Madeline Caron to them had Harry struggling to put all the pieces of the puzzle together.

If Maxwell Huntington and the men he'd just met were in any way related or close to her, why then was she in that state in Calais? Terrified and alone.

"It's a pleasure to meet you." Head whirling, he shook the hands held out to him.

As yet she had not looked at him, but the color riding high on her cheekbones told him she was as shocked as he at finding him here.

The next few minutes could only be described as mayhem as everyone surged forward.

Harry moved left until he could reach the wall, which he needed in that moment to hold himself up, and watched the goings-on. Half of the party had moved to one side of the room. The Huntingtons, Madeline Caron, Rose, Emily, Samantha, and the duke. The Sinclairs stood before Harry.

He needed to get out of this room, and yet his legs appeared to refuse the commands they'd been obeying since he'd taken his first steps.

This was all insanity, surely? Was he dreaming? Shaking his head, he attempted to focus. He watched the duke greet Madeline. She looked nervous, the duke happy.

"I am your brother, Madeline."

Christ! Suddenly it all clicked into place. She was of Raven blood? *Sinclairs marry Ravens, usually after saving them.*

He'd saved her. *It means nothing.* He was to leave London, and she had just arrived, Harry reminded himself. He was not part of this... whatever the hell this was.

People laughed and talked all over the top of each other, and as someone who had been raised in silence, he found it deafening. He saw by the look on Madeline Caron's face, she felt no different.

He closed his eyes, and when he opened them, he saw the room burst to life in color. It didn't happen often, but when it did, it was a shock.

"Close your eyes, count to ten, then reopen them. There are too many people in the room for that vision now, Harry, if you are unused to it." Dev gripped his arms. Standing before him, he then counted softly so only Harry could hear.

"Open them now."

Thankfully his vision had returned to normal and with it, his heartbeat.

"Better?"

"You have that?"

"I do, and Wolf. We see in color sometimes. We have control of it now, so Wolf and I can move between both. Do you see the white when someone is near death or sick?"

He couldn't speak as his throat was dry, so Harry nodded.

"I will teach you how to control it, if you'll let me."

"I should leave. I can't be part of this."

"No, you should stay. I will get you a drink. You look like you need one."

"It's morning" was all he found to say. He lived his life on board ships with sailors, for God's sake; he drank any time of the day. A sailor, a ruthless businessman, and someone who was not often thrown off balance, and yet today he was that and so much more. He felt like a child taking his first steps.

He watched his cousin walk away and thought seriously about slipping from the room while everyone was talking. His eyes went to her, Madeline. Her shoulders were back, chin raised, but those eyes told him of the panic she felt.

Looking down as someone tugged on his trousers, he saw Madeline Caron's daughter had approached. Unable to resist a child, he crouched, bringing their eyes level. Children, he understood, and often they grounded him when he felt adrift.

"Hello, do you remember me?"

She nodded.

"My name is Harry. What is yours?"

"Fleur, and I have an Uncle Rory and an Uncle Max. There is also a cousin called Luke."

"Well now, that's a good thing, surely. Are you happy to have new family?"

She nodded, then moved closer, wrapping an arm around his shoulder. The gesture was natural, and something he'd had happen often in his lifetime, such was his gift. The gift the Sinclairs had told him was like the one Wolf had with animals.

"They're noisy." She looked up at the people before them.

"Extremely, but I think they're kind," Harry said, wanting to make the child feel at ease even though he himself was not.

"She wasn't nice."

"Who?"

"The woman who made me call her grandmère. She was mean to me."

"Where is she now?"

"My home," she whispered in French.

"Well then, you have no need to worry about her again, as you are far away from there now."

"She made my mama cry."

"Hello again, Mr. Sinclair. I hope Fleur is not bothering you?"

Harry rose as Madeline Caron addressed him. He felt Fleur slip her hand into his, then she took her mother's in the other. Connecting them, he thought, then dismissed his thought as foolish. He was clearly not thinking straight, and who could blame him for that.

"No, we are just discussing her new uncles."

He wouldn't tell her what her daughter had told him. He had no right to be intrigued by this woman, not now he knew what family she was part of.

"My daughter doesn't usually talk to strangers. I cannot work out why she is different with you, as she seems to be with them." She waved a hand over her shoulder.

"Clearly she trusts us."

"She has trusted before, but rarely on such brief acquaintance."

"Because we are good people. Children can sense that in adults."

"If only adults were so intuitive."

"It would certainly make life easier."

"I can't believe you are one of them." The words rushed out of her mouth. "One of the family I had not realized I had. Reunited with a brother and then all this…" Her words fell away.

"How wonderful for you then, to find them and your brother once more."

"It should be wonderful."

"And yet?"

She gave her head a little shake. "Forgive me, I am not myself. I don't usually speak openly."

"With anyone or just me?"

"You are a stranger to me, sir, but to answer your question, I do not usually speak my thoughts freely."

Her features were fine, unlike her brothers'. Fingers slender. This close, he saw the freckles that marched across her nose and the soft pout of her lips.

"Surely not strangers. After all, yesterday I held you in my arms, and that was after traveling on my ship."

"You saved me, and that is why I was in your arms," she corrected him with a smile. "I had little choice in the matter."

"Neither did I. However, had I not held you, you would have ended up in the water or worse."

She closed her eyes briefly. "Forgive me, yes, you saved us, and I thank you again for that. Also the fares to England and paying for the hackney. What you did for us changed everything. I owe you a great deal."

"You owe me nothing. You were in need of help, and I could provide it. I am glad that you are here now, safe from whatever you were running from."

Her eyes shot to him, and if he'd been in doubt she'd been running, her look confirmed it.

"I was not running," she lied.

"Wrong choice of words. Forgive me, Mrs. Caron."

"My name is Madeline, and I would rather no one knew what took place between us, sir."

"Of course. We would not wish to worry them as to why you were there in that state in Calais or the fact that two barrels nearly squashed you."

She didn't know what to say to that.

"I am to leave England soon and travel back to France," Harry said, because he wanted to keep her talking and at his side. "But what of you, Madeline? Is this your home or France?"

She wore the same dress as yesterday, and hair the color of chestnuts was braided and pinned into a bun at the back of her head.

"I am unsure where my home is. Release Mr. Sinclair now, Fleur. Good day to you, and thank you again for all you have done for my daughter and me." She then walked away, taking Fleur with her. He followed the gentle sway of her skirts as she made for Mr. Rory Huntington's side.

Harry looked at the people that were his family. The resemblance was there in each. The eyes and hair. The love in this room was obvious to anyone who was looking. He wanted no part of that emotion—or Sinclairs.

Never trust a Sinclair, son.

"What am I doing?"

Suddenly his chest felt tight and palms sweaty. Panic, he realized. He'd been shot at by pirates who'd tried to board his ship, and stabbed, among other things, and yet this situation was making him panic. He'd not dealt with this much emotion in many years.

"Here." Devon held out a glass. "You look in shock, and for that I'm sorry, but there really was no easy way to tell you about all this."

Harry threw back the whisky, enjoying the burn as it traveled down his throat.

"I would ask that you give us a chance, Harry."

"I don't need a family, and this life is not for me."

"What life?"

"Society. I have never walked in it, and have no wish to."

"Not all of us walk in society."

He looked at the grandeur around him, then the people in the room.

"I have no wish for family, my lord. I vowed to my father that I would never trust a Sinclair or form bonds with the family that betrayed him. I will not change that now."

"That seems an incredibly harsh line to take when we are not at fault for your father's plight."

"And yet I promised."

"You know that's not rational, Harry, as do I. Everyone needs someone, and you are not the only Sinclair sibling who has suffered at the hands of this family's ancestors. My father wasn't a pleasant man."

He looked into the eyes and face so like his that it was like looking into a mirror.

"I'm sorry, I must go. Thank you for telling me what I am, but I'm sorry, I cannot be part of your life." He left without looking back. It was only after he'd run down the stairs and out the front door that he realized he was still gripping the glass in his hand.

Dropping it into his pocket, he thought it would remind him of this day when he struggled to believe that it had actually happened.

CHAPTER 7

Harry Sinclair was one of these Sinclairs.

"Harry is a cousin that the others knew about and yet had never met," Rory told Maddie. "He, I think, is in shock like you over meeting family he never knew existed."

She looked for the man who had given her passage to England, but he was no longer in the room.

"I want you to meet my fiancée now," Rory said, waving a young, dark-haired, green-eyed woman over. "This is Kate, Maddie. Kate, my sister."

Her smile was nice, and the look she threw Rory filled with love.

"It is lovely to meet you, Kate."

"Oh and you, Maddie. Rory has spoken endlessly about you."

The Rory she'd known had not spoken endlessly about anything, but she did not state otherwise.

Her eyes circled the room once more as Rory introduced Kate to Fleur. She had a new brother and three sisters. All had hugged her, and she'd remained stiff and unyielding because she could not take it all in. She'd tried to unbend, tried to understand that these people were her blood, but for so long there had been just her, Jacques, and Fleur. Now there were so many more.

"May we take Fleur with us to the nursery, Madeline?" one of the Sinclair twins asked. Maddie's instant thought was denial—she wanted to keep her daughter close—but the smile on her Fleur's face stopped her.

"Of course. Thank you for watching her."

"We love spending time with the children." She smiled, then led Fleur from the room.

For so long, Fleur had only her, and now that too had changed in such a short space of time. Listening to the voices all talking over the top of each other, Maddie suddenly felt the need for quiet.

Moving to the door, she slipped out unnoticed.

Wandering along the hallway, she studied cabinets and looked at paintings, letting the quiet settle around her. Never had she believed she would be in such a place, unless it was to work. There must be a dozen staff to run such a house.

Seeing the large dark-haired man with the piercing green eyes, Harry Sinclair, who had saved her and Fleur, had been another shock on top of so many. Rory had told her he too was meeting his family for the first time. There had definitely been something in those green eyes. Wariness, confusion; she could put many names to what he was feeling, as she felt it too.

She wandered until she found a set of stairs, then climbed. Stopping halfway up, the strength seemed to seep from her limbs. Slumping onto a step, she leaned against the wall and closed her eyes.

Were they safe here with these people?

Could she really allow herself to believe that she no

longer needed to struggle to feed her child? No longer needed to be scared?

"That rather austere gentleman above you is Dev's great-great-grandfather."

"Your Grace." Maddie saw the duke at the bottom of the stairs. "Forgive me for sitting here." She started to rise.

"There are plenty of comfortable chairs, Maddie, but if the steps suit you, then by all means sit. I am not here to censure you." To her surprise he joined her.

"I was just about to return."

"You looked like you were sleeping. Was your journey very taxing?"

This was her brother. She saw something of Max and Rory in him. The height and breadth of his shoulders. His hair and jaw too. A duke, a nobleman who had likely been born in a bed three times the size of hers. A man with ancestors that formed a long and illustrious line. How was it possible they were related? And yet knowing her mother, she could understand why. She and the late duke appeared to be kindred spirits in temperament, from Rory's description of the man.

"It was fine, thank you."

"I doubt that, as my brothers tell me you arrived exhausted."

"Traveling with a small child is never easy, your Grace."

"James. Very true. My children constantly test my fortitude."

Somehow she doubted much unsettled this man.

"What ship did you come across on?"

"Ah, I don't remember the name." She was reluctant to tell him she had arrived on Harry Sinclair's ship.

"I understand that meeting us has come as a shock to you, Maddie. I hope you don't mind me calling you that, but your brothers always have, and so I have come to think of you that way."

"Of course."

"Has Max told you how we met?"

She shook her head, keeping her eyes focused on the austere painting of Devonshire Sinclairs great-great-grandfather.

"When we first crossed paths, I did not know he was my brother. In fact, he was very much like you; he thought himself not good enough to be near me. Rory, too, reacted that way, as did both Emily and Rose."

"You have to understand that my life has been vastly different from this."

"I understand that, Maddie, but I'd like to explain some things to you if you would give me a few minutes of your time."

"Of course."

He had a nice voice. Not gruff, but calm. It was soothing, for all she'd never spent time with someone who spoke in such an educated way or was only a few steps down from royalty in the eyes of many. *A brother.*

"Our father was not a good man, and while I was born to wealth, I was not always happy. My life did not start until I found Samantha, and only then because of Eden."

"I don't understand. If she is your sister, how is it you found her?"

"Our father did not tell me about her. I found out after he died. When I met Eden, I was angry and confused and my sister hurting from the cruelty she'd suffered. When I married the woman I loved and began to collect siblings, I truly began to understand the meaning of love and family. I had nothing until then. Money and status, yes, but nothing more."

"I'm sorry you suffered, your Grace."

"I am your brother, therefore I really would like you to call me James."

"I will try."

"I did not tell you those things for sympathy, Maddie. I told you so you understand that I know what it is to suffer. I know how loneliness feels. You are of my blood, Maddie, and it is my wish that you never suffer again."

"How do you know I have suffered?" Her throat felt tight suddenly.

"Your brothers suffered, so it stands to reason you have also."

"Oh dear." She pressed a fist to her lips to stop the sob escaping. She didn't like crying; it achieved little but red eyes and a scratchy throat.

"It's my hope that if there is any suffering in your future, which there will likely be as it's the way of things, that you are surrounded by your family—me and the others, people who love and will support you."

He wore a large ring on the middle finger that was rested on his knees, and it was this she focused on. Huntingtons did not show weakness; they'd learned that lesson early, at the hands of their mother, and yet in that moment she could cry like a babe.

Too much emotion.

"I wish that for Fleur," Maddie said carefully.

"But not for you?"

Sometimes she felt she'd lived a hundred years, and none but a few had been easy. Her soul felt stained when she thought of the things she had done to survive. Until recently, she'd believed she'd never have to do such things again.

How wrong I was.

"Everyone needs to be loved, Maddie."

"And Fleur loves me."

"Do you not believe you are worthy of more love?" He looked at her with those steady gray eyes.

I am not worthy.

Looking at the elegantly dressed duke beside her, then the duck egg blue walls, it seemed almost unreal that she was here, when days ago she'd been in her house fighting for survival.

"I am unsure this life is for me, your Grace."

"James."

"I was not born to it, neither do I understand it."

"There is little to understand actually. It's merely the life you lived with a great deal more comfort and happiness. Your brothers have grown to love it, therefore I would ask that at least you give it some time before you decide it is not for you."

"I will try."

"Then that is all I can ask of you."

They sat in silence for a while, and it was surprisingly comfortable, considering where she was and who was with her.

"Should you wish to live somewhere else, there are other estates in our family and a drafty castle. It was there I met the Sinclairs, but that is a story for another day, as I fear you have already had too much thrust at you."

"My house was a small cottage in the country." Maddie wanted him to understand why this life was so strange to her. "We lived far from town, and half a day's trip to the nearest village."

"How did you survive after your husband passed?"

She'd answered the door when she shouldn't have and let the devil back into her life.

"We carried on living as we'd always done." *Without Jacques and Rory.* And for a while, she'd believed her mother had changed, gullible fool that she was.

"We are a close happy family now, Maddie, who welcome you and Fleur into our midst. But don't think things have been easy for any of us. The Raven and Sinclair families have suffered. Some more than others, but that is for them to tell you. Know this, though: I will always love each and every one of you and support you all in any way that I can."

The lump in her throat nearly choked her.

"You don't know me or what I am capable of." Those words had not come out as she'd planned. "I mean, I am different."

"I don't know you, you're right, but I know our brothers and what they have told me of you. I know it's hard to let go of what you've always believed. Let go of a past fraught with pain and anger, because here with us you are safe."

"I want to believe that." The words left her mouth before she could stop them.

He turned slightly, his eyes looking down at her. Maddie kept hers forward.

"Will you tell me what you fear?"

Maddie looked at her chipped nails. She was as different as night is to day from the man beside her. He talked about suffering, and possibly he had, but when it had been long and enduring, something inside you broke, and she didn't think it was repairable. She was damaged in so many ways, and not worthy of this man's company.

"I fear nothing."

"I am terrified of spiders."

She laughed as he'd meant her to.

"But like your other brothers, my shoulders are broad should you ever wish to confide in me, sister. You are no longer alone, and Fleur will be loved as all our children are."

"I want that for her, and she will adjust better than I, I'm sure."

"We are here to help you with that transition, Maddie."

"Hello." Max was now at the bottom of the stairs. "I wondered where you two had gone."

Like Rory, this brother had happiness radiating off him. She swallowed down the resentment that he had been living this life while she had not.

"We are getting to know each other, brother."

"Wonderful." Max climbed the stairs and sat on the one below Maddie, and suddenly she was trapped. The only escape route was up.

"I should go and check on Fleur."

"She is fine. I just saw her on Warwick's back as he galloped down the hallway. She is happy."

Fleur was happy. Maddie had done everything she could to ensure that happened and failed many times.

"What are you discussing?"

"Us, living here. How this is an adjustment for Maddie."

"Do you wish to leave?" Max looked at her.

"I don't know yet. I wanted to visit and for Fleur to see her family—"

"Where would you go if not here with us?" Max asked. "Surely not France. There is nothing for you there now."

"I don't know. It is too soon to make that decision. But eventually I will find work, and we will—"

"No, that will not happen. You and Maddie will stay here with us now. We have plenty, there is no need for you to work."

"Max," James cautioned.

"What I do is not your concern, Max." Her brother's jaw was set in that way she remembered. It meant he would not be moved.

"It is everything to do with me. You arrive in worn and old clothes with little but a single bag, Maddie. I saw the desperation etched in your face, and it broke my heart that I had left you to suffer. I believed you happy with your husband, and now I wonder why you weren't."

"I was tired from traveling and nothing more. Jacques was a good man, but we did not have this, what you have."

"And you resent me for that."

"I don't." Maddie sighed. "Mine was a good life until my husband's death."

"And then?"

James sat silently at her side, listening as the Huntington siblings talked.

"It matters not, as it is in the past."

"It matters to me," Max said softly. "I will not have you living in poverty when there is no need. You or your daughter. Surely Fleur deserves a better life?"

And that touched on the worry she'd battled since her husband's death. How would she support her daughter? How would she keep her safe?

"Your life is here now, Maddie, where you have family. Were anything to happen to you, Fleur would be cared for."

She didn't answer, and Max sighed.

"Just spend time here, sister, and get to know us all."

"I need to go to Fleur. Excuse me." Maddie turned and ran up the stairs and away from her disturbing brothers.

So many thoughts whirled inside her head. Could she stay, knowing what she had done? Would her past deeds follow her? She'd murdered a man and then fled France, and the only person who knew was her mother.

A woman so evil, even Satan could not compete.

CHAPTER 8

Harry whistled softly as he walked along the darkened street. He'd had a meal with his grandmother. Listened as she demanded information about the Sinclair family he had no wish to be part of. He'd dared not mention there was a duke and duchess; she would be unbearable in her need to visit them. When he could stand it no more, he'd left, lying about an appointment he did not have.

Deep in thought, as he'd been for the two days since he'd left Devonshire Sinclair's house, he contemplated his life as he walked the narrow street.

Faris had told him yesterday that his brooding would lead to badly written prose if he didn't take steps to pull himself out of the mood he'd fallen into, which was enough to give him pause. Harry did not get into moods. He knew his path, had set it himself, and never deviated. Those bloody Sinclairs and Ravens were inside his head, and he needed them evicted.

The problem was, no matter how much he fought against it, those people were his family, and he'd always wanted family even though he'd denied that very thing vehemently to Faris. However, he'd promised the man who'd raised him that he'd never have interactions with a Sinclair of his blood.

Harry had hoped to marry one day and have children of his own. They would be the family he'd secretly longed for. He'd never thought his actual family would appear to tilt his world upside down.

He wasn't sure what had him turning right when he needed to go left, and yet here he was. Looking at the sign of the building he was passing, he saw it was Faris's favorite tavern.

The Speckled Hen apparently had the best pies in London, and the ale was excellent also. Perhaps he'd sample some, Harry thought. What other reason could he have to walk along here? Unease trickled down his spine.

He was hungry. Maybe he just needed to eat? Harry did not function well when his stomach was gnawing at him to be fed.

"I blame them," he muttered. Those bloody Ravens and Sinclairs. All chatty and laughing, children and happiness. It was enough to throw a man off his stride, which it had. What he needed to do was leave England and go back to France. Once he was out at sea, everything would return to normal.

His meetings had gone well today… well, two of the three anyway. One had insisted on discussing Maxwell Huntington and that Harry should make contact with the man, as he would be an excellent person for him to have business dealings with.

"You'll be wanting to back away now, gentlemen."

The words came from up ahead. Harry searched the darkness and saw men.

"Well now, see here's the problem with that, governor. I want what's in your pockets. You toffs will have enough on you to make us very happy for quite some time."

"Three against five hardly seems fair numbers."

Harry knew that voice. He walked on quietly.

"We'd hardly have the numbers in your favor, now would we."

"I think you misunderstood me. The numbers are in our favor. Scum like you will go down easily."

"That will do, Cam."

He would know that voice too, if he hadn't already seen Devonshire Sinclair standing beside his brother. Plus, there was the small frisson of awareness that he now associated with his cousins.

Dev and Cam had their backs to him. Another stood with them also, but Harry didn't know his identity.

"I've known you two days, and already you're causing me trouble," Harry said as he joined their line.

"Take them!" one of the men opposite him yelled.

"Harry! Excellent timing, old chap," Cambridge said. Then with a roar he charged.

"Everything is always theatrical with him." Devonshire grunted as a man swung at him. He ducked, but it connected with his shoulder.

Harry had fought many dirty fights, and he could take care of himself, but these were noblemen. He would be bloody and bruised before this was over, as he held out little hope his cousins actually knew how to defend themselves. His job would be to ensure they walked away from here in one piece.

"Move your feet!" he roared as someone swung a beefy fist at Cam. "Hands before your face."

Cambridge swung his leg in a move Harry had never seen, and his foot connected with a man, sending him stumbling backward. "Just because we're gentlemen doesn't mean we're incapable," he added before pulling one of the men off his brother.

The other man was boxing, jabbing his opponent if he got too close. Harry swung and felled his man, then turned for another.

The fight was fierce, and the thud of flesh had him ducking and swaying. Dropping his man again, he spun to help his cousins. They were watching him, no longer fighting. Harry looked around for their opponents and saw they were groaning on the ground.

"Finish him, Nicholas!" Cam yelled.

The man he now knew as Nicholas was still boxing; he jabbed with his left, then shot out with his right, and his man staggered back, fell over one of the other men, and landed in a heap.

"You can't really say that was a knockout though, Nicholas," Cam said. "He tripped and fell."

"It bloody well was a knockout." Nicholas wiped the back of his mouth on his cuff. "I dropped him, and I'll have words with you if you say different."

"Perhaps this discussion could be undertaken in a more congenial atmosphere?" Lord Sinclair said.

"What the bloody hell are you lot doing in this street at this hour!" The words exploded from Harry.

They ignored him and started walking. He was forced to run to catch them.

"Harry, this is Nicholas. He is Lilly's brother and wed to Alice, your cousin," Dev said, looking like he had walked out of a ballroom and not a brawl.

"It's like looking at you and Wolf." Nicholas's eyes swung from Dev to Harry.

"He also has a rather nifty way with children."

"Nifty?" Nicholas raised a brow at Cam's words.

"Thank you, I don't think we need elaborate further," Harry added.

"Left, Harry. There is a large pile of something unpleasant

ahead."

Adjusting his steps, he did as Cam said, as now he could see the unpleasant pile of something.

"Explain to me, if you please, why you are here so far from home and what just happened?" Harry gritted out.

"We were in a fight." Cam smiled. "I do enjoy a good mill when no one has weapons. Perhaps don't tell our wives, however."

Devon and Nicholas grunted their agreement.

"But why were you here at this hour? Surely there is some social engagement you should be attending?" Harry looked at the men as they left the street and entered a busier one. There was lamp lighting here. "This is really not a place for the likes of you three."

"Us three?" Nicholas said politely.

"Are noblemen only allowed to socialize then?" Devon asked. "Are there certain parameters we should stay within? I had not realized this."

"He did seem to think we couldn't look after ourselves in a fight," Cambridge said. "Clearly his opinion of us is unflattering."

"Well, it took me a while to like you," Nicholas said.

"There is that. And you weren't exactly on any guest list of mine." Cambridge looked at Nicholas. "There was that annoyingly noxious habit you had after all."

Were they serious? Speaking as if the last few minutes had not happened, making light of the entire situation when even now those men could have been robbing them or worse? Okay, Harry had to concede they did appear to know how to look after themselves, but still.

"That I was an inebriated gambling wastrel with little or no sense?" Nicholas said.

"The very one."

"Why are you here?" Harry spoke the words louder this

time.

"We just had pies," Cam said.

"Pies?"

"The Speckled Hen has the best peas and kidney. We always stop there."

"Are there not pies closer to your homes? Can your cooks or chefs not create them for you so you are not thrust into dangerous situations?"

"Ah, I see the problem here," Devon added. "It's that business we discussed at my house. The noblemen behaving differently issue."

"What?" Cam's nose wrinkled. "God's blood, what is that stench?" Taking the handkerchief Dev held out, he pressed it to his nose.

"I don't envy him his sense," Nicholas said. "All those revolting scents about the place daily."

"Do you have one?" Harry asked the question before he could stop himself. He'd sworn to keep his distance from these men.

"I have visions about things that have happened, will happen, or need to happen."

"That can't be easy."

"No, but now I have this lot to help me, it is much more so."

"Come, we may need another pie now, as I just exercised and am once again hungry," Cam said.

"You ate two pies," Nicholas said.

"And? I did not have the apple one, so I shall try that now."

"I will leave, now you are safe." Harry turned. A hand on his shoulder turned him back.

"Get inside the Speckled Hen, Harry," Devonshire Sinclair said.

"I don't take direction from you, my lord."

"I'm not sure why you'd be any different; we're constantly forced to take direction from him," Cam muttered, entering the tavern. "It's our cross to bear."

"However, it is not mine," Harry snapped.

"Please come and have a pie with us, Harry," Devon said. "I do tend to dictate, but in my defense, someone has to lead this rabble."

"All true," Nicholas said, following Cam.

He nodded because he was hungry, as his grandmother had served him bite-sized morsels that would barely fill an infant's belly. It was his choice to enter the Speckled Hen, not theirs. A final drink would not hurt anyone, least of all him, and he could then leave and never see them again.

The interior was dark, the lamps doing little more than provide ambience. The hum of voices greeted them as they moved to a table.

"Back so soon, my lovelies?"

"We missed you, Hetty." Cam smiled at the waitress.

"Well now, that's sweet, and yet I know it's my pies that lure you back here, Cambridge Sinclair. Since you put that ad in your paper, we've been busy."

"I'm glad, and you deserve to be busy."

"Cam owns a paper," Dev explained.

Cam owned a paper. These people were full of surprises.

An order was placed, and Harry found his mouth was watering for the taste of pie.

"Harry is of the opinion that those who frequent society should behave as gentlemen. I think it's fair to say we are not conforming."

Harry could feel his collar tightening at Dev's words. Cam and Nicholas started laughing.

"He really has no idea about us then," Nicholas said when he could speak.

"Let me enlighten you, Harry," Devon said. "James,

Nicholas, and Lilly possibly have the bluest blood, so you are right about them."

"Oh now, I protest," Nicholas said.

"The stories of my family are not all mine to tell, but our story, that of the Sinclair siblings, was not an easy one. We were extremely poor—"

"And I was set on ruination through gambling and alcohol," Cam said.

"Like me," Nicholas added.

"Wolf was in the army, and nearly lost his life."

"Forgive me, I did not mean to judge you." Harry's words were clipped.

"Yes, you did. You're a snob, is what you are, Harry, but we shall set you to rights," Cam added.

"I have no wish to be set to rights, and I am no snob."

"It's reverse snobbery. There has been plenty of that in the family too."

He felt the words had some accuracy, as they had him wanting to shuffle in his seat. His father had convinced him peers were a shoddy lot of people not to be trusted.

"Maddie is the same," Cam said. "Won't unbend around any of us. She is convinced we are not for her and her life should be spent elsewhere."

"The woman I met the other day?" Harry said the words casually.

"The very one. There is a story there, and Max and Rory believe the same. She is scared and running, but as yet no one knows what from."

She'd been scared the day he'd first seen her, and heartbreakingly alone. Harry could clearly remember the vision of her holding Fleur in Calais.

"I'm sure her brothers will look after her."

"They will, but if there is an enemy, it is important to know from which direction it comes," Nicholas said. "Mind you, this family has faced its share of those. I'm sure they'll be ready."

He didn't want to think of her in danger; in fact, the thought made him nauseous.

"All we need now is for Harry to save Maddie and then the rest will fall into place," Cam said, then got an elbow in the ribs from Dev, which Harry doubted would shut him up.

"Tell me about this supposed marriage ritual?" He said the words out of curiosity, as he would not be marrying any woman of Raven blood, especially not the disturbing Madeline Caron.

"Our senses came about many years ago when a powerful Raven was saved by a lowly Sinclair," Dev said.

"Of course, we are no longer lowly," Cam added.

"King Edward III gave the Sinclair land, Oak's Knoll, our family land, and it sits at the base of Raven Castle. The heightened senses, we understand, developed from there as the Sinclairs became protectors of the Ravens."

"It is hard to believe," Harry said.

"Throughout history, there are records of Sinclairs saving Ravens."

"They're bloody reckless, is what they are," Cam muttered. "Eden saved James from drowning, and Dev saved him during the war. Essie pulled a bullet out of Max. I saved Em from drowning."

"Alice saved me from being attacked by men," Nicholas added.

"The list goes on, but the other twist to the tie we have is that Sinclairs marry Ravens. That is why I asked if you'd saved Maddie, as it then follows you'll likely marry her," Cam said.

They were looking at him, so Harry kept his expression blank. No way did he want it known that he'd saved Maddie and Fleur already.

"I'm afraid I must disillusion you there. I will be returning to France, so there will be no chance to save her, or indeed wed her."

"What color are they, Dev?" Nicholas asked.

"Color?"

"The colors we see, Harry. It's my belief you should marry only another of your color, then the union will be a strong one."

Dear Christ.

"What colors are they, just out of curiosity." Cam's eyes were deadly serious now as they locked on Harry's.

"I have not seen the shade before. They are both a deep shade of lavender." Dev was watching him closely too.

"Well, entertaining though this has been, gentlemen, I must go. I may not see you again, as my ship is due to sail shortly, so have, ah, have a good life." His chest was so tight, he could barely draw in a breath.

She had his colors.

"You wish to spend your life alone then, with no family?" These words came from Nicholas. "Believe me, if that is your sole focus, then I feel sorry for you. I was once like you, believing I needed no one and knew best. My sister suffered because of it."

"I need no one." Harry backed away. One thing he'd always vowed to do was never betray his father, and if he joined this family, he would be doing just that.

"His father told him never to trust a Sinclair and made him promise to never associate with us," Devonshire said, his piercing green eyes focused intently on Harry. "A father's wishes are heavy burdens to carry, indeed."

Amen, Harry thought as he left the men at a sprint. He would be leaving London now, as soon as it could be arranged. This was more than he could cope with. Family, colors. *She could never be anything to him.*

CHAPTER 9

Madeline could not deny knowing Fleur's tummy was full and that she slept in a warm and dry bed each night was a wonderful thing. Of course, when Jacques had lived she'd had that, just not to the degree or grandeur as now.

Her husband had been a good provider. They'd lived in the small cottage that his parents had once owned. But after his death, everything had changed. His brothers had wanted her to leave, but could not force her to do so, as Jacques had ensured she could stay. She had used most of their money before her mother had arrived, and then everything changed once more.

She was safe here.

She also couldn't deny that now the danger had eased, she was able to breathe deeply. The tightness in her chest no longer kept her awake at night.

And then there were the people she now called family. Over the seven days she'd been in London, she had tried to understand more about this new family she had. Sisters and another brother.

They wanted her to be part of their lives, and deep inside, she was coming to the realization she wanted that too. But Maddie feared one day what she'd left behind would catch up with her. The uncertainty was terrifying. She could feel the happiness within her grasp, but was scared to take it.

"Mama!" Fleur was running around Max's garden with Myrtle and Bran. The sky was cloudless, the sun showering them in warmth. She was happy; well, as happy as she could be with the cloud of worry that hung over her.

"She is happy today."

Looking over her shoulder, Maddie watched Kate Sinclair approach. Dark like the rest of the family, with those amazing green eyes, she was a lovely woman, and someone that made her brother very happy. They were to be married in a few weeks.

"Good morning, Kate. Fleur is having a wonderful time."

She wore a cream dress with blue satin ribbons around the bodice and hem. Her bonnet was blue, as were her shoes. She looked young, happy, and carefree. Maddie often believed she'd been born old and jaded.

"Kate!" Fleur's little legs pumped as she ran at the woman.

In only a few days, Fleur had come to love this family they'd landed in the middle of. She loved that they got down on her level and played with her. The other children had accepted her. Of course there were squabbles, but for all that, in the week she'd been here she had adjusted better than her mother had.

"Hello, Maddie." Rose and Emily appeared.

Sisters.

"Good morning." Maddie got to her feet and fought with herself not to curtsey. Both were dressed elegantly, as Kate was, and she, well, shabby was really the only word she could come up with.

Rory and Max had tried to buy her new dresses, and yet

she'd said she wasn't ready yet. Why? She was being stubborn and irrational for no other reason than Maddie had always controlled her own life, and now someone else wanted a hand in that.

"We would like you to come shopping with us today?" Rose said, leaning close to kiss Maddie on the cheek. She fought not to back away. These people were touchers, which was hard when you'd never been one. It was just one of the things that disturbed her in a list of many.

"I have no need of anything, but thank you."

Emily did not kiss her cheek, she just took Maddie's hand and gave it a gentle squeeze.

"We are celebrating, and I wished to do that with my sisters. Except Samantha, who is helping the twins in their office."

They were starting an investigative service. Maddie wasn't sure why the elder Sinclairs were allowing this, but nonetheless it was happening. The three youngest siblings would be open for business shortly.

Maddie had come to realize the Sinclair and Raven families were not normal. Cam and Emily ran a newspaper called the *Trumpeter*, and everyone else had business interests. They did not behave in the ways she believed noblemen should.

"What are you celebrating?"

"I am to have another child." Emily's smile was radiant. "Cam is strutting around the house crowing like a cockerel."

"Congratulations," Maddie said, genuinely pleased for this gentle woman.

Most of the families were loud and boisterous. Emily and Essie seemed the quietest, and it was those two Maddie felt most comfortable with.

"And I wish to go shopping with my sisters to celebrate. Plus, we will take tea in Rose's place."

"Rose's place?" Maddie looked at her sister. She was beautiful, her skin soft and creamy. Her pale green dress suited the red/gold of her hair. Even her lovely Scottish burr was easy to listen to.

"A teashop. The cakes there are excellent. It was where I worked," Rose said.

That shocked her momentarily.

"We were not all born in large beds with servants dancing attendance on us, Maddie. I thought you knew that?"

"I knew that some of you have had things happen in your past, but not what."

"Our stories would surprise you, and when you are ready to hear them, you will see that."

Rose had worked in a tea shop.

"So we will be off. Ah, perfect timing, here is Rory. He will take Fleur to play at Dev and Lilly's with the other children," Emily said.

"I have no wish to go shopping, Emily."

"And yet you will." Rory walked by her to Fleur and Kate. He then ran a hand down his fiancée's spine before picking up his niece and throwing her in the air. The shrieks were piercing. "Now, your mother is going shopping, and you're coming with me to Uncle Dev's house."

"Uncle Dev!" Fleur yelled, making him wince. "Bye bye." Fleur planted a loud kiss on Maddie's cheek.

"And I have no say in this? She is my child. I-I have always cared for her." Did that sound petulant? Maddie thought it likely did.

"And now you have us," Rory said. "We will see you later."

He'd gone before she could stop him.

"Come." Emily took one arm and Rose the other, and they were soon walking.

She didn't say anything further, just let them lead her back into the house.

Her bonnet was already waiting in the hands of a maid, as

were her gloves, so there was little she could do to waylay the inevitable. Minutes later, she was in the carriage.

"It won't be painful, Maddie, I promise."

"I have never been fitted for a dress before," she blurted out.

Rose clapped her hands, clearly excited. "How wonderful then, that we shall be there for the first time."

"I had never been fitted for a dress either before I went to live with James and Samantha. You see, I am an illegitimate offspring of the late Duke of Raven, Maddie, just as you, Rory, and Max are. I was raised in poverty."

"I'm sorry, Emily."

"And while it took me a while to adjust, I now have this family and Cam. I know this is hard for you, and the change so different from the life you've lived, but in time you will see it is worth it, Maddie."

It had surprised her that quiet Emily was married to the boisterous Cambridge Sinclair. Yet she could not doubt the love they clearly shared.

"Both Rory and I are very happy you will be here for our wedding, Maddie. He talks of you constantly, as does Max," Kate said. "Unfortunately, I was not raised in poverty, but my mother can be extremely trying, if that helps."

That had them laughing.

"I am so pleased you are marrying Rory." And she was. Her brother deserved happiness; they all did. Was there a small kernel inside her that actually believed that?

"Excellent! Well, you need a new dress for the wedding then," Kate said, opening the carriage door once it had stopped. "Come along, let us go shopping."

Maddie had been to Paris, she knew what fashionable ladies did and saw, but that was many years ago, and she'd never actually been into a fashion boutique.

"It will be fun, I promise. We will order some things for

Fleur also." Kate took her arm. "Rory wants you to do this, Maddie."

"We must walk up this lane, as the carriage will not be able to turn around down here. Madame Alexander's is a wonderful boutique with excellent seamstresses," Rose said.

The shop they wanted had a French look to it with a pretty shade over the window in lemon and green. A sign was written in gold denoting the name.

Inside it was bustling, and looking at the women present, Maddie wanted to slink into the background. Her dress looked shabby in such company.

"Hannah, how wonderful to see you," Kate said as an elegant dark-haired woman approached. Her skin was the color of milk, and she was exquisitely beautiful.

"Hello, ladies," the woman greeted them.

"Maddie needs an entire wardrobe, as does her daughter," Rose said.

"Well the seamstresses here will be able to help with that. Phoebe is here also."

"Brace yourself." Emily leaned in to whisper the words to Maddie. "This woman is likely the most beautiful you have ever seen."

A vision appeared in a deep emerald. The dress caressed her lovely figure, and Emily was right, she was exquisite with her honey blonde hair and lovely smile.

"Hello, Emily, Rose, and Kate. How wonderful to see you."

"Phoebe, this is our sister, Maddie. Maddie, this is Lady Levermarch, but we call her Phoebe," Emily said.

Everything about the woman was confident. The way she held herself and her voice. Every inch of her screamed noble birth to Maddie.

"Hello. Are you the one being fitted today?"

Maddie managed to nod.

"Well, you come along with me then. I know the staff here intimately and can expedite matters."

"Oh, well..." Her arm was taken, and she was forcibly yet gently led from the room. "I—ah, don't know what I am in need of," Maddie said when they reached the dressing rooms.

Lady Levermarch looked her up and down. "Everything is my guess, which is wonderful fun. Now don't look scared. My staff have yet to stab anyone and leave a permeant mark."

"Your staff?"

The woman made a tsking sound. "Botheration, I am not meant to bandy it about that I am a partner in this boutique. My husband gets quite snippy when he hears someone discussing the matter. It really is the most unkept secret in London." She laughed, and even that was lovely.

"Now you go in there, Maddie, and strip down to your chemise. I will return with material and pins, which I will try not to stab you with. I will also have that small hole in the back of your dress repaired."

"I did not realize there was one."

"There is." Phoebe nudged her into the dressing room. "I usually make my own clothes and those for my daughter," Maddie said. "This is all new to me, I-I..."Phoebe had been about to leave but stopped.

"I used to make all my own clothes too, and those for my sister. We were ridiculously poor, you see, Maddie. I'm married to a marquess now, which is nice, and I love him to distraction, but I will never forget how much I loved creating."

"You made your own clothes?" Maddie looked at the elegant dress she wore.

"I did. Now my suggestion to you is to stop thinking about the past and enjoy this moment, because there really is nothing quite like being fitted for new dresses. I promise you will enjoy it. And remember, your brothers are obscenely wealthy, and you will not cause their coffers any distress by having a few dresses made."

Maddie could do nothing to stop a nervous giggle at those words.

"Not all nobility are snobs. Some of us can be a great deal of fun." Phoebe then winked, and left with Maddie's dress.

She was fast coming to that realization, considering who she was now related to.

The materials were so soft, and the styles suggested beyond anything Maddie had ever believed she'd wear. Her clothes would not be serviceable but stylish. She could not stop the little shiver of excitement that ran through her.

Rose, Kate, and Emily were called upon to look as Maddie was draped in fabrics. Laces and trims were produced, and the number of dresses that were ordered was astonishing.

She tried to protest, but her heart was not in it. Phoebe had been right; this was fun.

"Oh, dear." Lady Levermarch appeared in the dressing room with Maddie's dress in her hand. There was a tear down the back of her dress now.

"What has happened, Phoebe?" Kate asked from beyond the curtain.

"What will I wear?" Maddie looked at the dress in horror. Visions of her walking about London in a chemise filled her head.

"Fear not, Maddie. I have a dress that a client ordered. It was the incorrect sizing."

"I can't—"

Phoebe disappeared before she could finish the sentence.

The dress was pale gray, almost silver, and had a black satin ribbon that tied beneath the bodice. Black flowers were embroidered into the hem and cap sleeves. It was so beautiful, she dared not touch it.

"I-I can't have that."

"You can, as the woman no longer wants it," Phoebe insisted. "Raise your arms, Maddie."

"I really don't think—"

"Thinking is vastly overrated." Phoebe cut her words off as she lowered the dress over Maddie's shabby chemise. It fell in a soft fall of cool, expensive material and settled around her body.

"Just a little loose, but hardly noticeable." Phoebe studied her. "But the color suits you."

She refused to cry as she looked in the mirror. How could a simple dress change the way she looked?

"Those boots need to go, and you need new bonnets, stockings, and undergarments also."

"They are next, Phoebe," Rose said from beyond the curtain.

Her brown bonnet looked so drab with the beautiful creation that Maddie didn't want to put it on, and yet knew she must.

"Now you go on, and I'll get the girls working on the rest of your things," Phoebe said, bundling her old dress into a ball and putting it under her arm. "This will be disposed of. And remember, Maddie, it is all right to enjoy what we've never had."

"I don't know how to thank you. I have said that so much lately." Maddie sniffed. "But I mean it, this is the most beautiful dress I have ever worn, Phoebe."

Phoebe simply patted her arm and swept the curtain aside.

"Oh my," Kate whispered.

Emily and Rose looked at her in awe.

"It's beautiful, Maddie, but you really must have a new bonnet to go with it," Kate said. "Come along."

After saying goodbye to Lady Levermarch and Mrs.

Hetherington, they left Madame Alexander's and took the carriage to Bond Street.

Wide-eyed, Maddie allowed Rose, Emily, and Kate to take her into the milliner's next. She choose a simple straw bonnet with a wide black satin ribbon that matched the ones on her dress.

"Change is good, Maddie," Rose said. "When you have been without, it does not mean that has to always be the way."

"Absolutely. There is no point in suffering just for the sake of it," Kate added.

"Is that what I'm doing?"

"Well, you are clinging to what you were when there really is no need. It's all right to embrace this change in your life, Maddie. You deserve it, and there is no reason not to," Kate added.

"I never dreamed of owning anything as beautiful as what I now wear."

She stood there looking in the mirror with her sisters and Kate, a soon-to-be sister, and thought that maybe some change was a good thing.

They went from shop to shop ordering clothes, undergarments, boots and shoes, and things for Fleur.

"No more. I will leave my brother with little money if I continue," Maddie said when she felt it time to stop. She'd purchased so many things, her head spun.

"He will not even notice it," Emily said.

"We are to visit that store there." Rose pointed to a shop that had lace fans in the window. "And then I promise you will have tea."

"Would you mind if I went there?" Maddie pointed to the one across the street. It had so many things in the window, but she'd seen a doll and some books. Her daughter had never owned any toys other than what she'd made her. She just wanted to look; one day she'd ask her brothers to buy Fleur something.

"Of course, and here is some money. Rory gave it to me this morning, but I was waiting for the right moment to give it to you," Kate said, opening the small bag she carried on her arm. A reticule, she'd heard Rose call it in one of the shops they'd entered.

"I don't need it. I was just going to look."

Kate simply removed the little bag from her wrist and handed it to Maddie.

"Go, and stop arguing." She made a shooing motion.

Clutching the bag, Maddie walked across the road, but now her eyes were raised. She looked as others did, and it was a good feeling.

Entering the store, Maddie saw it was crammed full of cabinets and shelves.

"Good day to you."

"Good day." A man stood behind the counter polishing a pewter mug.

"Please feel free to browse, madam."

She found a doll with brown hair like Fleur's that she would love. She then found the children's books. Maddie picked up one with fairies on the front. Opening the first page, she studied the drawings, as she couldn't read the words, and lost herself in the wonder of the pages.

CHAPTER 10

It was his grandmother's birthday tomorrow, and Harry always got her a gift because she reminded him to. A note had arrived this morning written in the bold letters of her companion.

It is my birthday; I expect a gift and your presence. There will be cake.

Harry never wandered aimlessly; in fact, rarely did he do anything aimlessly. Purpose or intent drove him to do things, and yet he had neither at the moment.

Bloody Sinclairs! He blamed them for entering his life and muddling his head.

It was annoying that he, the man who could dismiss things he didn't think were relevant with ease, could not dismiss them. *Because they were important.* He couldn't allow them to be, but as yet had not worked out how to achieve that.

Never trust a Sinclair.

He walked into another shop and out again minutes later, no closer to his goal of obtaining a gift. Looking down at the people before him, he saw Rose, Emily, and Kate Sinclair.

Coward that he was, he ducked into the closest shop to avoid them seeing him.

"Good day to you, sir."

"Good day." He walked past the proprietor and deeper into the long and narrow store. Actually, not a bad place to hide, as there could be something in here for Grandmère. It was one of those shops that had everything from toys to books and small knickknacks.

What are you doing? He was never a coward, and yet here he was avoiding three women who merely wanted to be his friend. One who shared his blood. Three women who had done nothing to him but be nice.

He'd had more headaches lately than he'd had in his lifetime. He was torn, conflicted as to what to do. Loyalty to his father warred with a need to be part of them.

A woman was standing in the book section as he neared that area. Her dress told him she was a lady. Harry looked at the delicate line of her neck as she looked down at the book in her hand. A deep chestnut curl had escaped the confines of her bonnet. The frisson of awareness that ran through had him moving to the left so he could see her face.

She was concentrating, lips moving as her finger moved across the page. Clutched under an arm was a doll.

"Hello, Madeline."

She turned swiftly, clutching the book. He already knew she was beautiful, but that dress and bonnet enhanced it. Her eyes seemed bigger, set in a face that was now flushed with color.

"Is that for Fleur?" He touched the head of the doll.

"Hers is made of rags, Mr. Sinclair. It is time she had a real one." Her chin elevated.

"I was not censuring you, Madeline. It was just a question."

She puffed out a breath. "Forgive me, and yes, it is for Fleur. She will love it."

Harry had never had a reaction to a woman like he had with this one. Was it simply because of how he'd found her that day? He'd felt protective of her, and that was a foreign emotion for him. Madeline Caron was fragile, even if she fought hard not to show it.

"Fairies, I'm sure, are popular for small girls," he said, looking at the book she clutched in her hands.

She nodded.

"Were you reading it to check its suitability?"

"I, ah, no."

"Do you like fairy tales also?"

She looked at the book, then back at him. Her eyes hid something from him.

"It looks like something a young girl would like."

"How would you know that?" She looked suspicious, and Harry had a feeling this woman did not trust easily. As he was the same, he couldn't fault her for that.

"It has fairies on it."

She looked at the book again. "I can't read." The words were flat and emotionless.

He was an idiot. Not everyone could read, he knew that, and yet he'd just made her uncomfortable.

"May I?" He pointed to the book, and she handed it to him. Opening it, he positioned it so she could see the pages and began to read. She listened carefully, her eyes following his finger as it moved over the words. This was how his tutor had taught him when he was a boy. When he was done, he closed it and handed it back to her.

"Thank you. I know a few letters and a word or two but have wanted to learn to read for some time. I-I had to make up stories for Fleur."

"I'm sure in that large family you have joined, someone could teach you, Maddie."

"Perhaps."

"But pride stops you from asking?"

"It is my cross to bear." Her smile was small but genuine. She seemed different today; the tension inside her had eased a little, Harry thought. "Strength was important to me and sometimes to my detriment."

Her candid reply surprised him.

"Being strong can never be a detriment."

"If it stops you from taking what is offered it is."

"I think that is called pride, Maddie."

Another small smile lit her lovely eyes.

"You look beautiful."

"Thank you. My sisters and sister-in-law-to-be thought it was time."

"Time?"

"To no longer wear my old clothes."

"You were beautiful before, Maddie; this dress simply enhances that."

Her face was close to his. Their eyes locked and held. He should walk away; it would be the sensible thing to do.

"I need to go," she whispered.

"I know." Everything he'd just told himself about her being vulnerable was forgotten as Harry leaned in and took her lips. Brief and so sweet. He wanted to pull her into his arms and take more.

"No." She backed away. "You should not have done that, and I'm not sure why you would."

She was right, he shouldn't have, but it would have taken several men to stop him. He'd been desperate to taste her lips, and now he knew how soft they'd felt beneath his, Harry cursed himself for allowing his impulses to get the better of him.

"Forgive me; I should not have done that. Your beauty captivated me."

"I am beautiful now I have a new dress and hat?" Her brows were nearly joined in the middle as she frowned at him.

"No, you were beautiful before, as I believe I have already stated."

"When?"

"What do you mean, when?"

"We barely know each other, Mr. Sinclair, and I was certainly not beautiful when I arrived in Calais dirty and weary with a child in my arms. I fail to see how you could believe otherwise."

"Maddie—"

"I will not be toyed with because I am a widow."

"I beg your pardon?" *Where the hell had that come from?*

"I have met men like you before." She was angry now.

"I have no idea what you are alluding to, but as it sounds unflattering, I assure you that stopping now is your best course."

"Don't threaten me."

"It was a simple kiss." *Which had nothing simple about it.*

"And do you do that often, simply kiss strange women?"

"Of course I don't kiss strange women!"

"Then don't do it with me ever again."

"I'm sorry, but you did not seem overly upset with my actions at the time. In fact, you leaned into me. Had you pulled away, then I would not have kissed you."

"So it's my fault?"

Harry sighed, as it seemed to fit the moment.

"I-I am not a loose woman."

"I don't believe I mentioned you were, and you are overreacting to a simple kiss, which I assure you I now regret."

"I have nothing further to say to you." She walked away from him.

He followed because it was the only way out of the shop and he wanted to. She was fighting with the ties of her reticule, attempting to open it when he arrived. Harry wrestled the little bag from her and untied the knot, then handed it back.

"I could have done that."

"Possibly, but as the proprietor does not have all day, I expedited matters for him."

She shot him a look that would drop any man to his knees, then muttered something that he thought may have been thank you but also could have been an insult, as it was not clear.

The proprietor told her how much the doll and book were, and she looked blankly at the notes now in her hands. Harry took two out and handed them to the man.

"Thank you."

With the package now under her arm, she left the shop. He followed.

"I bet that tasted sour on the way out of your mouth?"

"Manners are important, and sometimes all we have to differentiate us from animals."

"Are you suggesting I'm an animal, Madeline?"

"Go away, Mr. Sinclair."

"But I find you are such good company."

"Harry!"

He tensed as his eyes fell on the three women he'd been hoping to avoid. One of them had called to him. Placing a hand on Maddie's back, he escorted her to them, as he could no longer avoid the meeting. Her spine was so stiff, it was likely to shatter. She increased her pace to escape his touch.

"You can go now," she said out of those lush lips that had tasted of nectar. "Before we reach the others."

"I will say hello." Which he'd tried to avoid not long before. "It would be rude not to."

"Yes, let's not be rude."

"Stop being petty, Maddie." He nudged her the last few feet.

"Madeline," she snapped.

"I like Maddie," he said to be perverse.

"Harry." Kate looked pleased to see him, which should not make him feel warm all over.

Emily and Rose were at her side and looked equally as happy. They rushed forward, and he was greeted by each. Hands patted his arm and his cheek was kissed as if they had been doing this to him for many years.

Their brothers and husbands must be treated to this daily. He refused to be jealous.

"What has you out here, Harry, walking along Bond Street?"

"I have business nearby."

Maddie stood back slightly now, clearly uncomfortable after their kiss.

He watched two men cross beside her. They raised their hats, and Maddie was completely oblivious. He felt the ridiculous urge to smile.

She has your colors. He frowned instead.

"We have just ordered new dresses and clothes. It has been a happy morning, Harry, and now we are going to the offices to see how the renovations are going, and then tea."

"Offices?"

"Come, we will show you," Kate said.

He saw the horse rear from the corner of his eye, and in seconds he had Maddie in his arms, pulling her to safety before the animal could land on her.

"Control that beast!" he roared at the man who rode it.

Apologies were quickly uttered, and Rose, Kate, and

Emily let the man know they were not impressed with his negligent behavior.

"Are you all right, Maddie?" He could feel the rapid beat of her heart against his chest; it matched his own. Their eyes met, and Harry felt it again, the savage bite of need he had when she was near.

"I am, thank you. It seems you are always saving me."

All we need now is for Harry to save Maddie.

Christ! He released her and moved away. "Perhaps you should be more aware of your surroundings in the future, Mrs. Caron."

Her eyes told him she was surprised by his words, but Harry's only defense against her was to put distance between them mow.

"How was I to know that horse would rear?"

"Yes, well, had I not been watching, you would have been trampled."

"Which is hardly my fault, as I cannot control what others do!" She was frowning again.

"Well now, that was unsettling, but no harm done." Kate slipped her arm through Harry's before he could escape. Rose and Emily fussed around their sister.

"Let's go," Kate added.

"That man will be more careful going forward, I vow," Rose said.

"Yes, we certainly told him." Emily giggled. She then took Maddie's and Rose's arms and fell in behind.

"I think it best I get on," Harry protested. His efforts were futile, as Kate simply kept walking.

"Oh, but it is so lovely to see you again, Harry. We missed you."

"You don't know me."

"And yet we want to."

He gave up. "I shall escort you there and then leave." This

would be the absolute last time he spent in the company of a Sinclair. "What are the offices for?"

"Warwick, Dorrie, and Somer are going to start an investigative service."

Harry stopped walking. He got a prod in the back from Rose, so he continued on.

"Pardon?"

"They have had a few friends they've helped out, and have decided that with their senses they can help many more people. Nothing dangerous, as Dev would have conniptions, but they are going to have this office so people will know where to go for help."

"Surely that is not safe? You say they will not take on dangerous cases, but how can you be sure, and couldn't any investigative enquiry turn dangerous?"

"They will be watched, believe me. You do know who their brothers and sisters are, after all. There are also the Ravens and plenty of cousins," Kate said.

"Apparently there are many peers in need of investigative services for various things," Emily said. "Dev has a contact at the Watch who will work closely with them also. Plus, there is Mr. Spriggot, who has an investigative business the families use often. He has promised to send a few of the easier cases their way."

Harry actually shook his head. "I cannot believe—"

"And here we are," Kate said stopping before a narrow brick building. "In you go, Harry."

"I will leave now, Kate." He had seen who was waiting in the offices and had no wish to encounter yet more Sinclairs.

"I never took you for a coward, Harry."

"You don't know me," he said again.

"I do, as you are exactly like Wolf and Dev. Hard to move when set on a course. I would even dare to say obstinate." Kate kissed his cheek and then disappeared into the building.

"I am not obstinate," he muttered.

"In you go, Harry." Rose prodded him in the back again, which had him turning to face her. Maddie was looking at the building and avoiding his eyes.

"How is Ruben?"

Her smile was sweet. "He is much better, thank you, and stop changing the subject."

"I don't believe we were discussing anything."

"The twins would love for you to come and join us inside, Harry. Please think about it."

"I will come shortly," he lied. In fact, he wanted to run in the opposite direction.

"I hope you do," Emily said, passing him to enter the building.

"There may be cream cakes up there, Harry," Rose said. "Come on, Maddie."

"I should get back to Fleur."

"The carriage will arrive soon, but until then there is no way to return, so come and have a look."

"There is always walking," Maddie said, not moving an inch. "And that is something I am used to."

"I understand that, but as there is a carriage coming, there is no need. Fleur is having fun with her uncles, and you are having fun with us. Now come along." Rose waved Maddie to follow behind her as she entered the building.

Harry would go inside, say hello, and then leave and not return. He turned to face Maddie. She was frowning again.

"If I promise not to kiss you again unless you ask, will you stop frowning, Maddie?"

"That will never happen. I am a widow, and it is not right to do so."

"Kiss or stop frowning?"

"Both." Her eyes were still on the building.

"Just so I'm clear. Because you are a widow, you will never again kiss a man, especially me?"

"I have a daughter."

"And still I don't understand."

"You don't need to," she snapped.

"Very well." He wasn't going to push her, as he'd already come to the decision that kissing this woman again would be foolhardy in the extreme. "In you go, before they come looking for you."

"If I must, then so must you."

"I'm not sure where that is written or why you want me to when you just asked me to keep my distance."

"Well, certainly not anywhere I have read, as you know," she said, passing him. "And as I will never ask you to kiss me, I think I am safe."

"I do believe that was humor, Maddie."

"I am not cast in stone, Mr. Sinclair."

"Harry."

She had a stillness about her that he hadn't seen in the other women she accompanied. Madeline Caron never spoke unless necessary—or unless he'd kissed her. And then she had plenty to say.

She walked with a straight back, hands at her sides. Controlled and contained. Once they reached the top of the steps, they entered a room filled with people.

"Do you ever do anything singly?" he found himself asking. "Or are there always at least two of you wherever you venture?"

"Harry, how wonderful," Cam said. "And with Maddie, of all people."

"Safety in numbers," Warwick said.

"It is extremely lucky Harry was with Maddie today, as he saved her from—"

"There is no need—"

"A horse trampling her," Kate said, looking entirely too pleased.

"Saved Maddie, you say?" Cambridge stroked his chin like he was deep in thought and had a beard, when in fact he was clean shaven. Harry thought about punching him so he'd have good reason to cradle it. "Now that's an interesting turn of events."

The door was just inches from where he stood, so once again he left, rudely, without saying goodbye. Well, not entirely true—he did grunt a universal goodbye. The problem was, he turned, and the only person his eyes connected with was her, Madeline Caron, and the small smile on her face told him she knew he was running, possibly because she'd been running too not long ago. He just didn't know why.

CHAPTER 11

"It's the soaking in my special mixture that does the trick, Mrs. Caron. I leave it overnight."

Maddie sipped her tea as she sewed the split seam back together.

"Of course, you also have to boil them to get the stains out of the cloth."

She was sitting in Max and Essie's kitchens chatting with Mrs. Gripe, the housekeeper. Fleur was at the park with Essie and Luke, and she was doing something that had always been a part of her life. Maddie wasn't used to being idle, and here that was how she felt.

Three weeks, she'd been living in this house, and it was getting easier, but there was still wariness between her and Max, and a wariness of this life she was now living. It wasn't comfortable for her yet, but it was getting there.

She wasn't comfortable with servants looking after her—making her bed and cleaning her clothes—as this was something she'd always done herself.

"I used to light the fires in a grand house for a while. My

hands had so many burn marks on them by the end of the day," Maddie said.

Mrs. Gripe hadn't been pleased when Maddie appeared in the kitchen four days ago while she was taking tea with the other staff, but after she'd explained she merely wanted something to do, and why, she had unbent enough to let her do some mending.

"I've heard those Parisians can be quite risqué," Mrs. Gripe said.

"Oh, they can," Maddie agreed. "They wear pantalettes that have lace trim and embroidery beneath their dresses."

"No!" Mrs. Gripe looked suitably scandalized and the kitchen maid, Maisy, wide-eyed.

She dug a few more juicy tidbits from her memory and soon had more gasps coming from the housekeeper.

"Hello, ladies."

Maddie hadn't heard Max approach.

"Mr. Huntington!" Mrs. Gripe looked horrified as he stopped beside the table. She prepared to rise, but he waved her back to their seat.

"Enjoy your tea, Mrs. Gripe, and that delicious-looking cake. I was merely looking for my sister, and here she is."

Maddie noticed the lines at the side of his eyes when he laughed. She'd not seen him laugh often when he lived in France. Picking up the plate of cake, she held it out to him. Max took the largest piece and started eating.

"Is she annoying you?" He nodded to Maddie but spoke to the housekeeper.

"Oh, no indeed. Mrs. Caron has been a great help and sews a neat stitch. Of course, I told her it wasn't necessary she did so, but she insisted."

"I'm sure she did." Max took a bite but kept his eyes on Maddie. "What had you laughing when I arrived?"

"Mrs. Caron was telling us about Parisian society, Mr. Huntington."

"Was she now?"

Maddie knew why he'd raised a brow. She did not often offer conversation when she was with the family upstairs.

"I was just going to the park. Would you like to come with me?" He placed the last piece of cake in his mouth and made a humming noise that had Mrs. Gripe smiling.

"Of course, if you wish."

"Do you wish to?"

"Fleur is in the park, and I would like to see her."

"Then we shall do so."

Maddie nodded. She then placed the sewing she was doing in basket with the others she'd mended.

"Can I just add, that is a superb cake, Mrs. Gripe, and please thank Mrs. Smiley for it. I shall look forward to another slice later."

"I'll be sure to have some sent up on the tea tray, Mr. Huntington."

Maddie said goodbye and headed back upstairs with Max on her heels.

"I shall get my bonnet." She ran past him and to her room. Her room, she thought, walking through the door. It was large, with a big bed and two chairs. The colors were the softest peach and blue, and it was lovely and so far from what she was used to, Maddie was sometimes scared to sit on anything for fear of dirtying it. Fleur had moved to the nursery with Max's children, and loved it there also.

Maddie missed her but knew that this was making her happy. It would be mean of her to stop that happening.

"Are you happy in here?" Max had followed her.

"Thank you, it is very nice."

"But?"

"There is no but. I can never thank you enough for what you have given Fleur and me."

"I don't want your gratitude, Maddie, I want your friendship. I want you to be comfortable here with us, and yet seeing you with Mrs. Gripe, I realized you are far from that. In fact, that is the most relaxed I have seen you since you arrived looking scared and exhausted."

Maddie turned away from those eyes that clearly saw so much. The big brother who had now softened all those hard edges and become a gentleman. A father and a husband.

"This is a very different life for me."

"I understand that, truly I do. But I just want you to talk to me, tell me what you are feeling. Tell me what you left behind. You are closed up so tight, sometimes I fear you will burst."

"I talk to Rory."

"You're comfortable with Rory, but you do not truly talk to him. I know it will take you time to feel comfortable here with us, but it is my hope that you will."

"I am… mostly."

He laughed. "At least that is honesty."

"I do like it here, Max. It is just an adjustment. Before, there was just Fleur and me."

"And now she is being cared for by others, and you struggle with that?"

"It is change, and I am adapting. But this life you lead is as different as night is to day from my life in France. I am adjusting, but it will take time."

"It's my hope that soon you will have no need to go to the kitchens and sew to feel comfortable. You could achieve that state with any one of us."

"I do like it here, Max."

"Well, that is something, then, and pleases me greatly."

Soon they were walking out of the house into another sunny day.

"Will you tell me about your life after you left us, Max?"

"We will take a detour to the park, if you do not mind, Maddie."

"I don't mind."

She listened as he talked, really talked, for perhaps the first time since the day she'd arrived. There was a distance between them, but Maddie thought it was closing. He told her of arriving in England and how he had built his fortune.

"Essie saved me, really, and not just because I was shot and landed in her herb garden. She taught me what was important in life. Taught me that if you open yourself up to the right person, the rewards are vast."

"I'm glad she saved you, Max. She is a wonderful woman."

"She is, and my other half. Did you have that with Jacques? Rory said he was a good man."

"He was, and no, we did not love each other, but there was respect."

"You married him for safety and stability, didn't you, Maddie? To escape the life you'd always led?" Max's face was somber when she looked his way. "I should have come for you sooner, then you need not have wed."

"No. Jacques gave me Fleur and security. I can never regret that."

"Then for that I am glad. But I still should have come for you."

"I was happy." And she had been for a brief time. She'd had what she'd always craved. Safety and a family.

"I just want you to know that I am here for you and Fleur, Maddie, and always will be. I will never abandon you again."

"I understand why you left now, Max, even if it has taken me time to accept that what I always believed was not true."

"We are a family now," he said, taking her fingers in his. "A big, boisterous, happy one."

She let him swing her hand and enjoyed the contact when before she would have shied away from it.

"They are definitely boisterous."

"It is an adjustment." He laughed. "Thank you for speaking to me, Maddie. It means a great deal, as does having you and Rory here with me."

The fear inside her eased another notch. Slowly the knot of tension was unraveling, and Maddie felt the first kernel of hope grow. Maybe, just maybe, her past would not follow her to London and this life was a new beginning.

"As you know, the Ravens and Sinclairs live on this street, Maddie."

"It is most odd."

"Extremely, but we are odd, so it fits, and society has a lovely time laughing about it. They have named it Clan Close."

"And that doesn't bother anyone?"

"Some of us don't walk in society, and if we do it is a rare occasion, and the others have never really given a care for what people think."

They walked to the end of the street, where it curved around to lead off into another road.

"That house there"—he pointed to a tall white building that had black wrought iron fencing. Unlike some of the other houses, it was not quite as grand. Next to it were two more, butted up to each other—"is where Kate and Rory will live. I have as yet not told them that."

"It is a very grand wedding gift."

"I can afford it."

"Is there anyone left on this street who is not a member of this family?"

"Three houses actually, and they are not budging as yet."

Max smiled. "But they will not sell to anyone but me, I have at least got that promise from them."

"Are you so sure you will need more houses?"

"Society expects it of us."

"Hello, siblings." Rory was waiting for them when they arrived. His eyes went from her to Max, and he smiled but said nothing further. "What's this about, Max?"

Pulling out a bunch of keys, Max moved to the house Kate and Rory would one day live in and opened the door. He then disappeared inside.

"I guess he wants us to follow." Rory placed a hand at her back and nudged Maddie forward.

They walked through the door and found the house empty. Max was in a parlor, looking out the window. Rory went to stand at his side, Maddie stayed in the doorway.

"I have purchased this house and the one next door." Max turned to face her.

Her brothers were handsome men, she thought. Both tall and big men, they were so similar now. Their faces were no longer angular and drawn. Happy, Maddie thought, and that was a wonderful thing.

"This one is for you and Kate, a wedding present from Essie and me," Max said calmly, as if he was handing over a set of crystal goblets.

"Max, we—"

"I have not been a good brother to either of you."

"You had reason," Rory said.

"Perhaps, but that does not exonerate me from leaving you in her hands."

Her. No one needed to ask who that was. The evil, perfidious witch who had sold her daughter to the highest bidder.

"Maddie, what is it?" Max came to stand before her.

"Nothing."

"It is not nothing." He gripped her shoulders. "Your face has lost all its color. What did she do to you?"

"Who?"

"That woman who gave birth to us. I will never call her Mother, as she is not fit to wear such a title."

"It matters not; it is done now."

"It matters to us, Maddie," Rory said. "Tell us what happened to have you come to England. Only then can we fully move on."

"We are your brothers; lean on us," Max added.

Dare she tell them some of what transpired? Perhaps Rory was right, and this could help them move on.

"After Jacques passed, Fleur and I were still grieving. She came to the house."

"What? Why? I thought she wanted to never see any of us again after you married." Rory looked angry.

"Did she hurt you or Fleur?" Max's words were a soft growl.

"No, not at first. She said she was sorry and wanted a place to stay, as she had nowhere else to go."

"And you believed her? Oh, Maddie, no. How could you have been fooled," Rory said. "That woman always has an agenda."

"Maddie has always had a softer heart than us," Max said. "And she was vulnerable, and we were not there for her... again," Max said. "God, I'm so sorry, Maddie."

Could she tell them all of it?

"What did she do?"

"For a while, nothing. She seemed to have changed."

"Some people are just born evil, and that woman was one of them," Rory said. "She'll never change."

"The cottage was small. Two bedrooms. I gave her one, and Fleur and I the other, and then men started arriving."

Max cursed. Rory looked grim.

"She was living under your roof and having men pay for her services. Nothing has changed, it seems. She still has the morals of a gutter rat," Rory snarled.

"I hope you kicked her out?" Max asked.

"I tried, but she would not go and they kept coming. English and French men."

"Christ, it turns my blood cold to think of you alone with her," Rory said.

"I am no weakling, brother. I can look after myself."

"And while it is good to see you acknowledging that, you are no match for someone like her. She is a master manipulator, and because you are her child, she tugs on your heartstrings," Max said.

He was right there—Maddie had never given up hope that one day her mother would love her, even after all she had done to her children.

"I believe I have finally learned to expect nothing from her," Maddie said, remembering that night.

"What did she do?"

"It matters not, only that she will not have the chance to do so again. I will never allow that woman to come near Fleur or me again."

"We will ensure it," Rory vowed.

"But I still want to know what had you fleeing France," Max said.

"Hello."

Maddie wasn't sure if she was relieved or disappointed when Kate walked into the room.

"This conversation is not over," Max said. "We will talk more, and I want all the details, Maddie."

She nodded but said nothing more. It was not a time that she wanted to relive, especially considering what she'd done to escape.

"A note arrived stating you wanted to see me here, Max."

Kate looked from Max to Maddie, and then Rory. "I'm sorry, am I interrupting something?"

"There will never be a time when you are not welcome, my love." Rory took his fiancée's hand in his and pulled her to his side. Maddie saw the concern on his face as he looked at his siblings.

Max touched Maddie's cheek. "You are safe with us," he said, then turned to Kate.

"This is your new home. It's a gift from Essie and me. You need to tell your fiancé that you are happy to accept it, as I fear he is going to argue with me otherwise."

Thoughts whirled around inside Maddie's head as she walked from room to room behind the others. Should she tell her brothers what she had done? They would understand, but then what could they do about it? No, she was better off pushing it to the back of her head and hoping there would be no consequences to her actions.

"Seen enough?" Max asked, heading back outside.

"It really is lovely, Max. We cannot thank you enough." Kate kissed his cheek.

"Thank you, brother. It does not sit well, but we are grateful for such a generous gift."

"The house next door is identical, Maddie, and it is for you and Fleur if you wish it."

"Wh-What? I mean, pardon?"

He didn't say the words again, simply stuck his hands in his pockets and watched her.

"B-but I can't accept that." Her eyes were running over the facade.

"Well, it is in your name, so no one else can own it. If you don't want it, you can sell it."

Maddie had no words. Instead she walked through the gate and touched the front door. Number 17 Clan Close, and she owned it. Was it possible? She, Madeline Caron, who had lived in a cottage, milked cows, and sewn her own clothes.

"It is very grand."

"Not so grand compared to others." Max had followed her. He now stood at her back, a strong, steady presence, she was coming to realize. "You said Jacques gave you security, Maddie. This will give you and Fleur that also. I know you have no wish to live with Essie and me, even though we are happy to have you both. Here you will be close enough should you need us, but it will give you the privacy and solitude I also know you need."

"I-I don't know what to say."

"You have to say nothing, I only wished you to know that it is yours should you need it. I have also set up an income for you and Fleur."

She faced him. "Max, it is too much."

"Did Jacques leave you anything?"

"There was little left, only the house, and his brothers want that if they can get her out."

"I wish them luck. That woman always stays where she is not welcome."

Maddie shuddered just thinking about what had transpired over the last few weeks before she left France. Her mother ranting and throwing things when Maddie had asked her to leave. Fleur had been terrified of her grandmother.

"Unless something else is stopping you from staying here, then I see no reason for you not to move into this house, sister."

"Dear God!"

The cry came from Kate, who had wrapped her arms round her waist. Her face had leached of all color, and she was leaning against Rory.

"Who is it?" Max demanded.

"I-I don't know."

"Maddie, come!" Max took her hand, and soon they were running down the street.

"What is going on?"

"Someone is injured! Someone of Sinclair blood."

"How do you know?"

"They know." He looked grim. "They feel when another is in danger or pain."

She didn't understand, but the worry etched on the faces of the others had her keeping the questions inside her head.

Up ahead, Kate was sprinting with Rory. They reached Cambridge and Emily's house and found the others gathered there.

"I don't understand this. Everyone is here!" Dev roared. "Why are we in pain?"

Something stirred in the air, but when Maddie looked up, the sky was still blue and cloudless.

"Hands," Dev said.

Each Sinclair took another's hand until they formed a circle. Each person of Raven blood stood at their spouse's back. Maddie felt the hair on the back of her neck rise as the air thickened.

"Harry," Nicholas said. "I saw blood."

CHAPTER 12

*H*arry could hold his liquor and rarely got to a point where it took the edge off his intelligence. Today, however, he was drinking to put aside the memory of those Sinclairs and her... Madeline Caron, with her fierce eyes and beautiful face. He hadn't realized that fact until the man across from him went to fill up his glass again. Harry placed his hand over the top.

"Enough, thank you."

"'Tis just a drink to seal the pact between us," Braden Calloway said. "Long may it be profitable."

The man had a face women loved, but his temperament at best could be termed fiery.

Had Harry been thinking clearly, he would not have walked into this empty warehouse to meet Calloway with only Faris at his side. He was usually far savvier than that and never stepped in a direction without checking all exits and problems that may arise first.

"Harry, if I may have a word," Faris said from behind him.

"About what?" Calloway demanded. The man had a reputation for shoddy business dealings. He'd never crossed Harry, and that was what had lured him here today. That and the fact he'd wanted something to distract him from his thoughts.

Harry, you are an idiot.

He excelled at business, it was something he'd taken to with ease, and could often spot a charlatan at ten paces. Something in Faris's voice told him he'd had his blindfold on today.

"Just a few minutes, Mr. Calloway, and we will return," Faris said calmly. "I simply need to discuss a matter with Harry."

"You have no say in this, heathen!" Calloway stood now, hands braced on the desk.

And just like that, Harry was clearheaded. No one spoke to Faris like that.

"If my friend and business associate wishes to speak to me, then he will, Calloway, and I would suggest you think again before calling him a heathen in my company. He is, in fact, one of the most intelligent, articulate men of my acquaintance, and an astute businessman."

"He is a liar!" Calloway roared.

"How do you know he is telling a lie when he has not spoken a word other than to ask to speak with me?"

They were in a warehouse not far from the docks where the meeting had been set. They were to discuss Harry supplying the man with goods; the deal had gone well until now. Clearly he'd been too preoccupied to see something Faris had, and now he wanted to alert him to whatever it was.

"It's all right, Harry." Faris was always calm. In fact, Harry had never seen him lose his temper.

"No, it's not all right." Harry got to his feet also, feeling at a disadvantage still sitting. "If you wish to speak with me before the papers are signed, then speak to me you will, Faris."

"You would listen to him over me!" A vein was bulging in Calloway's neck now.

"He is someone I respect, so yes, I will speak with him."

"Which suggests you do not respect me, Sinclair. I would advise you to tread carefully. If you intend to sully my reputation, I will not stand idly by."

"I think we both know your reputation is already sullied, Calloway; however, until now you've not attempted to swindle me." Harry never backed away from confrontation.

"You've read the contract! Why have questions now?" Calloway glared at Faris.

"Because that is not the same contract that you presented two days ago on the *Charlotte Anne*," Faris said.

Harry grabbed the paper he'd been about to sign and began to read it. When he got to the pricing, he understood Faris's concern.

"These terms are different to what I agreed upon, Calloway. You're trying to cheat me."

"You dare to question me! You and that heathen are liars!"

"We do dare to question you," Faris said. "I too have checked the terms, and they are not as was originally quoted."

"They are not." Harry added his voice. "I think this meeting is over." Alcohol did not make Harry mean like some—it usually made him happy—but in that moment, he felt rage flood his body. Both at himself and the man who'd intended to cheat him.

"I dismissed the rumors about you, Calloway; it seems now that was remiss of me. You are someone I will never do business with again."

"You would take his word over mine?"

"It is not his word." Harry now stood beside Faris. "I can

see with my own eyes that you are trying to swindle me. After today, I shall ensure our paths never cross again."

Calloway had three men with him; until now they'd simply stood silently at the sides of the room. Harry had wondered at the need for their presence. It became clear as they moved to stand beside Calloway and pulled out their pistols.

"What are you going to do, shoot us?" Harry asked politely. "That would make an awful mess and need a great deal of explaining when I do not return to my ship."

"Your heathen has cast a slur upon my character, and I demand an apology. From both of you." The man was beyond reasoning with; Harry could see that. His face was almost purple with rage. They needed to get out of here now.

"I think you have that wrong. It was you who abused him and tried to cheat me, and I will ensure those I do business with know exactly what you are capable of. Of course, many already do, however I chose to ignore the rumors."

"I demand an apology!" Calloway's eyes were wild.

"Let me assure you, there will be no apology for the truth," Harry said. "Let's go, Faris."

He saw Calloway grab a pistol from the man beside him and aim it at Faris. Harry pushed him to the floor and took the bullet in his side. It dropped him to his knees.

Pain gripped him as he struggled to grab his own pistol.

"Bastard!" Faris was beside Harry now.

"Leave!" he heard Calloway roar, followed by the thud of footsteps.

"Harry, dear Christ, my friend." Faris pulled out his knife and slit the shirt open.

"That is one of my favorites," he said through his teeth as the pain made his head swim.

"Why must you always be the bloody hero?" Faris tore off his necktie and pressed it to the wound.

"That bullet was aimed at your heart," he gritted out as a wave of nausea swept over him. "A simple thank-you will do."

"We need to get you back to the ship before you pass out." Faris helped him rise, and each movement was agony. "Press your hand to the wound."

He was sweating when they reached the door.

"Stay with me, Harry," Faris said as they walked slowly down the road. "Not far."

It was in fact not far, but to Harry it seemed an effort of Herculean proportions. Each step jarred pain through him, and his fingers were soon wet from his blood that poured from his body. They reached the docks to find them full of people, as they always were.

"I'm giving you my ship and everything else."

"You're not going to die, don't be dramatic!" Faris's voice had risen, which it always did when he was scared.

"I am likely going to die, Faris." His voice sounded off. Weak and wavering. Harry hated being weak. "You will have it all."

"Shut up!" Faris roared. "I'm not letting you die."

"I-It cannot be stopped." Harry felt himself sway. Faris managed to keep him upright. "The infection will take me, if I last that long."

"Will you please be quiet and reserve your strength!"

"Tell my family I was glad to meet them," Harry rasped. Suddenly his need to stay away from them seemed foolish in light of the fact he was about to die. "And her... tell her I am gl-glad I met her."

"Who is 'her'?"

"M-Maddie. Tell her for me, Faris."

They were just about at his ship when the thunder of horses hooves filled the air.

"What fool would be galloping through here," Faris gritted.

Harry turned, attempted to focus, and saw Dev, Cam, Wolf, and Eden—in fact a gaggle of Sinclairs on horseback. Strange, he thought. Why were they here? A carriage stopped behind them, and out got Max and Essie.

They dismounted as one and ran to his side.

"What's happened?" Dev demanded, reaching them first.

"He's been shot in the side. That bastard Calloway did it because Harry was protecting me."

Faris's words seemed to come from a long way off now. Almost as if he was dreaming. Harry could feel his head growing foggy.

"F-family," he managed to get out. "S-sorry."

"Harry, let me see now."

"Essie." He made himself greet her, because, well, she was his cousin. "Ouch!"

She was touching his side, and fire burned through him, which had him panting in seconds.

"Let's go. We need to get him home to my supplies—and Lilly, should she be required."

Things got a bit hazy after that. He was jostled, and the pain intensified so much that he was close to blacking out. His curses were unpleasant, and yet he was a seaman, so hardly unexpected.

"It's all right, Harry, we have you."

Looking up into the eyes of Wolf Sinclair, who was above him for some reason, he noted they were unusually bright.

"I don't want to die."

"You won't, trust me. We will not let that happen."

"Because we're family?" Harry whispered.

"Exactly."

"I'm sorry."

"For what?" Cam was suddenly at his side.

Harry's eyes rolled back in his head, and everything went black.

He woke as they carried him inside, simply because the pain dragged him to the surface. Vicious pain that lanced through his body, robbing him of breath.

"Is he... I can't say it."

"Maddie?" He roused, hearing that voice, and latched on to it.

"I am here." She moved into his line of vision. Harry tried to focus and push back the darkness.

"Beautiful," he managed to get out, then gripped a handful of her skirt and held on. If he was holding her, he couldn't die. This thought took root inside his head. She would keep him anchored to this world.

"Walk with him. We need to get him to a bed."

Harry heard voices as he was carried, each step lancing pain through his body. There was blood, he knew that too, lots of blood.

"Not ready to die," he whispered. She leaned down, placing her lips next to his ear.

"Then fight, Harry, fight with everything you have, because we are not ready for you to die either."

CHAPTER 13

"Harry, let go of my skirt," Maddie said as she tried to prize his fingers from the material.

"No." The word was gritted out and filled with pain.

"Just sit with him, Maddie," Somer said. "He feels the need to hold something, and it happens to be you."

She didn't know what was happening, or indeed what she had witnessed earlier, but she knew it was odd. The air had felt different when they'd come together, and then they'd held hands and it had suddenly charged with tension.

"Of course, if you think I should."

"We do." Max came to her side. "It's all right now, sister, we just want to help Harry." He lifted her onto the bed.

How had Nicholas known Harry was in danger? Then some had gone in a thunder of feet, running toward the stables, leaving the others to prepare. For what, she'd asked Rory, and he'd said Harry was hurt and would need their help.

How had they known?

Emily had then dragged Maddie behind her into Max's

house, and soon they'd been running about the place, preparing a bed and helping Alice collect medical supplies.

Fleur had been put in the care of the nannies with any of the other children who were now here, which seemed to please her hugely.

Maddie had asked what was going on. The answers had been vague and unclear to her mind. What weren't they telling her?

Those thoughts had fled when they returned with Harry bleeding in Wolf's arms.

"How bad is he, Essie?" Lilly asked, entering the room they had taken Harry to.

"It's bad, but the bullet has gone through his side and is not lodged. I don't know the damage inside him, but for now we can try healing him the old-fashioned way first, as I fear this one will take a great deal out of you, Lilly."

"I will be here should you need me."

Old-fashioned way?

They all arrived again, the Raven and Sinclair families. Filing into the room, somber faced. Why were they here, when surely only Essie and Alice were needed, and a doctor? Had they called for a doctor?

Harry moaned, drawing her eyes away from the others and down to the man who had his face turned and pressed into her side. He still held her skirt in a surprisingly fierce grip, considering how weak he must be.

"Don't leave me."

Leaning over him, Maddie touched his cheek. It was ice-cold.

"It's all right, Harry, we won't leave you."

He lifted his head and looked at her.

"You," he whispered.

"Me?"

"Don't leave me." He hissed out a breath as Dev began

removing his shirt and exposing the mangled mess that the bullet had left. Harry was watching her, so she kept her face calm, though inside, fear chilled her.

Surely he could not survive such an injury. She rested a hand on his head, her fingers stroking his hair.

"I won't leave you."

"Harry, you must drink this for me," Essie said.

He clamped his lips shut as Essie handed the cup to Maddie.

"This will help with the pain and put him to sleep. Make him drink it."

"Drink this now, Harry." Maddie put her arm under his shoulders, easing him upright. "All of it." She spoke in the voice she used on Fleur when she was being naughty.

He did, choking, gagging, but she got it down him. He took her fingers as soon as the cup was drained and gripped them tight.

"Some of the things you may see will shock you, Maddie, but I will explain it all soon," Rory said before stepping back and away from the bed. "Trust that it is good and right."

"I don't understand."

Her brother's smile was small. "I doubt you ever will, but it is a miracle, Maddie, and a blessing to be part of."

"All right now, Harry, I am going to look at your side," Essie said.

"Hold his feet, Wolf. Cam, up beside Maddie. The rest of you make a connection," Dev said.

What are they doing? Her eyes went from Rory to the others. They were doing what they had outside.

The Sinclairs all moved closer to the bed, taking each other's hands. Dev placed his hand on Essie's neck. Lilly held on to Cam, and her other hand was clasped by her husband. Eden, the twins and Warwick, Alice and Kate—they were all there. Nicholas too.

Maddie felt it again, the stirring of something in the air. Ravens stood behind Sinclairs. Rose to Wolf, James to Eden, Emily to Cam. Max and Rory.

Maddie's heart thudded hard inside her chest. What was she witnessing?

Dev's and Wolf's eyes were a vivid, almost unnatural green now, the others were focused on Harry with fierce intensity. Nicholas had his eyes closed as he gripped his wife's hand.

"His color is pale, Essie," Dev said, "but still strong enough."

Essie worked quickly and efficiently, cleaning the wound. Harry did not make a sound, even considering the pain he must be in. The grip on her fingers was relentless, but Maddie didn't mind; it meant he was still alive.

As the bullet had left his body, Essie did not have to do an extraction. But still what she did was taxing on Harry's strength. Maddie felt the moment he slid into unconsciousness.

"It is best," Essie said. "He will not feel the pain now." She continued to clean the wound, then doused it in something and lastly applied a thick paste. "I think this will do, Lilly."

"And yet, just a bit of healing will expedite matters and ensure there is no infection."

"Lilly," Dev cautioned.

"The infection, Dev."

His nod was brief.

Lilly moved from her place, breaking the connection. Looking down, Maddie saw Harry's eyes were still closed, his fingers still holding hers. Stroking his hair, she prayed he survived this. Her stomach clenched at the thought of this large, vital man leaving them.

"Just a small amount, Lilly," Dev cautioned.

Essie moved, and Lilly took her place. The connection

was again formed. This time it felt different. The air was suddenly thick with something—the only thing she could call it was magic.

Her eyes found James, and he smiled; it was gentle and reassuring. Max and Rory looked the same.

Lilly put her hand on Harry's side, and he twitched, body jerking. Maddie felt the heat slowly fill him, as her hand was on his forehead.

Dear Christ, Lilly was healing Harry? Could that be possible?

"That will do." Dev pulled her hands free. He then placed an arm around his wife's shoulders, and they both left the room. Suddenly the air was normal once more.

Was this some kind of witchcraft? Looking at the faces around her, she didn't believe it was evil, and yet what had just happened?

"We will explain," Rose said, moving to hug Maddie.

"He will still have a recovery ahead of him, but Lilly has assured there will be no infection, and the damage inside is minimal," Essie said. "We must notify his grandmother too."

"I will go to the ship and speak with them, and they can pass on what has happened to the grandmother," Wolf said.

"Come away now, Maddie. Harry sleeps, and we will talk," Rory said.

"I will stay with him. I want to get a tonic into him now, to help with the recovery," Essie said. "Dorrie and Somer will keep me company."

The young ladies nodded their agreement.

Maddie tried to ease her skirt from the unconscious Harry, but his fingers wouldn't release her.

"Take off your scarf," Wolf said, coming to her side.

Maddie did as he asked, then watched as he leaned over Harry. Wolf pried open Harry's fingers and removed her skirts. Harry protested, mumbling something, and Wolf put her scarf in his hands.

"Tell him you are here, Maddie."

"I'm here, Harry. Rest easy," she whispered in his ear. He stopped moving, and his fingers gripped her scarf once more.

When she climbed off the bed, she saw that everyone still left in the room was focused on her, and the look in their eyes had her uneasy.

"What?"

No one answered.

"Come, there is much we need to tell you," James said, taking her hand. "But we all need sustenance to do so."

"Amen," Cam sighed. "This business always takes it out of me."

She let James lead her away from Harry. Maddie didn't want to go. In fact, she wanted to get back on that bed and watch over him, which was enough reason to leave.

"Will he be all right?"

"He will. Lilly has ensured that, and Essie will do the rest. Come away now, and we will talk about what you saw."

"What did I see, James?"

"Well now, sister, that is going to take some time to explain. Will you come and listen as we try?"

She nodded, her hand gripping his as they walked.

"Sit, you look like a ghost." Samantha took her other hand when she entered the parlor and led her to a sofa. She then sat at Maddie's side. "There is nothing to fear, Maddie, I promise you."

"I felt something in there."

"Yes, we all do, but it is those of Sinclair blood who are the magic among us."

"Darling, only you make it sound something wonderful." Cam smiled.

"But it is wonderful, Cam, and such a gift."

"Have you noticed Cam looks like a dog sometimes, Maddie?" Eden asked, interrupting them.

"He sniffs the air," Maddie said. "I have seen it. I wondered if he had allergies. Jacques sometimes sniffed a great deal at certain times of the year."

"If only it was allergies." Cam sighed.

"He can smell better than anyone," Eden added, "and that's why he will often press a handkerchief to his nose if a scent is particularly foul. He's not just being pathetic... although he does do that also."

"Rarely am I pathetic," Cam said around a mouthful of cheese.

"What you saw and we are about to explain will be hard to comprehend, and yet we want you to try, as you are family, and with you we are stronger," Dev said.

Maddie didn't speak. She couldn't, as she had no idea what to say or what they would tell her.

"Don't attempt to do anything you have no wish for anyone to see with Dev, Wolf, or Harry nearby," Eden said.

"Harry?"

"The eldest sons of the three Sinclair brothers all have the heightened gift of sight," Dorrie added. "'Tis most vexing, as we can get away with very little."

"One wonders when you will actually realize that fact," Dev drawled.

"As you can imagine, life was not easy for us as children. No one could do anything without someone knowing," Somer added.

"I don't understand. Are you telling me you see better than others?"

"We do," Wolf added. "We see a great distance, and at night. We also see in colors."

They talked. She listened and still could not take it in.

Surely it could not be true, and yet she'd seen it with her own eyes.

"Lilly?"

"Is now sleeping, as healing takes a great deal out of her," Dev said. "But she and Nicholas carry both Sinclair and Raven blood from many generations ago. That is why they are different."

"Odd, some would say," Cam added.

"We're odd," Nicholas scoffed. "There is no one odder than you."

"You saw Harry and the blood, Nicholas, when you did not know who was hurt earlier."

"I did. I have visions. They usually tell me what is about to be or what needs to be done."

"I don't know what to say." Maddie looked around the room.

"Their strength grows with each new family member, and that includes those of us with Raven blood. We make them stronger," James said.

"You make us stronger, Maddie," Dev said.

It was almost too much to grasp, and yet grasp it she must if she was to be part of this. So much had changed in her life, and now this. Looking around the room, she saw they were all waiting for her to speak. Waiting to hear what she would say about what she'd just learned.

"It will take some time to understand, but thank you for telling me, and of course I would never share any of this."

"No one would believe you if you tried," Rory said. "They'd lock you up and throw away the key."

"What you know about us should only make you feel safer to stay," Dev said. "You are family, and as such we will protect you should it be needed," he added solemnly.

"I don't know what you mean."

"We are very handy people to have around if there is a threat of danger."

"Our mother is a danger," Maddie said before she could stop herself. "But as she is in France, it's my hope that is where she will stay."

Rory moved to her side, dropping down before her.

"She will not hurt you again, Maddie."

"I know. I am stronger now that I am here and coming to the realization that I am not alone." She looked at the people around her. They had accepted her without question; perhaps it was time to accept them.

CHAPTER 14

He knew she was still there with him because he could smell her scent. Fire burned down his side when he moved, but because he could feel it, Harry took that as good sign that he may just live.

"Rest easy, Harry."

A soft hand pressed to his forehead, and he forced his eyes open but saw only the room bathed in a glow from the fire.

"Are you in pain?"

"Some." The word sounded rusty, and his throat was parched as he searched for her, Madeline. She was standing at his bedside, a gentle smile on her face.

"Here, let me help you. Essie said you should drink this when you woke."

"Where am I, and why are you here?"

Harry felt a hand slip under his shoulders, and then he was eased upright with surprising strength. He tried to help, but the breath hissed from his throat as pain seared through him.

"You are in Max and Essie's home, and I was checking on you."

She held the cup to his lips, and he gulped the cool, sweet liquid down. Madeline then lowered him back to the bed gently after plumping his pillows.

"What time is it?"

"2:00 a.m."

"Go to bed. I need no one watching over me." He gripped her hand as she tidied his covers. "I am not a child. You have no need to stay up and watch over me." He certainly sounded testy like a child.

"I offered to come and check on you, as I do not sleep a great deal and thought to let Essie get a good night's rest."

She didn't back away even though her pulse was now racing beneath his fingers.

"Why do you not sleep?"

She tried to tug her hand free, but Harry wouldn't release her. So she held her other palm to his forehead once more.

"You have no fever, which is pleasing."

She wore a shawl around her shoulders, and Harry couldn't be sure, but thought underneath was her nightdress. Her hair hung in a long braid, the ends tied with a piece of wool.

"Why is your hair tied up with wool when your brothers have as much money as they do? Surely they can afford a few ribbons for their sister?"

"They can, but as string does the job admirably and always has, I saw no reason to change. Now release me, please, Harry."

He didn't.

The firelight flickered over her face. She was incredibly beautiful and extremely dangerous to his peace of mind, Harry thought.

"Why do you not sleep, Maddie?"

He tightened his grip as she tried to pull away again.

"Don't strain, you'll open the wound!"

"Tell me why you don't sleep, and I won't have to strain."

"It doesn't matter why. Now, I need to check your wound. Essie said as long as there is no blood seeping through the bandage then I need not wake her."

Harry let her go and braced himself to feel her hands on his body.

"My hands may be cold, perhaps I should—"

"Just do it, Maddie."

She eased the covers slowly down to his waist. He wore no shirt, and when her fingers brushed his ribs, he could do nothing to stop the hiss of breath.

"I'm sorry!"

"It's all right. Just look at it," he gritted out.

She did, then raised the covers to his chest.

"There is no blood, so if there is nothing you require, I will retire."

"Tell me why you do not sleep."

"It is no concern of yours." She gathered the edges of her shawl closer, as if they would protect her from something.

"Please."

"What you took will help you sleep now."

"Excellent, but before I do, tell me what I want to know."

She looked to the fire, and Harry thought she would leave. He didn't want her to go.

"It started when I was a child. I have no notion as to why."

"Yes, you do."

She looked down at him.

"Why were you shot, Harry?"

"I wasn't thinking clearly and walked into a situation I should not have."

"Why weren't you thinking clearly?"

"What happened in your childhood to stop you sleeping?" he asked instead of answering her question.

Her sigh came from the soles of her feet.

"I was always scared, even with Rory and Max there. I couldn't sleep because of that, and now it's a habit."

"What were you scared of?"

Her laugh held no humor. "Noises, her and her friends, and so many things I could not recount them all or I would be here all night."

He wanted her to stay with him all night. Wanted to wake with her at his side so he could look at the firelight playing over her lovely face.

"When I was shot, I was thinking about them, Maddie."

"Them?"

"The Sinclairs."

"They are good people, Harry."

"I know that, but they can be nothing to me."

"Why?"

What the hell was wrong with him? He never spoke like this. Shared his innermost thoughts.

Harry released her wrist. "I'm tired now. Please leave."

She didn't move immediately, instead standing there and watching him. Then a soft hand touched his where it lay on the bed. The door closed quietly behind her seconds later; only then did he exhale slowly.

His chest had felt heavy when she told him she'd hadn't slept as a child. The fear of sleeping when there was danger had made her stay awake. What was the danger, and who was the "her" she mentioned?

Harry didn't feel things for people—well, maybe his grandmother, but no one else. He didn't want to feel when Maddie was near or his family. The hell of it was, he did.

Closing his eyes, he tried to remember what had happened when they'd brought him here today. He knew

Maddie had been there and that he'd anchored her to him, he just wasn't sure why he'd felt the need to do so. All he'd thought was that if she was close, he was safe.

Moving so he was comfortable, Harry thought the pain in his side was more a dull ache than the searing pain of before. He'd been shot, so it should have been a great deal worse. Had Lilly healed him?

How had they known he needed them today?

Harry let the thoughts come and go as whatever Maddie had given him took hold, and soon he was relieved for the reprieve from his thoughts as sleep dragged him under once again.

…

The next time Harry opened his eyes, he saw the light around the edges of the curtains. He remembered Madeline coming to visit him last night and telling him the reasons she did not sleep, as he'd told her that he'd been thinking about the Sinclairs when he'd walked into that warehouse and ended up being shot.

"Hello, Harry. How do you feel?" Warwick Sinclair appeared at his bedside.

"Sore and thirsty."

"I can fix the second, and my sister will likely be able to ease the first. I'll just let some light in now you're awake."

Warwick disappeared, and seconds later he saw the early morning light filtering into the room.

Harry tried to rise, and his side gave a vicious tug of pain.

"Let me help you." Warwick slipped his arm under Harry's shoulders, and between them, they got him up and resting on the pillows.

"Why are you here, Warwick? I thought this was Max and Essie's house."

"I slept the night so I would hear if you called out."

"I had no wish to put anyone out."

"It is what we do for family, Harry." The young man smiled down at him, and he saw his eldest brother in him.

"You have my thanks then." Harry's words came out gruff, but Warwick did not seem to mind.

"How about that drink?"

Harry drank deep from the cup Warwick handed him, the liquid feeling wonderful sliding down his dry throat.

"If you will be all right, I shall go and tell Essie you are awake. She wishes to look at your wound."

"Of course, and thank you, Warwick. Really, I am grateful."

The green eyes studied him in that way Sinclairs had. "I would have done it even if you were not grateful, Harry. Watching over family is not a choice, it is part of who we are." Warwick left the room, quietly closing the door as Maddie had done last night.

Harry closed his eyes and fought against what he felt. He was weak; that was why those simple words had touched something deep inside him.

"I need to get out of here." He pushed himself upright, but the pain forced him back down to the pillows. In a single day, he had lost his strength.

The door swung open suddenly, yet he could see no one. Harry heard the sound of running feet and eased slowly to the side of the bed. Looking over the edge, he saw Fleur with big sad eyes staring up at him. At her side was a large, shaggy hound.

"Bonjour, Harry."

"Bonjour, Fleur."

She scrambled up onto the chair beside his bed to look at him.

"Harry is sore."

"Harry is sore."

Her little face screwed up tight as she studied him.

"I'm all right, Fleur, I promise. Who is this with you?"

"He is Uncle Max, Uncle Rory, and Mama's dog, Bran."

The dog came closer, raising his nose to sniff the air. Harry reached out a hand and scratched the shaggy head.

"I will sit with you."

"Will your mother not be worried where you are?"

"No." She did not elaborate. He watched as Fleur climbed off the chair and pushed it closer to the bed. Once again, she climbed up. She then made shooing motions with her hands, which Harry thought meant he should make room, so he did, slowly edging across the bed.

She climbed onto the mattress and settled down beside him, resting her head on the pillow he leaned against.

"Story, Harry?"

"I don't know that many children's stories, Fleur."

She smiled up at him, then patted his cheek, which he had no idea how to interpret, but thought perhaps it was that she trusted him to tell her something she would enjoy.

Searching his memory, he remembered a story his grand-mère used to tell him.

"A long time ago, there was a hen called Camille who had two brothers and two sisters."

He adapted it slightly, as his memory was a little vague, and even managed a credible chicken voice, or what he thought they'd speak like. It was as he was drawing to the end of the tale that he looked at Fleur and saw she was sleeping.

Her lashes rested on her soft cheeks, and one of her hands lay on top of his. He'd never been this close to a child as they slept. It was a wonderful thing. Peaceful, Harry thought.

He rested there beside her, wondering when her mother would appear, as surely she would, looking for her daughter. Harry already knew she was protective of the child; he'd witnessed it that day in Calais.

The door opened, and there she was. This dress was in the palest peach, and unlike last night, today she wore no shawl. The material seemed to float around her body as she moved closer. No longer hampered by ugly, ill-fitting garments, he was able to see her lovely figure and wished fervently he did not.

"Oh, that's a relief." She pressed a hand to her chest. "I was just informed she was not resting in her bed where I'd left her. Essie's nanny is running about looking for her also."

"Perhaps you should have sat with her, as clearly no one had a close eye on her."

"There is little harm for her here. She slipped by the maid, and neither of us are quite sure how."

"She could have fallen down the stairs."

"And yet she did not. I will take her back to bed and am sorry if she has disturbed you." Her French accent was stronger when she was being excruciatingly polite.

His behavior was ill-mannered; he knew it, just as she did. Yet Harry didn't seem able to stop, which annoyed him. His head seemed to be all over the place.

Essie entered the room carrying a tray.

"I see you found Fleur."

"Yes, she and Bran made their way to Harry's room."

"Bran is a lovely boy and loves everyone in the family, but his special people are the Huntington siblings and their children," Essie said. "How do you feel, Harry?"

"I am well. Thank you for your care of me, Essie." He didn't know what had happened, but knew this cousin would have had a hand in it. "I will call a hackney and return to the ship."

"No, you won't. You're not going anywhere until I say so."

"I am strong enough to leave."

"No, you are not." Essie had a glint in her eye. "I will say when you can leave, and it will not be until then, Harry. You will not test me on this. I know what is best for my patients. Now, I'll alert the others Fleur has been found, Maddie. You give him his medicine, and don't take any of his nonsense. I'll return soon."

Maddie reluctantly took the tray that was handed to her, and who could blame her for that? He was being an ass.

"She is right. You cannot leave, Harry."

"I have been making my own decisions for years. This is no different."

She raised her eyes to the ceiling. "Lord save me from stubborn men."

"I am not stubborn," Harry said, sounding exactly that. "And keep your voice lowered, or you'll wake Fleur."

"Is there a reason you are behaving like an ill-tempered child, Harry?"

"I wish to return to my ship, as I stated before. I have men there who will care for and watch over me."

"Very likely, and yet here is where you will get the best care, and as you are not five years old, but an adult, perhaps you could try and understand that."

"Where did you get that dress?" *And those words were the ones that came out of your mouth?* Harry thought, disgusted with himself. He was an intelligent man; perhaps he should start behaving like one.

"I found it on the street. Quite a shock, and the perfect fit."

He wouldn't laugh at seeing this fire in her. Before, she'd been quiet and scared. That was changing.

"Now open up and take your medicine, and I will leave you to your misery and take my daughter with me."

"You've changed."

"Since last night? That was quick."

She moved to the other side of the bed, away from where Fleur slept, then slid her hand under his shoulders, which pressed him to her chest briefly. In his current state, his body should not be reacting as it was.

"Open up."

"I can take it myself."

"Very well." She handed it to him.

Harry swallowed it quickly, refusing to shudder as the noxious concoction slid down his throat.

"Tell me what happened yesterday."

"You were shot." She replaced the glass on the tray with a definite snap. Looking at Fleur, he noticed she still slept, snuffling softly.

"After that."

"You were brought here, and… ah, well, treated."

He gripped her wrist as she went to grab the tray once more, urging her to where he could see her clearly.

"What happened?"

Her cheeks had filled out, even in the brief time she'd been here. She looked healthier. There were still shadows under her eyes, but lack of sleep would do that.

"I know about what they can do. Do you?" Harry asked.

She nodded.

"And that shocked you?"

"I had never seen such things before. What I witnessed…" Her words fell away. "Are you… do you also…"

"I do. I can see like Wolf and Dev."

"When they told me, I did not want to believe it, and yet I witnessed it."

"Tell me what happened. Please," Harry added.

"The connection they have, the Sinclairs, and then the Ravens with them. They saved you. Essie cleaned the wound, and they all touched each other, forming a link between them. Lilly touched you, and I felt the heat as my hand was on your head."

"She healed me?"

"Dev would not let her do so completely, as it takes a toll on her, but yes, partially. So you would not get infected. I know what I saw, Harry, but I don't understand it."

"I have never understood it and yet always lived with it. Until I met them, I did not realize I was not alone in what I experienced."

"They are both wonderful and terrifying," she whispered.

"We are not terrifying, Maddie."

"We? Do you see them as your family now then?"

And just like that, he remembered. *Never trust a Sinclair.* He was betraying his father by being here, by trusting them.

"No. I will leave here soon, and then England. I will not come back." He released her.

"Of course." She hurried around the bed and scooped up her daughter before he could stop her. "Good day."

Harry rested his head again on the pillows after she left. He touched the place where Fleur had slept; it was still warm from her little body. His hand then slid beneath the blankets and gripped Maddie's scarf.

She was nothing to him, just as they were nothing to him. He could not allow that to ever happen. His life was not here in London with a woman who tugged at places inside him he had not known existed.

Sinclairs cannot be trusted, he reminded himself as his eyes closed. Sinclairs and brown-haired women with sweet-faced little daughters.

CHAPTER 15

The trouble with wanting to stay away from Harry was that Fleur refused to. If they took their eyes off the child for a second, she ran to his room, which meant Maddie had to go there to collect her.

Seeing him was not getting any easier. He created a feeling inside her she'd never felt before, and she didn't like it.

"Harry is in the small parlor resting today. It is sunny and will do him good to get out of bed," Essie said. "If you are looking for Fleur, I'm sure she's found him by now."

"Yes, one of the maids just told me she had found her there when she'd taken him a tea tray. I don't understand why she is always seeking his company."

They were taking tea together. Maddie had come to like her sister-in-law very much. She was kind and gentle but could be fierce when required.

"She likes him, as do the others. Claire had a sore belly this morning, so I took her to him, and he settled her."

"Why is he so good with children, Essie?"

"You know what we are, Maddie. Know how Wolf is with animals?"

"Surely not?"

"Harry is like that with children."

"Good Lord."

"It's his most redeeming quality," Essie drawled.

"Has he been very difficult?"

"Not extremely. He is just confused and wants to leave here."

"Why?"

"Change is not easy for anyone, Maddie, and for a man who had no one in his life to suddenly have all of us and what we are is, I should imagine, terrifying. Plus, by being here and accepting us, he feels as if he is betraying his father."

"Because his father was betrayed by the Sinclairs. Yes, James told me that."

"He is scared and fighting hard not to show it, Maddie." Essie held her daughter in her arms, patting her back while she slept.

"What do you fear, Maddie?"

"I fear nothing."

"That's not true. You are safe here with us. Surely you see that now?"

"I see it and have changed. Harry said as much."

"Did he? Then perhaps you are only different with him? Tell me, Maddie, did James tell you about what lies between the Sinclairs and Ravens?"

"I know about them saving each other."

"They also marry each other." The words had been softly spoken, but had they been shouted, the impact would have been no less. "Surely you have realized that by now?"

She hadn't, but now she thought about it, it was staring her in the face.

"Good Lord."

"Sinclairs marry Ravens, usually after a Sinclair has saved a Raven."

Maddie lowered her cup to the table, as her hand was shaking.

"Harry may be a Sinclair, Essie, and I have Raven blood, but we will never be anything to each other."

"Why?"

"Because I was married to Jacques. I will never marry again." *And because I murdered a man.*

"And you believe you will never care for another man?"

"Yes." Her words were a hoarse whisper. "I will never marry again." Maddie got to her feet. "I need to go now, Essie. I must get Fleur before she tires Harry out."

"He is strong, and yes, his side is still a long way from healing, but he can handle having Fleur with him. The other children visit him also when they are here. He draws them to him, which is funny really, considering he is an unmarried man with none of his own."

Hilarious.

"Yes, well, thank you for the tea."

She didn't run from the room, but it was a near thing. She did, however, run up the stairs with thoughts swirling around inside her head.

Sinclairs marry Ravens, usually after saving them. Harry had saved her twice. The legend would not be tying them together in a nice neat betrothal knot. Harry would return to France, and she would stay here.

That much, at least, she now knew. This was Fleur's family. Leaving them would be a wrench. Plus, if anything should happen to her, her daughter would be loved.

Reaching the parlor Harry was in, she heard her daughter's giggle. She would enter and take Fleur, then leave with only a few words spoken between them. As she had every day.

"Good day," Maddie said as she stepped through the doorway.

Fleur was beside him on a sofa, giggling at the story Harry read her. The vision would have pleased any mother's heart if the man was her husband. However, Harry was not.

"Come, Fleur, it is time to leave." Her words sounded clipped and angry. Harry noticed, because his eyes locked on her.

"No, Mama."

Her daughter was chewing a biscuit.

"I don't like her to eat too many biscuits." An outright lie, as Fleur had never had many treats, and she did not begrudge her them at all.

"Good afternoon, Maddie. Please join us for tea."

"Tea, Mama. Harry is reading."

"I have no time for tea." She was a horrid woman to speak to her daughter that way. It was not the child's fault the dark-haired man beside her looked like a rumpled god sitting there in a dressing gown made of green velvet the same color as his eyes. His hair was all over the place, and his jaw held stubble. He looked like a bloody fallen angel.

"Everyone has time for tea, surely?" He was teasing her.

Since that day she'd entered his room and he'd been curt with her, he'd changed. He was polite and kind when she retrieved her child. It put her off balance. She was even more so today, as apparently, Sinclairs married Ravens!

"Sit, Maddie. We have nearly finished the story."

She had no reason not to sit, and it would be churlish if she refused. She sat in a chair across from Harry. Picking up a biscuit from the tray, Maddie nibbled so she didn't have to speak if he asked her anything.

"The cat, who heard all this but pretended otherwise, said to him with a grave and serious air..."

His voice was lovely, deep, like smooth whisky. Not that

she'd tasted smooth whiskey, but still, she thought it could be like that. Maddie sat there listening to the story, eating her biscuit. She became enthralled, as she'd never sat and listened to fairy tales before.

"This book is *Mother Goose's Fairy Tales*," Harry told her when he was finished. "We are reading *Puss In Boots*."

"Thank you, she is enjoying them."

"Come closer and look, the pictures are lovely."

"I need to go." Maddie stood now.

"Come and look, Mama." Fleur waved her closer.

"Sit here, you will see better."

Harry patted the empty space beside him. She didn't want to. In fact, the thought of getting that close to this man made her go hot all over. His eyes laughed at her as if he knew what she was thinking.

She sat.

"We shall read the next story for your mother, Fleur."

"Oh no—"

"Sit." He pulled her back down as she tried to rise. "Once upon a time, there was a widow that had two daughters."

She followed his finger as he read each word, her eyes looking at the letters. A few she recognized. When she had been a maid, another girl in the house could read and had taught her in the evenings, but Maddie had been forced to leave after only a few lessons.

"See that letter there, it is an *A*," Harry said. he then continued on reading. He pointed out letters as he read, sounding them out, and Maddie would copy him in her head.

He read, and she watched and learned, and some of what Lucy had taught her in that kitchen many years ago came back.

"That is a *B*." She pointed at one of the first letters she'd learned.

"It is."

She sat and listened as he read page after page, and both she and Fleur were mesmerized. When he closed the book on the last page, she saw that her daughter had fallen asleep resting against Harry.

"You know quite a few letters and words, Maddie. Who taught you?"

He was so close to her now. She'd moved during the story telling, so the distance that she'd placed between them was no longer. Her thigh touched his. Their eyes were only inches apart.

"A friend."

"Which friend?"

"Just a friend I once knew. She could read and write in English and taught me a small amount before we parted.

"She should move, pull her eyes from his, anything to break the contact.

"I like this dress also." He touched the edge of her sleeve where it banded her upper arm.

"Thank you."

Harry leaned closer, so close she saw his eyes change to a deeper green, and then he was kissing her. His lips were soft, achingly soft. Only their mouths touched, and yet she felt it through her entire body. Each brush of his lips made her body tighten. *More.*

Her hand touched him, and he grunted in pain.

"I'm sorry!" Maddie leaped to her feet. "I touched your injury."

"It's all right."

"No, it's not. None of this is all right. This... It can't happen again." She hurried to pick up her daughter.

"If I promise it won't, will you let me teach you to read while I recover? After that, I will return to France."

His words stopped her at the door.

"I can't."

"Yes, you can. This is for Fleur as much as it is for you. You saw how much she enjoyed the stories. Think of her."

"Harry!" Dorrie burst into the room. "Your grandmother has arrived. I have come to warn you, she is not far behind me."

"God have mercy on us all," he muttered.

"Grandson!"

Maddie watched a short, round woman enter the room. She could find only one word for the colorful vision who had entered: Imposing.

"Hello, Grandmère." Harry said. "You will forgive me for not rising, as I am still sore."

Clutching Fleur, who had woken at the commotion, Maddie moved to where Dorrie stood watching the reunion.

"I could not come earlier, as I have been unwell." The woman stomped closer to Harry with her cane.

Her clothes were orange. Not a soft shade, nor even a peach like Maddie's dress; no, these colors were loud and almost hurt the eye. The dress was made up of many seams and layers, each a different shade of orange. Over the top she wore a shawl that was the most hideous color of all. It was pinned together with a large brooch in the shape of a bird.

"She looks like a many-layered exotic fruit," Dorrie whispered.

"And I thought I had no idea about fashion," Maddie said.

"How is it you were shot?" The words were fired at Harry.

"The usual way, Grandmère, with a gun."

"Don't be flippant with me, grandson!"

"This is Miss Dorset Sinclair and Mrs. Madeline Caron, Grandmère. The sleeping child is Fleur Caron."

It wasn't easy to curtsey with a child in your arms, but Maddie stumbled through it.

"Ladies, my grandmother, Mrs. Heloise Paquet. Don't be fooled by her demeanor; she is actually a nice person."

Shock had Maddie's eyes shooting to the woman who was seating herself beside her grandson. How would she take him speaking to her like that?

"'Tis true I can be, but only if I like you. Bring me some tea and biscuits, which I believe you English excel at, and we shall see how it goes from there."

"I'll go!" Dorrie ran from the room before Maddie could.

Drat.

"You come and sit with that babe. I wish to visit with the sweet child," Heloise Paquet demanded.

Maddie hesitated.

"You won't escape, so you may as well give in," Harry said. "Take a seat, Maddie."

"Down, Mama." Unlike Maddie, who woke slowly, Fleur was always ready for action. Lowering her daughter to her feet, she took her hand and moved to a chair.

"You have cared for my grandson, Mrs. Caron?"

"I and others, Mrs. Paquet."

"And he has behaved?"

"Oh, yes." Maddie shot a look at Harry. He had a knowing smile on his face. He knew she was uncomfortable, and from more than just that kiss.

"As a child, he did not like being ill."

"Grandmère."

"Harry does not like to be dependent on anyone." She ignored the warning in his voice. "He is strong, that one." Heloise looked at her grandson, and while it was not exactly a tender moment, Maddie knew there was love between these two.

"Yes, thank you, I don't think Maddie wishes to hear more, Grandmère."

He appeared such a strong man. A man others respected, and yet he had a grandmother who could still embarrass him. Why did that make him more appealing?

"He needs a woman to set him to rights. A woman and a family. He needs a home."

"Grandmère." This time Harry's words were a growl. His grandmother harrumphed but said nothing further.

"A home is not always just four walls, Mrs. Paquet." The words were out before she could stop them.

Fleur moved away from Maddie and closer to the older woman. She then stared at her.

"Your bird is pretty, Harry's Grandmere."

"*Oui*. I found it in a little store right here in London. I'm glad you like it."

Harry's eyes met Maddie's as Mrs. Paquet undid the bird and handed it to Fleur.

"There was another in the shop. I shall purchase it, and then we will match each other."

"No, really, she does not need such generosity." Maddie tried to refuse. Fleur however, had clasped it to her chest and moved to the side of the chair Heloise Paquet sat in.

"It is a gift, and therefore unable to be returned, Mrs. Caron."

"Oh, well then, thank you. Say thank you, Fleur."

She did, with a sweet smile. One thing that had changed in her daughter since arriving in London was that she smiled a great deal and used it to effect when required.

"Such a sweet child." Mrs. Paquet patted her cheek.

"And knows how to be so when required," Harry drawled.

"You are a nice grandmother," Fleur said. "Not like my one."

Maddie felt the tightness in her chest again. She'd hoped her daughter had not suffered overly and would forget what had happened. It seemed her hopes had been in vain, and she hated that she had subjected her child to the venom she'd received as a child.

"Well then, you may call me Grandmere, Fleur, and you will forget about the other one."

"Thank you, Grandmere." Fleur looked happy. She then proceeded to tell Heloise Paquet all about her new family.

"Maddie?"

She turned as Harry called softly to her.

"Are you all right?"

"Of course."

"You look worried."

"No, I am fine." Maddie could and had handled most things that life had thrown her way, but her mother had never been one of them.

"The color has left your cheeks."

"It has not."

"It has, and before your daughter mentioned her grandmother, you were fine."

She didn't reply, just focused on her daughter, who was having a lively conversation with Harry's grandmother.

"Where is home to you, Maddie, if not four walls?"

"You answer first."

"I'm not sure I've ever really wanted or had one." He did not seem overly worried about what he'd just said, but his words made Maddie sad. Perhaps he was good at hiding what he really felt?

"Everyone wants a home, Harry."

"What is a home to you?" Those green eyes were alive with color as he looked at her.

"Somewhere to belong, where you're safe."

"Grandson, I asked you a question!" Heloise thumped her cane. "What is being done about catching the man who hurt you?"

"He will be caught, Grandmère. There is no doubting that, as I will ensure it is done."

"Good. No one shoots my grandson and walks away."

"Exactly my thoughts."

The familiarity between them was real, as was the love, and it softened his face.

She felt the longing then. The need to be special to someone for herself. Not as a sister, or mother, but to be loved with passion.

Dear Lord, where had that come from? The thought had her getting to her feet.

"Excuse me, I need to do something. It is nice to meet you, Mrs. Paquet, and thank you for Fleur's brooch. Come." She held out her hand, and Fleur reluctantly took it.

Harry was watching her; Maddie could feel his eyes. She didn't look his way as she bobbed another curtsey and left the room, and this time she would keep her distance from him, because if a simple kiss had made thoughts of passion and love enter her head, heaven help her if he did so again.

CHAPTER 16

They all came, as Harry had known they would. The first to arrive was Dev, the head of the family.

"Mrs. Paquet, how wonderful to see you again." He wandered in as if this was his house, which Harry had noted they all seemed to do. Family members living in each other's pockets. The thought should horrify him. He was a man who'd lived a solo life and had never needed anyone, and these people seemed unable to do a solitary thing without first checking with someone.

"Lord Sinclair." His grandmother held out her hand like a princess, and Dev dutifully bowed over it.

Next came Cam, and Harry wondered if they were coming in order. Oldest to youngest.

"Ah, Mrs. Paquet, how wonderful it is to see you again. As you see, your grandson is receiving excellent care from us, his other family."

By the time Warwick, the youngest Sinclair sibling arrived, Harry had a fair understanding of just what it was they were doing. Staging a show for his grandmother, to ensure she realized that Harry was one of them, and only he as yet had not understood that fact.

"We would be more than happy to show you the sights of London, Mrs. Paquet," Eden said to his grandmother, who was reveling in all the attention.

Preening, actually, if he had to put a word to her behavior.

"In fact, we would love to take you to see James's castle too, should you be here long enough."

The parlor he'd sat in with Maddie and Fleur was not overly large, so Harry, his grandmother, and the seven Sinclair siblings, plus Wolf, who had just arrived, were quite a squeeze. No one seemed overly concerned, such was their comfort in each other's company.

Tea was replenished—and cake, which had Cam smiling.

"The castle may actually work," Harry said to Eden, who was seated beside him now. "She's a terrible snob."

"Work?" Eden raised an elegantly arched brow.

"You're all thinking you can get to me through my grandmother, Eden. I'm not a fool."

"A man, yes, fool, often."

"Meaning?"

"Pride gets in the way of what is best for you, as it does for the other men in our family."

She wore rose today and looked every inch the duchess she was.

"I have no need of more family. I am here and grateful for what you have all done for me, but I will be leaving soon."

"You will give in," Wolf had told him yesterday. *"We work as a pack and overwhelm you until you simply have to."*

Harry was made of stronger stuff, he'd told his cousin. Wolf's reply had been to snort.

"We felt you, you know." Warwick moved to his other side. "All of us knew you were hurt and came running."

"Grandson, we are going to visit a place called Crunston Cliff!"

"One day, Grandmère," Harry replied while he grappled with what Warwick had told him.

"We feel pain when another is hurting or in danger. It's swift and fierce, depending on the degree of hurt."

"You're serious?" Harry said, giving himself time to understand what they were saying. *They'd felt his panic.*

"Absolutely. We had to find you," Eden added. "Then when we did, we brought you here, and Essie did what she could, then Lilly healed you."

"And that's why you are not dead or lying in a pool of infection," Warwick added with a calm that Harry was not feeling.

"A castle, grandson!"

"Oui, Grandmère." He looked from Eden to Wolf.

"You leave us, and you will feel the pain but not be able to reach us," Eden said.

"I won't. I have not yet, so doubt I ever will."

"But now we have a connection," the duchess added.

Luke wandered in with Dev's eldest son, Mathew, and James and Eden's daughter, Isabella. The children looked immaculate, which was at odds to how they usually appeared when he saw them. This too was clearly a statement. A selection of children who could behave would be paraded before his grandmother. In Isabella's arms was Fleur. Of Maddie there was no sign.

Harry told himself he was happy about that. Seeing her face when Fleur mentioned her grandmother had told him that her relationship with the woman had not been a happy one.

The children smiled and allowed his grandmother to pat their cheeks, and Fleur even sat on her lap, her new brooch now pinned to her dress.

"I love Harry," she said to his grandmother.

"Well now, so do I, so that's nice. We will share him, as he is sharing me with you."

He felt the family's eyes on him as he watched the conversation between child and woman.

Harry had always known he was loved by his grandmother; his father too in some small way, but that had come wrapped up in a pile of rage connected with him leaving England disgraced. But Heloise Paquet had been a constant in his life.

He'd told himself her love was enough and hated that now something inside him was yearning for more. Yearning for what he'd never believed he could have, but had deep inside always wanted. That dark little place that he'd shut away as a child because he'd known that kind of warmth was not coming his way.

Family.

Harry schooled his features. He wouldn't be taking what these people offered. He couldn't for so many reasons, and possibly none of them were logical ones, but they were what he'd lived his life by. Besides, his life was in France.

Finally, after they'd talked, taken tea, and behaved like polite, well-mannered society folk, which they absolutely were not as far as Harry could see, they left. Kissing his grandmother as they did so, and begging her to return.

"She'll see through you all," he muttered to Dev. His cousin's smile flashed all his teeth, but he left without speaking again.

"Grandson, you must keep these people, they are good ones." The door had just closed when she spoke.

"They are not pets, Grandmère."

"Do not be glib with me!"

"Apologies, but I have no wish to make connections with these people."

"And yet you are, as you are here, with them. They are the ones who helped you when you needed it. They did because you are of their blood."

He didn't add anything to that, as every word was the truth, and he could dispute none of it.

"Family is important!" She stomped her cane on the floor.

"Yes, and I have you."

"But you do not have a castle." She glared at him.

"And that is important to you?"

Her smile was small, but he knew the signs a lecture was coming. "Open your heart, Harry. They love you. Why is it you choose to fight this?"

Why indeed?

"My life is in France, and Papa had no wish for me to associate with his family."

"You father was a bitter man. Do not live your life as he did."

"Grandmère—"

"I am leaving now and wish to speak of it no more. You will do what is right."

She hugged him, which was a shock. They loved each other but were not terribly demonstrative. Then she left, leaving the strong scent she chose to bathe in in every corner of the room.

"You need to go back to bed now, Harry." Essie had returned. "You are not healed, and rest will aid in that."

He did as she said because he wanted to, and yes, he was tired, but he'd admit that to no one but himself. He took the medicine she gave him when he was settled, because she was surprisingly fierce when required.

"Now sleep. That too will help you heal," Essie said, pulling up his covers. She kissed his forehead before leaving, as she always did, as all the women did, and he hated how much he loved that too.

Harry needed to leave this place and return to the man he was. He was betraying his father by being here. There was also the fact that the longer he stayed, the harder it would be to leave. He could feel himself changing. Exposure to all this love and kinship was wearing him down. And then there was Maddie and Fleur.

He'd kissed her, and he could never regret that, no matter that he was a fool for doing so. He felt his eyes close and welcomed the oblivion of sleep. Freedom from his disturbing thoughts, if only briefly, would be a good thing.

"My life is in France," Harry murmured as the waves of exhaustion pulled him under. *That is where I am returning to.*

CHAPTER 17

*A*nother four days passed, and still he made no plans to leave.

Essie had told him that to leave before he was ready was folly and would likely prolong his recovery. Usually Harry would not have listened, but for some reason, he did.

His ship would be fine, Faris would ensure that, but he was seriously concerned for his ability to leave if he didn't do so soon.

This was a house filled with love and family. Family that he had blood ties to but was torn about accepting.

They'd all come to visit him, and often. He'd tried to pretend he was sleeping; they'd simply waited for him to open his eyes. They played word games with him, read him stories, and gave him their time, and it was humbling and disturbing in equal measures.

Yesterday he'd played whist with Wolf and Eden; the latter, it turned out, was a cheat, but would sell her firstborn before admitting that fact. He'd laughed, and Harry was not a big laugher. He'd then had the twins, Samantha, and Warwick visit, and they'd discussed their investigative service with him. He'd questioned them, because he wasn't entirely comfortable with the concept, not that it was anything to do with him, but still… they were his cousins.

"Another question, please, Harry, and try harder, if you please."

"I shall try harder, Isabella."

At the moment he was throwing questions at Isabella, Luke, Hannah, and Mathew. All were sitting on his bed, legs crossed, waiting for his next question. So far, they'd answered every one correctly.

"What is a Binnacle List? And where on a ship is it kept?"

"That's two questions, Harry." Hannah sucked her bottom lip in as she thought about his words.

"Well, if it's too hard…"

"It's not," Luke said. They then leaned in, heads together, and started coming up with ideas.

"Do you need a clue?"

"No!"

"Don't feel bad, it is a tough one," Harry needled them.

He was even starting to talk like the others, Cam and Dev. They always teased and challenged their children.

"It's something to do with a ship," Hannah said, frowning.

"One point only for that," Harry said.

One by one, they climbed off the bed.

"Where are you going?"

"To the library. We'll be back with the answer soon," Mathew said.

Harry settled down to wait for Fleur, who should be arriving soon. Maddie's sweet little daughter insisted on visiting him every day for a story and her nap.

Maddie came too. They'd formed a truce, and he had to say he enjoyed her company. She was happy here, and that had brought out the woman she should have always been, to Harry's mind. She smiled freely and snuffled her soft laugh often now. Hers was a gentle nature that, if he had to guess, through necessity had been hardened.

Harry knew hers had been a difficult life, but he'd not asked anyone for the details, as it was likely they would not give them to him. Plus, that would signal his interest in her, which he could not allow. Because in this case, a Raven would not be marrying a Sinclair.

When she came, Maddie sat and watched him read and mouthed the words and letters he taught her. Having her that close was both torture and pleasure.

She had a scent about her that seemed to linger in the air long after she'd left.

True to his word, he'd not kissed her again. The hell of it was, he wanted to… desperately. There was an innocence about the woman that had touched him. He felt the need to protect and ravish her at the same time.

The Caron women were slipping into his heart, and that was no good for anyone.

He needed to leave here now. He was strong enough, and had told Faris when he visited him two days ago that he would be back on the *Charlotte Anne* by the end of the week.

"How are you feeling?" Cam's head appeared around the door.

"Better, thank you."

"Excellent. We are all going to the park for a picnic. I thought I'd visit before we leave."

"You need not check on me." His words had come out curt.

"And yet, that is what family does." One thing Harry had noticed about Cambridge Sinclair was that it was not easy to offend the man. "I brought you the latest copy of *The Trumpeter*."

"Did you call it that?" He took the paper as it was held out to him.

Cam sighed. "No, and Em and I considered changing it, but there was quite a protest from the regulars who read it, so we're stuck with it, I'm afraid."

"It's an odd name, but I guess it's better than the bugler."

Cam snorted. "There is that. Now, I need to ask you about this man who shot you, Harry. I've been elected, as apparently I have a way with words, and Essie tells me you are strong enough to have this conversation."

"Elected?"

"We do that when there's a particularly sensitive subject that needs broaching." Cam fell into the chair beside Harry's bed. "We usually riddle for it."

"I beg your pardon?"

"It's a game we play with words. Take the words cherry cake, for example."

"Please do."

"Cherry has six letters."

"Your counting is excellent."

"You must make up a sentence using the letters in the word. For example, Cam had edifyingly round roulades yesterday."

"That made no sense."

"Roulades are round," Cam protested.

"Edifying is providing moral or intellectual instruction or used to express disapproval, as in, it is not edifying to watch someone make a fool of themselves," Harry pointed out and wondered why he was bothering. This entire conversation was ridiculous, and yet, he was enjoying it.

"I didn't give that sentence a great deal of thought as it was just an example."

"Not a very good one," Harry needled his cousin.

"You're just like them." Cam exhaled loudly.

"Them?"

"Wolf and Dev. Annoyingly proper and nauseating."

"Thank you, I'll take that as compliment."

"But as I was saying, I lost the game."

"Can't have been easy, as I'm sure there is something of a competitive streak in all of you." Harry had only really competed with Faris.

Cam laughed. "Something of a competitive streak. Harry, Eden once locked herself in the chicken coop for an entire night because I said she wasn't brave enough to do so. I knew she was there, of course, and stood watch where she couldn't see me, but she did it. Such is the ferocity we have for besting each other."

"And yet you love each other very much," Harry said quietly. He felt it then, the ugly monster that was jealousy.

It's right there if you want it.

Sinclairs are not to be trusted.

"I would give my life for any of them, and what we are merely strengthens that." The laughter fell away, and suddenly there he was, the man behind the facade he wore. The strong, loyal family man.

"As you should" was all Harry could manage around the lump in this throat.

"You are now part of us, Harry."

He looked away. "I cannot be that. I will be leaving soon."

"And yet you will always be so. But enough of that for now. I was sent in here to discuss the man who shot you. Is he a continued threat?"

"I will deal with him." Harry had many ideas on what he would do to Calloway when he was fit and strong once more.

"You are one man; we are many. Let us help you."

"I need no help."

"Why are you fighting us?" Cam got out of the chair and began to pace. "You have no family save your grandmother, who, I might add, loves us. Her visits have been wonderful. She fits right into the family with her colorful personality."

His grandmother had told him repeatedly during her visits that he needed to open his heart to this family.

"It's the castle. She's always wanted one of them."

"Raven Castle is special, for all that it's a drafty old place," Cam agreed. "But I digress. Is there a chance your father was wrong about us?"

The door burst open, and in ran Fleur. She hurried to the chair.

"Not today, Fleur." Harry said the words as she prepared to climb. "I am weary and have no time for reading."

She stopped, looking up at him with those big eyes.

"I want a story."

"And yet I have said I cannot read stories today. There are plenty of people here; go and find one of them. In fact, it is best you do so from now on, as I am not staying." He hadn't meant his words to come out gruff and spiteful, and yet they did. Cam had said he was now one of them, and he'd hated how good that had felt. He felt as if his world was tilting on its axis, and he had no idea how to right it.

Sinclairs are not to be trusted.

Harry now knew that was wrong, but what he didn't know was how to handle what he felt. He'd always run from emotion.

Fleur's lip quivered, and tears formed in her eyes. She turned and ran at Cam, who caught her as she lunged at him. Lifting her into his arms, he hugged her close. Harry wanted to get out of bed and take her back. Have those arms wrap around his neck.

"I can tolerate many things from my family, Harry," Cam's face was hard now, "because most often I have deserved them, but one thing I will never tolerate is anyone hurting one of our babies. That was mean and uncalled for. Good day."

Cam left, taking Harry's sweet little bundle of sunshine with him—and he let him.

"It's for the best." Harry got out of bed slowly. His side still burned but was nowhere near as bad as it should be, because Lilly and the others had saved him. Guilt had him picking up his clothes. Wolf had given him some, along with the nightshirt and dressing gown.

He pushed aside more guilt as he thought about how these people had accepted him in their lives and he'd given nothing in return.

"Why can't I accept what they want to give me?" Harry had no answer to the question, only that he needed to get away from here and them so he could think.

He'd just been horrible to a child, and he never did that. He could be mean when required, there was no getting around that, but children were exempt. They were special, a gift of innocence that so many people tried to break. He was not, until now, one of them.

The pain was there, nagging away at him as he pulled on the breeches and boots. By the time he had his shirt tucked in, he was sweating. He sat on the bed until his heart stopped thudding.

When he was calmer, he once again stood and tied his necktie. It looked like a child's knot, but he had no strength to worry about that. Slipping his arms into the jacket, he went back to the bed. Lifting the blankets, he grabbed Maddie's scarf without giving himself time to think about why and stuffed it down his jacket.

Making his way through the house, he nodded to servants but saw no family. Cam had said they were all going to the park, so that worked in his favor.

"Can I be of assistance, Mr. Sinclair?"

"I would like a hackney, please, George. I am returning to my ship."

The butler studied his face, no doubt seeing the sweat and pallor. But like any well-trained servant, he simply nodded, then left. Harry found a chair and fell into it with a groan.

Harry had always been strong. He'd loaded cargo alongside his men for years, and yet today a simple walk was taxing his strength. Essie had told him his side would make a full recovery, but it would take time.

He did not have time.

He sat there waiting for the hackney, letting thoughts come and go as he told himself over and over he was doing the right thing. This life was not for him. His life lay over the Channel, far from here.

Why cannot I not have it all?

Never trust a Sinclair.

"Your hackney is here, Mr. Sinclair."

He should leave a note, but someone might return while he wrote it.

"Please tell the family I have returned to my ship."

"They are in the park should you wish to tell them on the way out, Mr. Sinclair."

"I don't, thank you, George. And thank you for my care while I have been here."

"It was an honor, Mr. Sinclair." The butler bowed, and the hell of it was Harry thought he would miss him too.

He walked slowly out the door, his eyes searching but not finding a Sinclair or a Raven. The step into the hackney was not easy, but he pulled himself in, then tapped on the roof.

Harry did not look at the house as he rolled away, because he was suddenly consumed with a feeling he was leaving something of huge importance behind him.

He saw the park as they approached, saw the families sitting around on blankets. He could be part of that if he wished it. Part of a family, something he'd never had or expected to have.

She was there. Harry found her straight away. She sat with her legs folded under her in a cream muslin dress. In her lap was Fleur, and the little girl rested against her mother. He saw the sadness in her eyes and knew it was he who had put it there.

"This is for the best," he reminded himself, and yet the argument was no longer convincing.

Sinclairs could be trusted; they'd proved that to him. The father he'd never doubted, in this, had been wrong.

CHAPTER 18

"He's leaving."

Maddie's heart dropped at Dev's words. Surely Harry would not be so foolish as to leave?

"What? He can't do that." Essie got to her feet.

Maddie saw the worry etched there as her sister-in-law's eyes scanned the carriages on the road, passing the park.

"We have to let him go. Only then will he understand what he is leaving behind," the eldest Sinclair said, his voice solemn.

"He's a fool." Rory shook his head. "But you are right, it took me some time to learn what we have."

"He is not strong enough." Essie sighed.

"He is strong. That man has run a business dealing with cutthroats and gentlemen alike, and done so with only his grandmother for support," Dev said. "He is possibly the strongest of us all."

Us all. Harry was a Sinclair, and as such, family. He was the only one who did not understand that yet.

"Harry has gone, Mama." Fleur looked up with solemn eyes. "I liked Harry. I wanted him to be my papa."

She knew those close had heard the words, but Maddie didn't look up, instead focusing on her daughter, who sat cuddled in her lap. Fleur had been talking a great deal about finding a father lately.

"Harry is not your papa, darling. He has his own life. We just borrowed him for a while. He now has to return to his ship and his people."

"I want to be his people," Fleur said with a sad little sigh.

"Out of the mouths of babes," Dev said. "He'll be back, little one."

"Fleur, come and play!" Meredith shrieked.

Maddie lifted her daughter to her feet, and soon she was running around with her cousins. Needing to walk, Maddie wandered along the path that ran to the pond.

Harry leaving was a good thing, she told herself. He made her feel strange things inside. All quivery and warm. Jacques had never made her feel that way.

Plucking leaves as she walked, she listened to the squeal of children at play. Would he be all right away from the family? He still had to heal, even though Dev had said he was strong.

The path ran alongside the road, and she looked in the window of the closest carriage rolling by. Her heart almost stopped beating. She only saw the side profile, but it was enough to have her turning away. She stood still, pretending to look around her. Every muscle clenched as she heard the carriage wheels roll on.

Why would she be here? She hadn't seen the face, but that profile had looked the same. You didn't forget the face of the woman who had tormented you most of your life. Shuddering, Maddie made herself walk back to the family. There, she was safe. There, no one could harm her.

Suddenly she was back there in France with that man on top of her, his voice whispering horrid things in her ears.

"Maddie?" Rory came to meet her. "Are you all right?"

"Of course. Why do you ask?"

"Wolf said he could see your face and you looked scared."

She made herself laugh; it was high-pitched and squeaky.

"I was just thinking about things; there is nothing wrong. Sometimes I get sad thinking of Jacques, and sometimes I get scared thinking of her, our mother."

Rory grabbed her, hauling her close. "She will never touch you again."

Maddie let him hold her, felt his strength, and the calm came. Rory was right, their mother could not harm her or Fleur again. She must be mistaken; no way was she here in London. Maddie had left her behind in France with the man she'd killed.

"I'm all right now."

"I'm not. Thinking of that woman makes me tremble."

"Men don't tremble." She eased out of his arms.

"Some men do." He took her hand as they walked.

"Is everything all right?" Max and her sisters arrived. Samantha's face was clenched with worry.

Emily had told her how she had suffered at the hands of their father, and that she hated to see any of her people that way.

"I am well, Samantha." Stepping closer, she put her arms around the young lady who shared her blood and instigated the first hug she'd shared with anyone but Fleur since arriving in London.

"Well." Max cleared his throat. "We are about to play hide-and-seek. I believe you are it, Maddie, as you are last to the blanket," Max said. She was then left standing alone as everyone sprinted in the direction of the picnic.

"Mama! You're it!" Fleur screamed as she arrived.

They played, and for her this was a first too. She'd never

just laughed and played freely; there had always been something to do.

Harry had gone, and the mood of the adults was somber for all they tried not to show it. But still they played, and perhaps because of it, Maddie found herself loving these wonderful people even more.

She'd hugged a sibling and played hide-and-seek and eaten the picnic that was brought by James's staff. She pushed thoughts of the woman in that carriage aside. No one could hurt her here. She was safe with her family.

...

Two weeks to the day after Harry had left, not that she was counting, Maddie woke with streaming eyes and a sore throat. Today they were all visiting a display in Hyde Park where a man was exhibiting velocipedes and various other inventions that Maddie doubted would ever amount to much but her family wanted to see.

Her family. They were that now, and each day she learned how to be part of them. Fleur loved them, and the heart that Maddie had believed could only love her child had now increased to accommodate them.

Dragging herself out of bed, she washed and pulled on clothes, attempting to ignore the aches in her body.

Fleur asked for Harry daily and, like Maddie, missed the laughter she'd forced from him and the smiles he'd given her whenever she'd visited him. The children had taken up Maddie's lessons, and she learned to read each day in the schoolroom. This, she loved, as soon she'd be able to read to her child, something she'd longed for.

"Hello, Maddie." Essie and Luke approached her as she left her room.

Maddie's reply to Essie was a loud sneeze.

"Oh dear, you don't sound good." Essie pressed a hand to Maddie's forehead. "You have a fever. Get back into bed at once."

"Oh, no, I'll be fine."

"Now, Maddie."

"I was just going to the nursery to see Fleur and prepare for our outing." As this produced another round of sneezes, Essie handed her a clean handkerchief.

"I will watch Fleur, Aunty Maddie."

"That is very sweet of you, Luke, but I don't want to trouble you."

Meredith had become fast friends with Fleur, and while she was happy about the connection, as it was helping her child get over Harry's departure, she wasn't sure the high-spirited Sinclair wouldn't lead her much younger cousin into trouble. Just yesterday, she'd found them sliding down the banister together. Her heart as yet had not recovered.

"She will have plenty of adult supervision. Now, I insist you get back into your bed at once, Maddie. We will take Fleur with us and give you some peace," Essie said, opening Maddie's bedroom door. "Let's go." She urged her inside. "Undress and get beneath the covers; I will bring you something to make you feel better."

"I'm not really—"

The door shut behind her.

She sat in the chair by the window and pulled a rug over her legs. Maddie had never taken to her bed during the day before, and it didn't feel right doing so now.

"Here you are." Essie bustled in. "I don't mind you sitting there as long as that is where you stay. Now drink this, and I have a rub for your chest."

She took the medicine and the chest rub, then Essie left and joined the family for their outing, promising that a maid would check on Maddie often and bring her tea.

An hour later, she was sick of sitting in the chair. Maddie didn't read, so she couldn't lose herself in a book. Pulling a shawl around her shoulders, she headed downstairs to find George. He was always pottering about in the front entrance doing something.

A knock on the door when she arrived had her moving to answer it. George would surely appear, but as she was here...

Two gentlemen stood there.

"Good day to you. We are here to speak with Mrs. Madeline Caron."

Had she not been a bit fuzzy in the head from whatever Essie had given her, she may have asked why they wanted her. Instead she said, "I am Mrs. Caron."

Yapping had the men turning, and in through the door shot Wolf's little ugly beast, Hep. He skidded on the floor, then hurried back to Maddie to sit on her foot.

"What can I help you gentlemen with?" Maddie said, bending to pick up the dog.

"We are from Bow Street, madam, and have a warrant for your arrest."

CHAPTER 19

Harry returned from a torturous visit with his grandmother, where she'd spent the entire time talking about Sinclairs and Ravens. He'd tried to deter her by changing the subject; she hadn't budged.

Oh, what manners. How sweet the children are. They have a castle, you know.

His grandmother rarely annoyed him. He found her amusing and loved to battle wits with her. She censured him when she felt it necessary and threw out small doses of love when she felt that was required also. Today, however, she'd annoyed him with her constant chatter about them, with a special focus on Maddie and Fleur, who Harry missed desperately. They were like a deep ache inside him that he couldn't reach to soothe.

Even the dainty nibbling of the cakes she'd ordered had driven him crazy. So he'd left when he could and arrived back at the ship to sit in his office and stare at the papers that he should be reading.

In the days since he'd left them, Harry had tried to convince himself he was done with the Sinclair and Raven families. His wound was healing, and the delay in leaving was simply because some supplies he had ordered had yet to be delivered.

He told himself he was chaffing at the delay. It was a lie.

He couldn't stop thinking about them. He saw Maddie as she tried to say the words and letters he had taught her. The line down her forehead as she frowned. The smile of elation when she got a word right.

Harry threw his pen across the floor in frustration. What would it take to get them out of his head? He needed a woman and would ensure he found one on his return to France.

His life was on this boat, where he was free and in control. Running a hand through his hair, he wondered why that thought didn't give him the pleasure it usually did.

"How is the injury today?" Faris entered his rooms without knocking.

"It is customary to be asked into a person's cabin, I believe." Harry was seated at his desk, staring at the same set of figures he had been for the last ten minutes, now minus his pen.

Why had they not come for him?

Faris turned around and left, closing the door behind him. He then knocked loudly.

"Enter." Harry felt like a fool.

"Good evening, Harry. How is the injury today?"

It was fair to say that Faris had the patience of a saint, and this Harry knew as he'd tested him constantly in the days since he'd left Essie and Max's house.

"Better, thank you. I am healthy once again." Was it nighttime already? Harry wondered how many hours he'd been sitting here staring at nothing, thinking of her and them.

"That was a swift recovery."

"It was."

"I had not believed it when I saw you. You took a shot to the side, Harry, and yet you were sitting up, looking if not exactly healthy, a great deal better than I had thought you would."

Harry grunted something. He couldn't tell Faris the truth, that his family had healed him.

Faris did not speak again, and Harry could feel his eyes on him.

"What?"

"You are a bear, Harry; a very unhappy one. You have torn strips off me and everyone who comes near you since your return from your family."

"I don't want to talk about them."

He'd thought they would come for him, simply because they were persistent and had said they'd cared. And yet they hadn't. Such was his perverseness, he was hurt by this, even though he'd chosen to leave.

I am unraveling like my grandmother's shawl.

"Your men are drawing wood splinters to see who will speak to you if an issue arises. The shortest one loses."

"Christ, really?" Harry lowered his head to the desk and banged it softly. "Life was easy before we came to England, Faris."

"It was, but was it fulfilling, Harry?"

He looked into the eyes of the man he trusted more than anyone... Not quite true, he thought, thinking of a few more he could add to that list.

"I thought it was." He decided on honesty. "My father told me to never trust a Sinclair, Faris. How can I betray him? He made me vow that I would never become one of them."

"Perhaps he was wrong, Harry, and not all Sinclairs are bad. Or Ravens for that matter. I spent a few hours talking with those people when you were unconscious and out of your head rambling and dribbling in pain."

"As you just said I was the picture of health, I fail to see how that was possible." He raised his head with a piece of paper now stuck to it.

"They are good people, Harry. A little odd, and far too involved in each other's lives, but the best type of people."

"What type of people are they, Faris?"

"Good and loyal. Harry, they are your people. Even your grandmother likes them, and she doesn't like anyone."

"Grandmother and you are the only people I need."

"And we will always be there for you, as will my family. But these are your blood, like your grandmother, and the real surprise here is they seem to like you." Faris smiled, and Harry threw a ball of paper at him.

"Go and see them, Harry. We are to sail soon, and you must make amends by then."

"How do you know I need to make amends?"

"A hunch. Do you?"

"Perhaps."

He'd left without a word. Just walked out of the house after what they'd done for him.

"You must decide whether England or France is to be your home now."

"France!" Harry said with force, because he really wanted to believe that.

"Perhaps, but then perhaps not."

"Well, which perhaps is it," Harry snapped.

"Only you can decide that."

"You want to return to France without me?"

His friend reached across the desk and held out his hand. They clasped as they had that first day when they met as young boys.

"Brothers," Faris said softly, "and that we will always be, my friend. Any distance between us will never change that."

"You just want me out of the way so you can marry Natalie. We both know she loves me best."

"Very true. And no matter where you are, I expect you to return to France for the wedding."

"I will be with you on this boat when it leaves London."

"We shall see."

He felt it then, tension, so strong his teeth snapped together as a knock sounded on his door. Anxiety settled heavily inside his chest.

"What?"

"I don't know. I'm suddenly tense."

"Enter!"

Barney, his boson, entered.

"What is it?" Harry barked.

"Pardon for the interruption, Mr. Sinclair, but something odd has just happened." Barney's face was wrinkled with worry. "I was out getting a few supplies and passed the Watch House on my return."

Harry had to stop himself roaring at the man to get to the point. The look Faris threw him said that he needed to be patient. Not easy when acid swirled inside his gut.

"It was right odd, but as I passed I watched two men take a woman inside, and she held a little black dog in her arms."

"And you're telling us this because?" Harry snapped.

"The woman was the same one we took on board in Calais. Her with that sweet little girl."

"What?" The word erupted from Harry as he surged to his feet.

"She was being led in there by two men, and to me it looked like she was in some kind of trouble," Barney added. "I came right here to tell you."

"Call me a hackney, Faris, I must go!" Harry could feel it inside him. Something was very wrong. "You did well, thank you, Barney."

Faris did not argue and left the cabin behind his boson. In seconds Harry had retrieved his jacket and hat. He stuffed the book he'd recently purchased into his pocket and followed. His side was healing, and he was getting stronger, but he still tired if he walked too far. Right at that moment, he felt stronger than he had in weeks.

Walking down the gangway, he nodded to Faris, then climbed into the hackney and gave the address Barney had given him.

The trip was twenty minutes in traffic, and the entire time all he could think was why had she been there alone? It made no sense. Her brothers would never have allowed Maddie to fall into the hands of the Watch. They mustn't know, he realized. That could be the only reason for this.

But why? Where were they?

"I'll pay you double if you get me there as fast as you can," Harry bellowed at the driver through the opening above his head.

The tension was nearly choking him as finally they pulled up outside a gray stone building.

After paying the driver, Harry stopped outside the door. Switching his vision like Dev had taught him to, he searched for Maddie. She was in there; he saw the flash of lavender. The little dog, Hep, too.

The relief that she was, as far as he could see, unharmed nearly had his knees buckling. Drawing in a large breath, he exhaled slowly. No good would come from storming into the Watch roaring. He needed to be rational, no matter if inside he was anything but.

Maddie needed him, and he would not let her down.

CHAPTER 20

The Watch House was as he'd expected it to be: bleak, sparse, and uninviting. The thought of Maddie anywhere near this place made his anger climb.

Walking to the front desk, he nodded to the man seated there.

"Good day. I am Mr. Sinclair."

"Constable McDagger, sir," the man said.

"I believe you have a friend of mine in here, and I would like her released at once. Her name is Mrs. Caron."

"We do, sir, but I'm afraid she can't be released." The constable's expression never changed.

"Can you tell me what possible reason you could have to bring her to such a place?"

Stay calm, Harry.

"I'm not sure as that's your business, Mr. Sinclair."

The man was doing his job, Harry understood that, and also that it wouldn't get him anywhere if he leaned across the desk, grabbed his collars, and shook him.

"I wish to speak with your superior officer, please."

"He won't tell you any different."

Harry leaned on the desk and looked the man in the eye.

"Do you have any idea who that woman is related to?"

The man nodded. "Mr. Huntington, a wealthy businessman."

There were many who weren't overly impressed by wealth unless it came with a lofty title. It appeared Constable McDagger was one of those.

"Her brother is a duke."

That got him twitching. McDagger jerked in his chair. He then leaped to his feet.

"I suggest you get your supervisor out here now before he arrives."

Harry checked on Maddie once more after the constable had left; she was exactly where she'd been when he'd arrived at the Watch House, and her color was strong.

The injured muscles in his side pulled as he paced the room. He ignored them.

"Mr. Sinclair, I am Sergeant Gavell."

The man was short and round, with a great deal of bushy facial hair.

"Sergeant, I wish to know why you have detained Mrs. Caron."

"We have charged her on theft of jewelry, Mr. Sinclair."

"On whose word?"

"I'm not at liberty to say."

"And yet Mrs. Caron has been in this country for a short period of time and lived with her family since her arrival. I fail to see who she could have stolen from."

Sergeant Gavell made a show of looking at the papers in his hand.

"I wish to have her released at once."

"We can't do that, as there will be a trial."

Someone very well-established and with a great deal of power had to be behind this. He just had no idea who or why. None of it made any sense. Maddie had only made the connections with James and the others since arriving in London. None of this rang true.

"I wish to see her."

"We can't do that either," Sergeant Gavell said.

"Do you know who her family are, Sergeant?"

"Constable McDagger said a duke?" The man raised a brow as if Harry was lying.

"Her brother is the Duke of Raven; her closest friend is Lord Sinclair. Her other brother is one of the wealthiest men in the United Kingdom, Mr. Maxwell Huntington. Do you really want me to leave here and tell them that you wouldn't let me see her? That I cannot reassure them that she has been treated fairly by you and your men?"

The man's face didn't change, and Harry battled the need to punch him.

"I want to see her now!"

"I'll have to ask you to leave—"

"If you do not allow me to see Mrs. Caron, I will do everything within my power to make sure you pay for what you have done. I will bring the full weight of her family and mine down upon your heads. Your reputation will be in tatters, and you will never work in London again." Harry's words were a growl. "One of her family owns a well-respected newspaper in London. I will have your name splashed all over the front pages if you do not let me see Mrs. Caron now."

Something in Harry's words had the sergeant shooting the constable a nervous look. He was not quite so smug now.

"I'll allow you to see her, but she's not leaving here with you, sir. No matter who her family is. The charges against her are serious, and as such she must face the full weight of the law."

Harry thought he could take both men, even contemplated it. He'd seen no other colors inside, which told him they were alone. He could knock them out and take the keys in seconds.

"Whoever put you up to these trumped-up charges will be made to pay alongside you, Sergeant Gavell," Harry said.

"We don't take kindly to threats, Mr. Sinclair."

"I don't take kindly to my friends being incarcerated!"

The man swallowed loudly, and Constable McDagger was now looking ill.

"Yes, well, if you'll come this way, Mr. Sinclair." Sergeant Gavell opened a door.

They walked down a corridor, and then he opened another door, and Harry found three wooden cell doors with squares cut out of them and replaced with iron bars.

"I can't let you in to see her. She's in the last one."

Heart thumping, Harry looked through the square. He found Maddie seated on a chair cuddling Wolf's ugly black dog.

"Maddie."

"Harry!" She hurried to the bars.

"It's all right." He put his hand through and cradled her cheek. It felt hot to touch. "We will get you out, but I need your brother to achieve that. Are you all right?"

She sniffed, then sneezed.

"You're unwell?" Her brown eyes were red and watering.

"I want to go home, Harry. I don't know why I'm here."

"I know, sweetheart, and I'm working to make that happen."

Shrugging out of his jacket, he forced it through the bars. "Wrap this around you."

"I-I am all right." She pulled it around her shoulders. "I don't understand this, Harry. They said I stole something, but I didn't."

"I know. Something is off, and I will find out what, Maddie. But you have to be brave now. I will need to go and find some of your family, the more powerful ones, to get you out. It seems I don't have blue enough blood to do so."

"Hep is helping me be brave. He wouldn't leave me when they came for me, but you should take him now."

"I doubt that podgy little dog will fit through the bars."

That made her snuffle.

"Yes, take the dog. He should not be in there, but we have not been able to part him from her," Sergeant Gavell said from the doorway. "I will allow the door to be unlocked so you can remove the beast from the Watch House."

"Her?" Harry said. "She is Mrs. Caron to you, Sergeant. Pray never forget that. The dog stays," he added, looking at the way Maddie held it close.

Ignoring the scowling sergeant, Harry talked to Maddie.

"Where are the others?"

"At an exhibition in the park. Fleur will wonder where I am if I'm not there when she returns, Harry."

"You have to leave now, Mr. Sinclair," Sergeant Gavell said. "Your time is up."

He didn't want to leave her. It went against everything he felt inside. He'd felt protective of this woman since he'd found her vulnerable and alone that day in Calais.

"I don't want you to go, Harry." He heard the fear.

"But you know I must, Maddie. Just as you know I will return to you. I would never leave you for any longer than I had to, sweetheart." He gripped the hand she held out to him. "Stay strong, and I will return soon, and then we will leave together."

She nodded. Eyes streaming, standing there clutching the ugliest dog in all of Christendom.

"I do not like small spaces, Harry. Please get me out before the dark comes."

"I don't like snails," Harry said, which made her laugh again.

"Don't they eat those where you come from?"

Harry shuddered. "I am a constant disappointment to my grandmother."

"Come back soon, Harry," Maddie said softly.

"I will, I promise. Ask them questions while I am gone, Maddie. Demand answers as to why they have you here. It is your right, sweetheart. Be brave and strong, as I know you can be."

"You don't know that about me."

"I do. You are brave and strong to have risen above what had you fleeing to Calais."

Her eyes caught his. "How did you know I was fleeing?"

"I see a great deal, as you know."

"I can be strong," she whispered to him.

"Because you've always had to be so?"

"Yes. Because it was the only way."

"Then call on that now, Maddie. Be strong until I return, and know that I will, and with me will be vengeance in the form of your family."

"Yes, I know they will come. I am no longer alone."

"You'll never be alone again, Maddie." He touched her cheek. "I brought you something. It is in the pocket of my jacket, Maddie. I bought it for you and Fleur."

She found the book and pulled it out.

"Practice your words until I return."

Their fingers touched, and then he turned and walked away from her, and it was the hardest thing he'd ever done.

"A word of warning," he said to Sergeant Gavell before he

left the building. "If I come back here and she has not been treated like the lady she is, then someone will pay... and dearly. I want a blanket and tea brought to her at once. Then, Sergeant, prepare yourself to face hell, because when next you see me, I will have an angry duke at my side, and he is only one of the men you will face."

CHAPTER 21

*L*eaving Maddie, Harry took a hackney to Max's house. He hoped the family had returned before he arrived. Rapping on the front door, he tried not to think about Maddie in that cell and focus on what he needed to do to get her out of it.

"Mr. Sinclair!" George looked shocked the see him.

"Where are the family, George? I need to speak with them at once."

"I will take you to Mr. Huntington."

The pain in his side was barely noticeable as he took the stairs up. The need to get Maddie out of the Watch House superseded anything else. He saw the flash of colors as he approached the room they were in.

"Mr. Harry Sinclair," the butler announced him.

He stepped through the door.

"Harry!" A little figure climbed off Emily's lap and ran at him. Bending, he scooped Fleur up and held her close. "I want Mama." The little girl was crying into his neck, her arms wrapped around him.

"Shhh now." He patted her back gently. "All will be well,

Fleur, trust me."

"Why are you here?" Dev came forward, the look on his face stony.

"I came about Maddie."

"Where is she?" Max's words were raw. "We can't find her; she was not here when we returned. None of the staff saw her leave. It is as if she has disappeared."

"What do you know, Harry?" Rory demanded.

"One of my crew passed the Watch House as they were leading her in."

"What!" The roar came from Max.

"I went there immediately and demanded to see her. They have arrested her on charges of theft."

"Theft!" Max stalked to where Harry stood, as if it was he who had put her in the Watch House.

"That's what they said. I demanded to see her, and she is holding up, but scared and clearly unwell."

"She was sick this morning. That's why she stayed home." Essie looked worried. "This will not be helping."

"Your dog is protecting her," Harry said to Wolf.

"Hep? I wondered where he was. Likely Bran sent him to go with Maddie."

"You're serious?" Harry said when no one else questioned these absurd words.

"Deadly. Animals are very intuitive," Wolf added, to which Harry simply shook his head.

"But what would she steal?" Rose asked. "She has been here with us from the day she arrived."

"Jewelry, the sergeant in charge said. He would give me no more details."

"From where?" Rory demanded.

"That I don't know."

"Where is your jacket?"

"I left it with Maddie," Harry told Essie. "I told them I

would return, and with me would be her brothers, one of whom was a duke."

"Excellent." James stepped forward. "I'm feeling mean, so let's go."

"This has to be done right, and until we know what is going on, you have to stay calm," he said to the brothers. "I have threatened the men already, and they looked frightened enough that I believe they will treat her well until we return, but to get the information we need and her discharge, we must remain rational and calm."

"She is my sister—"

"Think, Max. You know what these men are like. If you charge in there demanding answers, that will put them on the defensive. We must act calm to ensure Maddie is released," Dev said.

Harry stood rocking Fleur and gnashing his teeth. Maddie needed rescuing, and she needed rescuing now. She was sick and scared. "We need to go now," he said softly, so as not to upset the child growing limp in his arms.

"We cannot all go in," Cam said. "James, Dev, Max, Rory, Wolf, and Harry," he added. "Size, wealth, title, and menace. You will intimidate them. More will confuse things."

"We will take Warwick also, as he will hear what is being said."

"As will I." Eden stepped forward.

"And you are a woman, and therefore, according to some men, have little or no sense," Dev added. "Stay here, sister, please."

"You're lucky you added the bit about 'some men,'" Eden muttered.

"I value my life," Dev returned.

"Give her to me," Emily said, taking Fleur. "She is sleeping. You have calmed her, so she will get some rest."

"She missed you, Harry," Rose said. Harry didn't reply to that. He'd missed her too.

Soon they had everything they needed and had left the house. They travelled in two carriage, as James and Dev wanted to make a statement. Somber-faced, Harry shared the carriage with the Huntington brothers and Dev.

"And she is all right, Harry?" Rory said for the fifth time.

"She is. Cold and clearly unwell, but all right." *Please let her still be all right.* "I put the fear of God into Sergeant Gavell that if she was not cared for while I was away, there would be hell to pay."

"Sergeant Gavell?" Dev said. "He and I have met before. I shall look forward to our reacquaintance."

"What I want to know, Harry, is how your crewman recognized Maddie." Max's eyes narrowed.

How would he answer that?

"Yes, I wondered that." Rory's expression matched his big brother's.

Christ.

"Harry is an honorable man," Dev said.

"You don't know that," Rory said. "You know nothing of him."

"What are you suggesting he did?" Dev asked in a polite voice. His eyes, however, were anything but. He was standing up for Harry, and it was an unsettling feeling.

"I gave her passage from Calais to London," he said before the matter escalated.

"Why didn't one of you tell us?" Rory asked.

"I found her in Calais. She was exhausted and sitting on a crate holding Fleur, who slept. I asked Barney, the crewman who saw her outside the Watch, to speak to her."

"Why?"

"I could see she was desperate." Harry thought the time

for honesty was there. Her brothers needed to know their sister had been scared and alone before she reached them.

"I then gave her passage to London."

Rory and Max looked devastated.

"You surely saw how she arrived?"

"We did. I asked what ship she came on, but she said she could not remember," Rory said. "There is still so much she will not tell us. Things that happened that I know hurt her. She hurt her again. We're just not sure how."

"She?"

"She who gave us life," Max said in a tone that suggested he had no love for the woman.

"We know she stepped back into Maddie's life after Jacques, her husband, died, and wouldn't leave when Maddie asked her to, but the rest she will not speak of."

This must be the grandmother Fleur was scared of.

"Thank you, Harry." Max held out his hand. "Were it not for you, our sister would not be back in our lives."

"She would have found passage. I just expedited matters."

"For a cheap fare," Dev said, studying him.

Harry did not reply. They traveled the rest of the way in silence. *What had the mother done to her?*

Doors opened when the carriages stopped, and they all stepped down and gathered outside the Watch House. Harry was sure someone had seen them, and that the fear of God was about to rain down on those inside.

"Stay calm. No yelling or threats unless what I propose does not work," James said, straightening his jacket. Harry now wore one of Dev's, which fit as if it had been made for him.

"What do you propose, James?" Warwick asked.

"You lot may not respect my title, but I'm not a duke for nothing, Warwick. I plan to use that to the full effect."

They entered the building. James first, as the highest-ranking peer, then Dev. The others followed, and they approached the reception desk.

"Constable McDagger, I said I would return," Harry said. "And as promised, I am not alone."

The constable got to his feet, eyes wide as he took the men in. They were big, Max the biggest, but the others were close. Plus there was the look in their eyes that would surely terrify most people.

"Good evening. I am the Duke of Raven. This is Lord Sinclair, Mr. Warwickshire Sinclair, Captain Sinclair, Mr. Huntington and Mr. Rory Huntington. I understand you know Mr. Harry Sinclair?"

"Your Grace." The man's shoulders shot back. He then bowed so low, Harry lost sight of him beneath the desk.

"I wish to speak to your superior officer at once." James used a voice Harry had never heard before. "Now." The word held the right amount of bite to it.

The man ran. They heard doors open, and then a slam.

"He's talking to someone and saying that it was the truth, you did bring a duke back with you, Harry, but more than that, there's a lord also and others," Warwick said.

Harry switched his vision and found Maddie again. She was where he'd left her, her color still strong.

"I hear another voice. He's angry, demanding that Sergeant Gavell stand strong. That Maddie did steal from that jewelry store and the owner has laid a complaint."

"What jewelry store?" Max asked. "She's never brought jewelry in her life and would never steal. Maddie has always been far more honest than us."

"We know it's not true, Max, but what we need to find out is why and who is charging her," James said.

"He's coming," Warwick said.

The man Harry had spoken to appeared. "I am Sergeant

Gavell. Good evening, your Grace, Lord Sinclair." The man addressed James and Dev.

"There are others with me, Sergeant," James said.

"Of course. Good evening."

"I believe it is customary to bow in the presence of a duke," James added in a voice that would slice through glass.

The man disappeared under the table.

"We meet again, Sergeant," Dev said, his eyes glowing green. "And under equally unpleasant circumstances."

"Ah, indeed, my lord."

Sergeant Gavell was doing all he could to remain unaffected by the men in his Watch House. It wasn't working. He was nervous, it was there in his eyes as they shot from Dev to James. His forehead beaded with sweat.

"Now, my friend, Mr. Sinclair," James pointed to Harry, "has informed me my sister, Mrs. Caron, is being detained here. I want her released at once. If my wishes are not adhered to, I will bring the full force of every magistrate I know down upon you. I would also like to point out that I am a confidant to the King, who will not be pleased when he is notified of what has occurred."

Harry couldn't be sure, but was fairly confident that was a lie. However, if anyone was going to get away with it, it would be a duke.

"Mrs. Caron has been charged, your Grace. She is—"

"I don't think you understood me, so let me make myself clear." James leaned on the desk, cutting the man off. "If my sister is not brought to me in the next few minutes, I will make your life, and the lives of those who have any hand in these trumped-up charges, hell. In fact, I will ensure that by morning you have no position here and are on the next boat to some far-off uncivilized place. And Sergeant, I will not let you pack for the journey."

The man gulped loudly.

"It is my duty to see the l-law is fulfilled and each charge investigated, your Grace. I cannot simply let Mrs. Caron go because you wish it."

"I do not wish it, Sergeant, I demand it and will not be leaving this facility until that has happened," James added.

"Why have you not searched the house she lives in, if in fact you believe she has stolen something?" Rory asked. "Surely that is the first course of action you should have taken?"

Harry hadn't thought of that.

"Well, now, we were getting to that," the sergeant rushed to add.

"Excellent point, brother," James said. "You simply took my sister from my brother's house without first issuing a warrant to search the property. She was then left in a cold jail cell, unwell and shivering. What I want to know, Sergeant, is why? And also who laid these charges, because something about this entire thing has a nasty stench to it."

The man was sweating now. "If you'll excuse me, I must confer with my colleagues."

"Warwick," Dev said as the man ran away, "listen to every word."

Dev looked at Harry and Wolf and held up three fingers. Yes, there were three others beside Maddie in the building now. He nodded.

"Gavell is talking to the other man again. His voice suggests he's from our world," Warwick said. "Gavell is angry that the man did not tell him Maddie had powerful people at her back. Says that this has got out of hand and now his position is in jeopardy. He is stating he has no wish to go on a voyage or for the King to find out what has been done to the duke's sister."

"Stroke of genius, bringing the King into it," Dev said.

"We need to see who that voice belongs to," Max said. "As

I have a feeling it's he who laid the charges." He pushed on the door that would lead to where Maddie was, but it was locked and sturdy.

"His color is an angry red," Wolf said. "He's in the grip of a fierce rage. I have rarely seen anything like that before."

"I have," Dev added. "The man killed me."

"Gavell is now arguing with the man, demanding the charges be dropped," Warwick said. "And that he wants no part in this anymore, or the money."

"Ah, now we understand," James said. "Someone is throwing money around, but what we need to ascertain is why?"

"He has to be who is behind this entire thing. I'm going outside to see who leaves. I'll walk around the building," Dev said. "Wolf, come with me."

The cousins left, and Max tried to get through the door again with little success.

"Clearly it is reinforced for just that purpose," Rory said.

"Gavell is returning. Move back, Max," Warwick said.

"Where is my sister?" James demanded when the sergeant appeared.

"The charges will be dropped, your Grace." Gavell looked nervous. "Constable McDagger is bringing Mrs. Caron now."

"How convenient," Harry said. "But why the hell were they placed to start with?"

"Mistaken identity," the sergeant said quickly. "We've, ah, we've charged another."

"And you think that is enough to pacify us?" James snapped.

"We apologize, your Grace."

"This will not end here," the duke growled softly, making Sergeant Gavell swallow several times. "I smell something rotten, Sergeant, and when I uncover what that is, those responsible will be very sorry."

"You have crossed the wrong family," Max said, "and someone will pay."

The door opened, and there she was, still with the little dog clasped in her arms and the book he'd given her clutched in a hand. Pale, shaking, but courageous. She made his heart ache. Harry wanted to hold her, and yet it was to her brothers she went... all three of them.

He had no rights to this woman, no matter that Ravens married Sinclairs.

CHAPTER 22

Maddie saw Harry first; he stood back slightly from the others. It was Max who reached for her as she walked through the door.

"Maddie, dear God, I'm so sorry." He wrapped his arms around her. "We failed to protect you again."

"You could not have helped, Max." She let him hold her. Rory then patted her back. She just closed her eyes and leaned into all that strength. The fear was now gone. She was safe.

"Are you all right?" Rory asked her.

"I am." Maddie sneezed. "I just want to go home."

"Then we shall. Harry, take Maddie to the carriage," Rory said. "We just have a few more things to say to Sergeant Gavell."

"Are you all right, Maddie?" James came to her side briefly. His hug was all-encompassing, as the others had been, and she enjoyed that too. "I'm so sorry this happened, sweetheart."

"I'm all right. Thank you all for coming to get me."

"Did you think we wouldn't?" His smile was gentle.

"No. I knew you'd come once Harry told you."

"We are not finished talking yet, Sergeant Gavell," James barked. Maddie turned in time to see the sergeant trying to escape.

"Come." Harry took her arm and guided her out of the Watch House. "The carriage is close, just a few more steps."

"I'm all right now, Harry."

"I'm not," he muttered.

Opening the door, he simply picked her up and stepped inside, lowering her to a seat. Hep, understanding all was well now, leapt off her lap and onto the opposite seat. He then turned a circle and settled down with a loud sigh.

"The book you gave me, Harry—it is wonderful."

He sat across from her, his green eyes so bright in the dim interior of the carriage. He'd found her, and for that she'd be forever grateful. Once again, it was Harry who had rescued her.

"Thank you for bringing my family. I knew you would come back."

"I told you I would." He moved to the edge of the seat, so close to her now, their knees touched.

"H-How is your side? I forgot to ask you—"

"You had quite a lot on your mind." His smile was small.

"How did you know I was there?"

"Do you remember in Calais, the crewman who came to see if you were all right?"

She nodded.

"His name is Barney, and he was passing the Watch House when you were being led inside. He came to my cabin and told me."

"Please thank him for me. Had he not been there—"

"We would have found you."

His eyes were running over her face.

"Maddie." He took her hands in his, pulling her closer. "I knew something was wrong. I felt you; I felt your fear."

"How?"

"I don't know how, but it was not a pleasant feeling."

She had never willingly touched a man, not even her husband. He'd been good and kind, but there had been no hugging or gentleness. The hand she lifted to Harry's cheek shook. Maddie traced the edges of his cheekbones and angle of his chin. Felt the roughness of the growth of his beard. She'd touched him when he was ill, but not since.

"Maddie." He whispered her name.

She leaned closer and kissed him. Just a brush, but that soft touch ignited something inside her. Need bloomed. She wanted him, and so much more than a mere kiss.

He let her take the lead, the kiss soft and slow—and over in seconds when they heard voices outside the carriage.

"I won't apologize for that," Maddie said.

"I would not ask it of you."

She would not regret it. She felt something for this man, and yet knew that anything between then would be fruitless. She was… well, she was a widow and a mother, and Harry's life was in France.

But for now, she would simply enjoy that kiss and hold the knowledge deep inside her that he had too.

The door opened, and Dev appeared with Wolf and Warwick. Hep leaped off the seat and into the arms of his owner.

"What a good boy you are for watching over Maddie."

"A carriage had pulled up around the rear of the building, and a man walked out and into it before we could see his face." Dev entered the carriage. "I would know his colors anywhere, however."

"Evil," Harry said. "I also."

"Colors?" She'd heard them speak about this, but as yet did not understand it.

"Everyone has a different color," Dev said. "Harry, Wolf, and I can see them when we change our vision. I know you are aware of what we are, Maddie, just not all the nuances of it."

"No." She still couldn't grasp what she'd been told, and yet had seen the miracle of the Sinclairs for herself.

"Illness and near death weakens the color to white, and evil darkens it," Dev added.

"It is almost more than I can believe, and yet I do not doubt what you say." Maddie sneezed.

"Here." Harry handed her a large handkerchief. "We need to get you home to Essie before your condition worsens."

"It is only a sniffle. I shall be fine now I am out of there."

"They come," Warwick said. "James, Max, and Rory, I mean."

"Is that hard? Hearing things that sometimes you don't want to."

The young man smiled at her and tapped his ear. "Those of us with strong hearing wear earplugs to mute everyday sounds."

"Put them in now, Warwick," Dev told him.

"We will take the other carriage," James said from the doorway. "Gavell told us nothing of interest, only babbled about how they'd made a mistake. It took all my strength to pull Rory off him, as Max was urging him to pummel the sergeant. Luckily we escaped without any more charges being pressed against the Huntingtons."

He closed the carriage door, and soon they were on their way. Maddie sat with Harry's jacket wrapped around her and watched the darkening sky as the carriage took her home.

It was that and so much more for her now.

The Sinclairs talked, discussing what had happened.

Maddie listened but did not say much, and every now and then her eyes caught and held Harry's and she felt that little thrill travel through her.

She was a widow, a woman who had known the touch of a man, but not a touch like Harry's. He would show her passion, and for the first time ever, Maddie wanted to know what that felt like.

"We are here. Prepare yourself, Maddie, everyone will be inside waiting," Warwick said as the door opened.

"All of them?"

"It is our way. When one of us is hurting, in danger, or needing support, the others are there," Dev said.

"All this is hard to accept when it has only ever been you and another to care for," Harry said as they prepared to follow the others from the carriage.

"I fought against it."

"And now?"

"Now I think I would be a fool not to take what is offered," Maddie said. "I was guarded because that is always the way I had to be, but they don't allow that."

Harry's laugh was a small huff of breath. "It is indeed hard to maintain distance when they don't understand that concept."

"Will you accept them, Harry?" Maddie took his hand and stepped down.

"I don't want to. This is not my life, and I have no wish for it. But I must tell you something, Maddie. They know you sailed here on my ship. I had to tell them when they asked how my crewman recognized you. But that is all I told them."

"I understand, and thank you again for today, and finding me."

"Come." Max was waving to them from the front door of his house.

"They are good people. Surely you can see that now, Harry?"

He didn't answer, just placed a hand at her back and nudged her forward.

Would he stay for long? She wanted to ask him that, but it was not her place to do so.

Fleur saw her as she entered the parlor where the others waited and ran at her. Little legs pumping, wide smile on her face. Maddie dropped to her knees right there on the floor inside the doorway and scooped her daughter into her arms.

She felt hands on her head.

"Mama, I missed you," Fleur whispered into her ear.

"I am here now, and will not leave you again, I promise." Maddie rose with her daughter in her arms.

"Come, sit, you must feel terrible." Essie waved her to a chair. "I will have a tisane prepared for your head, as I'm sure it aches."

Several people moaned.

"I will add honey," Essie added, glaring at them.

Food was brought, and the entire story recounted. Harry explained his part for those who had not heard it.

"Let me help you with that headache." Lilly approached Maddie.

"I am well, Lilly, I promise."

"I'm not sure how you can be, considering what you have endured."

She felt Lilly's hand pass over her head briefly, the touch light. She felt the heat, and then the pain had gone. It was bliss.

"Thank you."

"You're welcome. I always say there is little point in suffering unnecessarily."

"But I have no wish to tire you also."

"Oh, that doesn't tire me; it's saving lives that does that." Lilly smiled at Harry, then went to sit next to Dev.

They loved, as did all the couples in the room. She saw it in the small gestures and looks. Maddie had never received such a look before. Her eyes went to Harry. His were on her.

"And now I must return to my ship," Harry said.

"Stay, Harry, we are to take tea," Cam said.

"I won't, but thank you." He nodded, his eyes settling on her and Fleur. She thought he'd approach, instead he nodded again, and then he was gone and she told herself that was all right, as she had all of this now.

CHAPTER 23

Harry threw cargo out of the hold and up into the hands of a crewman. He needed the manual labor. Needed the hard work to make him forget what had happened to Maddie and in that carriage two days ago.

Maddie had kissed him. She'd leaned in and placed her lips on his, and he felt as if she'd given him so much more. She'd trusted him and felt safe. She would never have kissed him otherwise. It had taken every ounce of his self-control not to pull her onto his thighs. He wanted her straddling him, wanted her body pressed to his.

She was a widow, and yet still an innocent. He hated that any man but he had touched her, and yet he knew that jealousy was unworthy of him. Fleur was the result of her marriage, and she was a blessing.

"A letter has arrived for you, Harry." Faris's face appeared above him.

"I'll read it later."

"What are you doing down there?"

"Knitting. What the hell does it look like?" Harry grabbed another barrel and threw it up, nearly hitting Faris, who pulled back just in time.

"Is your side up to such strenuous exercise?"

"Yes, thank you, Father."

"Your stupidity knows no bounds." Faris appeared again. "You took a bullet, and not that long ago, and yet you are down there hurling large objects around like an idiot!"

Faris was rarely angry, and usually it took a great deal to get him there. Harry had perfected the art over the years.

"Go play with your doll house." Harry's words had his crew snickering.

"Imbecile," Faris muttered.

Harry made kissing noises and felt a great deal better for needling his friend, which was beneath him, but anything to improve his spirits.

He'd wanted to stay at the Huntington house after they'd returned with Maddie. Wanted to eat, then talk about what or who had had Maddie arrested. He'd wanted to sit and have Fleur climb into his lap. She would then kiss his cheek, as she had often done, and produce a book for him to read.

He'd wanted that so much, he'd left.

Hell of a mess, Harry. But the point was, what did he want to do about it? That he wanted to do something suggested there were changes happening inside him.

It was hard to break the habits and beliefs of a lifetime.

"My brothers have the same streak of foolish disregard for their well-being that you are currently displaying, Harry." A pretty face appeared above him this time, and then another, this one not so appealing. Both he knew well.

"All true, sadly, and it's most definitely a Sinclair gene, and male dominant," Cam added. "But I think Wolf, Dev, and Harry are the most stubborn."

"Oh, I'm not sure about that. I think the Raven gene shows a strong streak of imbecilic behavior also," Eden said.

"Duchess, you will end up covered in dirt if you kneel there." Harry looked up at his cousins. Cam had that look that said he was mischief bound.

"Grime does not bother me, Harry. Idiocy, however, does."

"I protest," Harry gritted as he lifted another barrel. His side gave a vicious tug that had him dropping it.

"Get up here at once, you fool!" Eden snapped.

"Leave him, sister. We can watch him prove to us he is well, and then when he drops, say I told you so," Cam drawled.

Harry glared up at them. "Is there a purpose to your visit? Or do you just wish to fire insults at me?"

"You were shot in the side," Eden snapped. "Honestly, Harry, you are lucky it is Cam and I and not Essie, Wolf, or Dev. They would not have been so nice."

"This is you being nice, is it?"

Harry knew his crewmen were watching avidly and enjoying the production.

"Of course. Were we not, you would be weeping piously into your cargo," Cam taunted.

"I have never wept piously and have no plans to start now," Harry gritted out. "Now get to the point before I throw some cargo at you."

"Come up here, and we'll tell you." Cam's nose wrinkled. "The smell is not pleasant."

"No, really, that saddens me greatly," Harry said with no sincerity at all.

"Harsh, cousin, but it pleases me that you are becoming one of us." Cam smiled. "Insulting is an important part of Sinclair daily life. I have high hopes for you now."

The man really was impossible to insult.

"Don't you have a paper to run? *The Bugler*, I believe?" Harry needled him.

"Oh, I like that name!" Eden looked pleased.

"I'm thinking of doing a piece on sea captains, Harry. Can I interview you?" Cam said. "Apparently you're a salty bunch."

Harry picked up a smelly rag, balled it up, and lobbed it at him. Cam disappeared. What did it say about him that he felt happier than he had in days, seeing two of his cousins?

"Maddie is doing well, but…" Cam and Eden reappeared.

"But?" Harry prodded.

"But you will have to come up here, as my skirts are getting grimy, if you wish to hear the rest," the duchess added.

Both Sinclairs then disappeared, and Harry gnashed his teeth. He wasn't playing their games.

He lasted five minutes before climbing out. His cousins were standing by the railing. With them was James, holding their youngest daughter, Katherine. She had chubby cheeks, a sweet little smile, and a riot of brown curls.

"Hello, Harry," James said.

"Duke." He bowed deeply.

"He certainly understands his place better than you lot," James drawled. "But family really don't need to bow that low, Harry. Just so your nose is level with my waist."

"I don't think I've ever bowed to you," Cam said.

"Shall we hug?" Harry moved closer to the Sinclairs, and as his smell at best could be termed rank, Eden hid behind her brother.

"Is the ship named after your mother, Harry?" Cam said, stepping to the right, thereby exposing Eden.

"She is."

"Go and wash, old man—you stink—and we can talk," Cam added, pinching his nose.

As he could smell himself, he did just that. Once inside his cabin, he stripped off his clothes, scrubbed his body, and washed his hair. When he was clean and dry, he pulled on clean clothes. Picking up the narrow, flat, rectangular stone off his desk that he'd found on a beach one day, Harry scrubbed it clean too.

Wandering back out on the deck, he found them where he'd left them, but talking to Faris. None seemed overly concerned to be speaking with a man far below them on the social ladder. Harry battled the swell of pride.

Pride for the fact that these people carried his blood and showed no bias. He didn't want to feel himself softening toward them, but the simple fact was, he couldn't not. They were part of him, the family he'd secretly always craved.

Not that he'd tell them that.

"There he is, our handsome and sweet-smelling cousin," Eden said, moving to kiss Harry's cheek.

"So now I'm worthy of your attention?"

"Of course. We are nothing if not fickle."

Katherine was wailing when he arrived, and lunged at him, out of her father's arms. Harry took her, settling her against his shoulder.

"Her teeth are sore. This will help." Harry held the stone to Katherine's mouth, and she began to chew on it.

"He's always had a way with children"—Faris frowned—"and yet has none himself. It is the same with my siblings' children. They crowd around him when he comes to visit. And when one is unwell or upset, it is he who can calm them."

"I think it is because he communicates on their level," Cam said. "Intellect wise."

"Perhaps you're right." Faris laughed. "Now I must be off, as there is work to do."

"That will make a change," Harry muttered.

"We thought to bring you up to date on the matter of Maddie's arrest," Cam said.

He'd started making investigations of his own and gotten nowhere. No matter how much money he was willing to throw around, no one was talking about who'd laid those charges against her. Harry was not happy. Someone knew something.

"Mr. Brown from Bow Street and Mr. Spriggot, who runs an investigative service, have worked with our families before. It is they who are looking into the matter," James said. "Thus far they have turned up nothing, which both are finding odd, as there is usually a way to gain information, if not through money then some other means."

"Warwick, Dorrie, and Somer, are doing some of the investigative work for Mr. Spriggot also," Cam added.

"You cannot be serious? Surely that is far too dangerous?"

"We would not allow that, Harry, you must trust us in this," Cam said.

"I have been unsuccessful also," Harry said.

"You? How interesting that you would want to investigate Maddie's arrest also." Cam wore that smile that had his hand itching to remove it.

"I did not like that entire situation. There was something off, and I thought to see what I could uncover," Harry said calmly. He'd learned already not to show any weakness in front of a family member.

Family.

"Very well, we will leave that subject alone for now. We are going to Mr. Rolland's Circus of Strange and Ridiculous Curiosities," Cam said, looking excited. "The eldest of our children are at an age where we can now unleash them on poor Mr. Rolland, as we did when the twins and Warwick were small."

"He must be quite an age now though, Cam? Perhaps he is

no longer in charge?" Eden added. "I will be sad if that is the case."

"I doubt Mr. Rolland will have retired. We burned down his theatre once, you know." Cam smiled at the memory.

"And he allows you back?"

"He likes to have a duke and duchess in the place, so he forgave us. And the funds we gave him rebuilt the place entirely," Cam added.

"Someone else who respects me more than you lot," James added.

"Was there a particular purpose for your visit other than to yell insults to me from above the cargo hold?"

Katherine gnawed on the stone, her cries now eased to sniffles. The fingers of one of her little pudgy hands were wrapped around the lapel of his jacket.

"How did you know she was teething?" James asked.

"Sometimes I get a twinge where the child's pain is. It's only mild with Katherine, but in more severe cases it can be quite painful."

"Wonderful. We have plenty of children who need soothing from time to time." Cam added, "You will be the one to tell us what is wrong with those that don't speak. Now, let's be off."

"Off where?" Harry looked at Cam, completely at sea.

"To the circus, as I have just explained."

"I shall pass on the joys of Mr. Rolland's circus. However, I would like you to finish explaining what is happening with the events of the day Maddie was arrested. Has it been discovered who laid the charges?"

"We will tell you in the carriage," Eden said as James opened his mouth to speak. "Come along."

"You do know that outside our family, I'm quite well respected," the duke muttered. "People even listen in awe when I speak at the House of Lords."

"Of course they do, darling." Eden patted his cheek, which had the duke's eyes rolling.

"Tell me what I want to know or you don't get your child back," Harry said.

"We have two others." Eden flicked her wrist. "Plus she is very weepy at the moment. I'm happy for her to stay with you."

"Heartless wench," James said. "But really, Harry, we would like your company."

"Oh, all right," Cam said as James nudged him. "We have missed you."

"No, really, cousin? I had no idea how much you cared." Katherine yawned in his arms, and he looked at her swollen gums. "Has Essie nothing you can give her?"

"She is making something today."

Harry grunted his approval.

"So will you come?" Eden asked. "Please. Fleur asked to see you again this morning, the poor little girl, and of course she's only just starting to recover—"

"From what?" Harry's heart started thudding. "What's wrong with Fleur?"

"Just a sniffle, but the poor wee thing, she'd been quite miserable," Eden said.

James looked over the side of the railing, and Cam simply smiled. He was being played, he knew it, as did they, but the hell of it was, he really wanted to go with them.

"Very well, but only because you seem desolate without me."

"Oh yes, desolate," Cam said as they all headed for the gangway. "I've been weeping since you left."

The Raven carriage was waiting for them, and he knew his men were watching and by now would know he had connections in places a great deal more elevated than he'd had when he arrived in London.

"She's sleeping, Harry," Eden said. "I shall step inside, and you can pass her to me. I cannot thank you enough. The poor darling is exhausted."

It was as he lowered the babe into her mother's arms that Harry felt the first shiver of awareness roll through him.

CHAPTER 24

"What is it, Harry? Your eyes have become more vivid," Cam said as he left the carriage.

"Do you feel anything?" He looked at Cam, who shook his head. "It's a child then."

Stepping away from them, he opened his senses. Now he knew what he was doing, the shock was still there, and the colors rocked him back on his heels, but he understood it.

"Easy." Cam's hand grabbed his shoulder. "What do you see?"

"I hear the sound of a child begging for someone to stop," Eden said from inside the carriage. "To the right."

Harry looked that way and found a pale pink color. They were in a building, on the second floor.

"Do you see them?" James asked him.

Harry nodded and started running in that direction.

"Stay in the carriage, Eden," he heard James say. "Henry, watch over the duchess and my daughter!"

The bottom floor of the building was a large store selling shipping supplies like ropes and rigging.

Entering, Harry didn't bother with the man who asked

what he wanted, he simply walked behind the counter and into the rear of the building. Once there, he took the stairs up.

He knew Cam was on his heels, could feel him. Behind him he also knew would be James, simply because that was their way. Ravens and Sinclairs were there for each other.

Reaching the top, he heard a slapping sound. Opening the door with enough force that that it banged on the wall, he entered.

"Who are you? Get out!" A woman scurried away from the child cowering on the floor. Her hands were over her head.

"Cease!" Harry bellowed, stomping forward. He wrenched the piece of leather from the woman's hands. "You will not strike that child again!"

"How dare you enter my premises!" The woman wore black. Dress, bonnet, and boots. Her face was tight with anger, lips drawn in a straight line.

"Why are you beating this child?" Harry didn't allow himself to look at the girl again, because he could feel her pain, the heart-wrenching fear of what she was enduring. Strangely, his eyes were itching now too.

"That's no concern of yours."

"Try that again," Harry said, very aware of the two men at this back. The woman was looking from him to them and back again. "Why are you beating that child with a piece of leather when she cannot defend herself?"

"I'm purging her," the woman spat.

"I beg your pardon?"

"My husband and I, we take these children and rid them of the evil they were born into. They are limbs of Satan reared by women of no morals. It is our calling to put them on the right path."

"By beating them. Hardly sounds a Christian thing to do,"

Cam snarled, moving to Harry's side. "Children are God's blessing and should be treated as such."

"Where are the other children?" Harry asked. "I see none but the girl."

The girl moved so quickly no one saw it, and in seconds her arms were wrapped around Harry's leg, her face pressed into his thigh. Harry rested a hand on her head.

"Charity Thrice!" The woman went to grab the girl, but Harry held out a hand to ward her off.

"Touch the child again, and I will take that piece of leather to you."

"Charity Thrice?" Cam asked. "Presumably there is Charity Once and Twice?"

The woman pressed her lips together.

"What's going on?" The man who had been downstairs arrived.

"These men entered our premises, Mr. Blythe, and stopped me doing God's work!"

Harry saw right off Mr. Blythe was not quite as committed to God's work as his wife, because he winced as she spoke.

"God's work is not beating a child," Harry snarled.

"It's what we need to do to make them see reason, then we can put them to work." Mr. Blythe moved to his wife's side. "Good, honest work that will see them stay on a righteous path."

"Work?" James stepped forward. "What kind of work?"

"Splicing ropes and working on supplies needed for my store. We pay them, of course," Mr. Blythe added.

"And the children all come from where?"

"The orphanage and off the streets," Mrs. Blythe said. "We are doing the Lord's work!"

"The Lord, to the best of my knowledge, never told anyone to beat children or purge them because they are limbs of Satan. To enjoy beating a child because you believe it is your calling suggests the problem lies with you, not them!" Harry thundered.

"Take up that switch, James, and show them how much it hurts," Cam snarled.

"I will not meet like with like," the duke said in that tone he'd used on Sergeant Gavell.

"I am guided by the highest authority to do my work," the woman stated. "You have no say here."

"I am the Duke of Raven," James said slowly.

"One step below royalty," Cam added. "So he tells us," he said out the side of his mouth.

"D-Duke?" The man went pale.

"Did you buy this child so you could put her to work?" James snapped.

The man dropped his eyes. The woman sniffed.

"Where is this place of labor?" Harry asked. The child was sniffling into his leg, which just about broke his heart, She couldn't be any older than four or five. Harry rubbed his eyes; they were watering now. Maybe he had caught something from Maddie.

"I demand you answer Mr. Sinclair's question," James said.

"A warehouse. Old Beamouth Road," the man rushed to add.

"We will be visiting this warehouse in three days. My suggestion is that what we find is a clean facility with plenty of air and light. I will also need an assurance the children are served meals each day," James said.

"Of course." The man nodded quickly.

"I will then visit it each week on a different day to check you are indeed doing what I have demanded."

The man and his wife paled.

"You have no right to interfere in God-fearing work," the

woman said. "The Lord says defend the rights of the poor and needy, and Mr. Blythe and I do just that. We offer them a home."

"He also states 'do not exploit the poor because they are poor,'" James snapped back.

"How much did you buy this child for?" Harry asked the couple.

The sum enraged him. A child's life was worth a pittance to the Blythes.

Taking money from his pocket, he threw it at them.

"You own her no more," Harry said.

"We will come to that warehouse and expect everything is in order," James said. "Make sure it is so, Mr. and Mrs. Blythe, or we will make your lives hell."

Picking the little girl up, Harry left the building with his family behind him.

"Sometimes I forget, and then something like this happens and I am reminded of just how evil some of those who walk among us can be," Cam growled.

"Amen," James and Harry said.

Once they reached the carriage, Harry looked at the other two men.

"I will take her with me onto the ship."

"It is no place for her. We'll take her home and decide what is best there," James said. "Get into the carriage, Harry. We are drawing attention."

Harry stepped inside.

James explained what had happened to his wife, who still held the sleeping babe.

"Is she all right?" Eden looked worried.

"I'm not sure." Harry settled on the seat, and the girl clung to him.

"What is wrong with your eyes?" Cam asked, handing

Harry a handkerchief. "They look bloodshot and are watering."

"It happened when I was in that room."

The carriage rolled through London, and Harry held the child to his chest with one hand and the handkerchief pressed to his eyes with the other. She never moved, just kept her head in his shoulder, arms around his neck.

"James did the duke thing again." Cam pulled out a blanket and tucked it around the girl.

Eden sighed. "He does it well, but it can be tiring."

"If I may protest," the duke in question said. "I do the duke thing when the duke thing is required. You should all be bloody grateful you have one you can trot out when it's convenient."

"We're extremely grateful," Eden said, handing him their child. "You have the bigger arms for her to sleep in, also handy. I think there is a special place in hell for people who mistreat children. I know a few people who are already there. James's father for one, and mine also."

"The Blythes have just booked a spot," Harry said. "We shall visit that warehouse in three days. I want to ensure those children are all right. If not, we will have to help them in some way."

"We will," Cam said. "Max has houses, as does Lilly."

"Houses?" Harry lifted the handkerchief briefly to look at them.

They explained about Lilly's house for children on the streets, and Max's house for the boys who had been mistreated on ships. It humbled him to hear they did these things.

He'd been wrong to believe they were not good people.

"I have a warehouse in Paris. I had beds put in there and other necessities," Harry said. "Children who have nowhere to go can stay there for as long as they need. Sometimes there are not enough beds, the need is so great."

"With every word you utter, your place in this family is confirmed, and yet still you don't believe it so," Cam added.

"My life is in France."

"Can it not be in England and France?"

They looked at him, three pairs of eyes, all wanting him to say yes. Instead he looked away and out the window with the child still clasped in his arms, confusion muddling his thoughts once more.

CHAPTER 25

Maddie had taken Fleur and Bran and gone to see the house Max had said was hers. She'd stood outside and imagined herself living in such a grand place. A place that would give them a home again. This would be very different from the cottage she'd shared with Jacques; it would also be hers alone. Max had said so.

Rory and Kate would live next door, so if she needed them they would come. Here, Fleur had family and safety. It would be selfish of her to walk away from this now. There was also the fact that she no longer wanted to.

"It is a nice house, as is the one next door, and I hear exceptional people are moving in." Rory joined her. "Hello, Fleur." He bent to place a kiss on her head, then scratched Bran's head.

"We're looking at a house, Uncle Rory."

"I can see that, sweetie."

"It is a nice place, but I had heard the man moving in next door is something of a braggart."

"Surely not." Rory dropped his arm around Maddie's

shoulders, and it felt right, standing there close to him. His hand was on Fleur's head. She was changing, opening up to other people slowly.

The fear was easing, and that made her want to step out of the shadows.

"What are you doing here?" she asked her brother.

"Kate wants to look through the house once more, to see what furniture we will need."

The smile on his face was like many she'd seen him give his fiancée.

"You love her very much, don't you?"

"Very much. She has made me warm, where once I was cold."

Maddie laid her head on his shoulder. "I could not have asked for more for you than that."

She left him when Kate arrived, with the promise that they would see each other later.

Walking slowly back down the road, Maddie enjoyed the sun on her face and the small hand of her daughter swinging at her side. She started singing a French ballad, and Fleur joined in with her sweet little voice. Right in that moment, Maddie could almost believe the hell she'd left behind on that night in France was a distant memory. The arrest still niggled at her, but her family was looking into that.

Mistaken identity, they'd said, and yet who had identified her? She had not been here long enough to get to know anyone but family. It all sounded odd and shady. Max wondered if it was someone wanting revenge on him. But surely no one knew she was his sister yet? Essie would have been the likely target in that case.

As they approached James's house, she watched a carriage pull up. The crest told her either the duke or duchess was inside.

Cam stepped down first.

"Uncle Cam!" Fleur loved all her new uncles.

James and Eden were next, and in her brother's arms was Katherine, sleeping. The looks on their faces had her hurrying. Something was wrong.

"What has happened?"

"Harry found a child being mistreated and has brought her here," Eden said.

Looking in the carriage, Maddie found him rising, a little girl pressed to his side.

"Is she hurting in any way?"

When he looked at her, she was shocked to see his eyes were bloodshot and watering.

"What has happened? Your eyes, Harry, they look painful."

"They are." His words were gruff. "Step aside now, Maddie."

She did as he asked, and Harry was soon on the road with the others. The little girl had auburn hair cut short and was dressed in a gray smock. She could be no older than five.

"I will get Essie." Cam ran off in that direction.

"Go to my study, and Eden and I will return shortly." James waved them inside, and they took the stairs up with Bran on their heels. "Buttles, bring food, please."

"And a clean cloth damp with water," Maddie added, thinking of Harry's eyes.

James's office had been a wonderful surprise to Maddie when first she'd seen it. The ceiling was high, with the farthest wall holding floor-to-ceiling windows that made it seem as if she were stepping into the sunlight. Books lined two walls, high enough that a ladder would be needed to reach the top ones. She'd asked James if he'd read them all; he'd said not all, but that Emily, Samantha, and the others had read most of the ones he hadn't.

She'd secretly vowed to add her name to that list.

The furnishings were of rich, deep reds and blues with woven patterned rugs scattered on the polished wooden floors. It was alive with a feast of color and light.

Harry took a seat on the sofa with the child still clinging to him. Fleur tugged her hand free from Maddie's and stood before him.

"You are hurting, Harry?"

"My eyes are sore, Fleur, but I'm sure it will pass soon."

She patted his knee.

"Who is that?"

"I'm not sure of her name yet. Perhaps you could ask her?"

Fleur climbed on the sofa beside him and patted the girl's hair.

Maddie sat next to her daughter. "Has she spoken to you, Harry?"

"Nothing." He blinked, trying to clear his eyes.

Maddie lifted Fleur into her lap. Bran crept over and laid his head on Harry's lap

"Hello, my name is Maddie." She touched the girl's shoulder. "Would you like to meet my daughter, Fleur?"

Maddie talked softly to the child, rubbing her back. Harry sat silently with his eyes now closed, clearly in a great deal of discomfort. The little girl moved her head slightly.

"Hello," she whispered in a gruff little voice.

The head rose and looked at Maddie, but there was no focus, eyes empty and sightless. The lids were puffy and swollen. She also had a nasty welt on her cheek.

"She can't see, Harry."

"What?" His whisper was ragged.

"Your eyes are hurting because she is blind, but there also seems to be some kind of infection there," Maddie said softly.

"Dear God." He raised her chin, studying her eyes. "You

are safe here now," he said, stroking his thumb over her chin. "No one will hurt you again."

The girl remained silent.

"I am Harry, and this is Maddie." He took the little girl's hand and touched it to Maddie's cheek. "And this is Fleur." He did the same with her daughter, and Fleur sat still, allowing it. "And this shaggy creature is Bran, who wants to meet you." Harry lowered her hand to the dog, who was still as a statue now while the girl touched his head.

"How long have you been without sight?" Harry asked her.

"Not long. They were sore, and slowly I lost my sight."

How terrifying that must have been for her, Maddie thought. She wondered if anyone had been watching over the girl.

The butler arrived with a laden tray of refreshments, and after lowering it to a table, he handed her the damp cloth.

"What is your name?" Maddie asked the girl.

"We're changing that," Harry said. "No child should be called Charity Thrice." She heard the rage in his words.

Maddie folded the cloth into a pad and placed it over Harry's eyes. His sigh told her it felt good.

"No, indeed. What would you like us to call you?"

"I am Daisy," she whispered. Her hand was stroking the soft fur on Bran's head.

"Well now, that is a lovely name. Fleur, this is Daisy."

Her daughter seemed happy with that. "We are both flowers."

"Will you come and sit with me now, Daisy? I am a friend, and there is absolutely no need to be afraid anymore, I promise you." Maddie lifted the girl into her lap beside Fleur so Harry could rest. His side was surely sore along with his eyes.

Bran followed and now rested his big head in Daisy's lap.

Harry lowered the cloth. "It's like he knows something," he said, looking at the dog.

"He does." Maddie watched Daisy's hand creep to Bran's head again.

"Thank you for the cloth. The pain in my eyes is easing."

"You have a gift, Harry, and yet it must also cause you a great deal of pain." She touched his cheek. It felt natural and right. He was special to her; she could no longer deny that, even if nothing came of the feelings inside her.

"It is just something I have always lived with. I had not thought it special until I met this family."

She lowered her hand as Essie, Eden, and James entered the room.

"I want to introduce you to some other people now, Daisy. They are family, and I promise you they are good people too," Harry said.

She listened but kept her eyes lowered, saying nothing. Fleur took Daisy's free hand in hers and held it close, and Maddie had never loved her child more than in that moment.

"This is Daisy," Harry said. Maddie watched him place a hand over his eyes and point to the little girl.

James mouthed the word blind, and Harry nodded. The shock on the duke's face soon turned to anger. Eden's matched it, and Maddie wondered just how badly Daisy was being treated when they found her.

"Hello, Daisy, I am Essie."

Her sister-in-law came forward and dropped to her knees before them. She then took one of Daisy's hands and rested it on her face.

"Are you hurting anywhere, Daisy?"

"My eyes are sore," the little girl whispered.

"Let me see?" Essie touched her chin raising it so she could see Daisy's eyes. They looked red and swollen..

"Well now, I have something that will make the pain ease." Essie chatted as she opened a jar and smeared the contents onto a soft piece of cloth. She then folded it, and held it to the girls eyes. "Where is it you are from, Daisy?"

"The Haleigh Orphanage."

"And you were there for some time before you went to live with Mr. and Mrs. Blythe?" Harry asked.

"I knew only the orphanage."

The words were spoken in a subdued, serious tone.

Essie wound a bandage around her head, holding the pad in place. Tending her gently, drawing out answers to questions that Harry and she asked the little girl. She did not know her age and had been in the hands of the Blythes for only a short time… thankfully.

Fleur handed Daisy a biscuit and explained that it was yummy, then broke some of her own off to feed Bran, which Maddie had often told her not to do.

Around them the adults watched solemn-faced, all aware of the suffering this child must have endured.

"Excuse me, your Grace," Buttles said from the doorway. "A Mr. Brown and Mr. Spriggot have called at the Huntington residence. A note has arrived requesting your presence."

"Thank you, Buttles," James said. "It will be about Maddie's arrest."

"I will take Fleur and Daisy, and we shall read a book," Essie said, lifting the little girl into her arms. Holding Fleur's hand, she walked away to the bookshelves with Bran on her heels.

"I think she'll be scared if we both leave," Harry said.

"You're right. You stay." Maddie got to her feet.

"I was thinking you should stay."

"Why?" Maddie looked at Harry, who was now on his feet too. "This is about my arrest."

"And I want to know what is being done." He frowned at her through eyes that were a lot clearer now.

"We will all go," James said. "Come along."

"Just a moment," Harry and Maddie said at the same time, both heading to where the girls now sat in a chair with Essie.

"We will return soon." Maddie kissed Fleur's cheek and touched Daisy's, not wanting to scare her. The little girl still had her head down and was clutching Fleur's hand.

"I will get them some more food and stay with Essie. We can take them up to the children in the nursery," Eden said.

"The noise may be too much for her," Harry said.

"Then we shall make sure it is not," Eden added. "Now go, both of you."

Daisy did not look overly distressed, but how could they tell? The girl had clearly had a traumatic life thus far and knew how to hide that. As someone who'd suffered her fair share of traumas, Maddie understood about hiding.

...

Max and Rory were with two men when she arrived with Harry and James.

Mr. Brown was big, with blunt features and a bald head. He had sweet smile, however, when he bowed before her, which still shocked Maddie. No one had bowed to her before she came to London.

Mr. Spriggot was the opposite of the Runner, thin, pale and with hair that seemed to be long on one side that he had somehow managed to coax over his head to cover the bald areas.

"Mr. Spriggot has come to report his findings in regard to the investigation into your arrest, Maddie," Max said, motioning her into a seat. "Proceed, please."

"I'll let Mr. Brown start," Mr. Spriggot said. "I'm afraid the news is not what you would want to hear, and some of a grave nature."

"Oh, dear." Maddie sat.

"After we got no answers with our initial questioning, I thought I'd start leaning on the staff in the Watch House who arrested Mrs. Caron."

"Leaning means putting pressure on, Maddie," Harry said from his seat beside her.

"I know what it means, thank you, Harry."

"I found something interesting," Mr. Brown said. "Both Constable McDagger and Sergeant Gavell have left."

"Been dismissed?" Harry asked.

"No, they simply didn't return to work the day after Mrs. Caron was released."

"Which tells us what?" Max asked.

"Well now, we can't be sure, but the word from the two other constables I spoke with is that there was some kind of shoddy dealings going on with regards to Mrs. Caron's arrest."

"I asked Mr. Brown to demand to see the arrest records, and they have disappeared," Mr. Spriggot added. "I have since asked my contacts why something like this would happen, and all said it was likely bribery."

"Someone bribed Constable McDagger and Sergeant Gavell to arrest Maddie!" Harry roared.

"It appears that way, but of course there is no proof," Mr. Brown said calmly, even in the face of Harry's and her brothers' obvious anger. "Mr. Spriggot and I also think that there is a possibility that whoever did this knows of Mrs. Caron's connection to you, Duke, and Mr. Huntington."

"Revenge of some kind?" James asked. "Yes, we thought of that avenue also."

"But I'm afraid we have more to tell you, and it is of a grave nature indeed." Mr. Spriggot spoke now.

"Go on," Max said.

"A body was pulled from the Thames this morning, and it was that of Sergeant Gavell."

"Dear Lord." Maddie suddenly felt cold. To her mind, there was no one in London who held a grudge against her so strong that they'd do this. In France, however, that was possible. Surely her past had not followed her here?

CHAPTER 26

They forced a promise from him that he would attend Mr. Rolland's circus of strange and unusual curiosities before he'd left. They'd got him in a weak moment, as he was still feeling on edge after what had happened. He'd then received many letters stating that Daisy and Fleur missed him and Maddie was gravely ill. That one had arrived yesterday. It gave his heart a jolt, even though he knew it was not truth.

He would have felt her if she'd been gravely ill, and those were the simple facts that he had no wish to examine too closely.

So here he was, walking along the street to where a line of carriages waited.

"Your mount, Mr. Sinclair." A groom walked forward, leading a large bay as he reached Dev's house.

"Pardon?"

"Lord Sinclair thought you may like to ride today and had a horse brought for you."

He didn't gnash his teeth, which was his first thought;

after all, it wasn't the groom's fault that his cousin was high-handed.

"Thank you." He took the reins and mounted. It felt good to be on a horse again, but he wasn't telling his bossy elder cousin that. Nudging it forward, he approached the first carriage.

"Harry!"

Meredith was hanging out of a carriage window.

"Get back inside now, Merry." He moved to where she was. "It's not safe. You could fall."

"I have the back of her dress," her brother Mathew replied from inside.

"Are you coming with us to Mr. Rolland's Circus of Strange and Ridiculous Curiosities, Harry?" The question came from Dev and Lilly's other daughter, Hannah. She wasn't hanging out the window; just her head appeared.

"I said I would, so here I am."

"Wonderful! It will be so much more fun with you accompanying us." She smiled up at him and batted her lashes.

"How many carriages are actually needed for you lot?"

"Many!" Merry shrieked. Seconds later, her brother had tugged her back inside.

"Meredith, what have I told you about talking to strangers?" Dev drawled, riding up beside Harry.

"Cousin." Harry nodded. "Thank you for the horse."

"You're welcome."

"How did you know I'd actually come?"

"You promised, therefore you would. And I'm glad you did, Harry."

He grunted something neither of them understood.

"Your grandmother visited us yesterday. I did invite her to accompany us also, but she declined due to the fact she had a shopping trip planned."

"Grandmère was here?" He'd wondered why she hadn't been in her hotel when he called.

"She said she liked loud and boisterous people and that we needed to encourage you to be part of our families so she could spend more time with us. She then added that our children could be better behaved, but as we have a castle, she will overlook that issue."

"Now that, I can imagine her saying. I'm sorry if she inconvenienced you, Dev."

He laughed. "I like her, as do the others. Besides, I doubt there is anything she could say that would inconvenience us, considering who we are."

"You have a point. How is Maddie? I think it extremely callous of you to go out and leave her on her deathbed. I thought the illness was ravaging her and she was not eating and growing weaker every day?"

Dev showed nothing more than his usual calm facade. "Indeed, quite a remarkable recovery really. She woke this morning healed completely. Essie said it was a miracle."

"Have you no shame, lying like that?" Harry sounded testy.

"I would never lie about such a thing." Dev placed a hand on his chest. "Is your father not the most honorable person you know, Hannah?"

The girl blew her father a kiss. "No one is more honorable, Daddy."

"To teach your children to lie on your behalf at such a young age is beneath you, my lord," Harry said.

Dev laughed.

"Your women are all in one of the carriages farther to the front," Dev said, waving a hand in that direction.

"As I have no women, I'm not sure who you could possibly mean."

"You'll beg my pardon, cousin, I seem to have that wrong

then."

He didn't react to the smug look on Dev's face and absolutely refused to move to where he knew Maddie and the girls were.

"Merry, take your hands from around your brother's neck," Dev said, leaning in the carriage window. "You shouldn't allow her to do that, Mathew."

"You try and stop her" came the muttered reply.

Harry moved away while Dev wasn't looking.

He greeted various family members and their progeny as he walked his horse along the line of carriages.

"Cousin! This is a surprise," Cam said. On his lap was Beth.

"I said I would come. You lot are entirely too manipulative and have absolutely no shame." Harry glared at the smirking man.

"Everything we do, we do out of love, Harry."

He wanted to reach in the window and smack that pious look off his cousin's face.

"Next carriage, by the way."

"Pardon?"

"Maddie, Daisy, and Fleur are in the next carriage," Cam added.

"Daisy is coming. Is that wise?"

"She is blind, not ill, Harry. I'm sure Mr. Rolland's Circus of Strange and Ridiculous Curiosities will not present her with too many difficulties. Her eyes are no longer infected. Essie believes that this is what has caused the blindness. The infection was severe and left untreated, the eyes deteriorated.

Harry didn't reply, simply nudged his horse to the next carriage and dismounted. Looking in the open doorway, he found Maddie dressed in lavender with a matching darker spencer. His heart *did not* thud harder inside his chest at seeing her.

Seeing him, a smile lit her face, and he could do nothing to stop responding in kind. Beside her sat Daisy on one side and Fleur the other.

"Harry!" Fleur launched herself at him. "Daisy, it is Harry!"

The little girl he'd rescued three days ago from the Blythes was almost unrecognizable. She wore a white dress that matched Fleur's. Her bonnet was pink, as were her cheeks. Healthy, Harry thought. In three days, she looked healthier. The tightness too had gone from her face. Her eyes still look puffy, but the redness had gone.

"Hello, Fleur." He accepted the hug she gave him. "Hello, Daisy."

The girl turned her head at his voice, and a small smile tilted her lips.

"Daisy is happy now, Harry, and Bran is her constant companion. She holds his fur, and he leads her around the house."

"Does he now? Well, that is good to hear."

"I love Bran," Daisy said, still with that little smile on her face.

"Are you coming with us today?" Fleur asked him.

"I am."

"Uncle Rory and Uncle Max and Uncle Nicholas could not come with us."

"They must be devastated." He saw Maddie smile at his words.

"Come and sit now, Fleur. We are about to leave," she said. "We will see you soon, Harry."

"Of course." He mounted, and then let the carriages roll out before falling in behind the last with Wolf, Dev, and James, who also rode.

"Have you any more details on Maddie's case?"

"None. It's extremely frustrating," James said. "But like

Max and Rory, we don't believe it is a case of mistaken identity. They knew her name, and she has not been here long enough to have become acquainted with anyone for that to happen. Therefore the conclusion is someone is trying to get at us through her. We're just not sure why or who."

"Do you think it could be someone who has followed her from France?"

"Why do you ask that?" It was Dev who questioned him.

"You know I saw her in Calais and gave her passage to London?"

They nodded.

"But at the time, I had a feeling she was desperate and maybe running from something. It was merely a hunch, but given what has happened, perhaps it is more than that."

"No one has even considered that," James said.

"We just thought that she came because there was nothing left for her in France after Jacques's death. Although Max did mention briefly that their mother had shown up on Maddie's doorstep."

"And that was a bad thing?" Harry knew it could not have been good, as Fleur had told him how much her grandmother scared her, but he wanted to hear what the others knew.

"She's an utter bitch." James looked grim. "Did any number of atrocious things to her children. Maddie was grieving, and she took advantage of that weakness. As yet, we're not sure what happened, but what I know about that woman suggests it would not have been a happy time."

Harry thought about that as they rode through the streets. To think of Maddie vulnerable and at the mercy of such a woman made him want to roar. Could this woman in some way be involved in what had happened here? It seemed farfetched, but something that would be looked into.

She wasn't going to suffer again.

CHAPTER 27

Mr. Rolland's Circus of Strange and Ridiculous Curiosities stood before them in all its tattered glory. Flags flew, and a faded sign hung over the door of the small wooden building through which a few people were wandering.

"Hold the hand of an adult if you are a child that comes to below my armpit," Dev said. Mathew snickered as Merry stood on her toes and still did not reach the correct height. "No touching, pushing, or shrieking."

"This particular lecture has remained unchanged since we brought Samantha, Warwick, Dorrie, and Somer here many years ago as children," Cam said to Harry. "He's a pompous prat."

"Someone has to take charge of you lot, surely."

"Harsh but true. Now I must hand out the sweets, Harry, so don't try and distract me."

He watched Cam distribute the treats to the children while he continued to listen to Dev's lecture about behavior and how it was important they did not act like a pack of heathens. He then bent to speak with Daisy. She was pressed to Maddie's side and must be nervous, as this was all so new to her.

"Are you all right, Daisy?"

She nodded.

"Are you enjoying your time with Fleur, Maddie, and the others?"

She nodded again.

"Shall I carry you now, until we get inside?"

"Yes, please."

Harry picked her up. People were everywhere, and Daisy had no idea where she was, so that had to be terrifying. One of her arms went around his neck.

"Thank you for saving me, Harry."

The words were whispered into his ear. That small, raspy voice made his heart melt.

"I love Maddie and Fleur and the others. They are all so kind to me. Bran is my special friend."

"I'm glad you are happy, Daisy."

"Harry has Daisy, Fleur, he cannot pick you up also," Maddie said from beside him.

"I want to hold his hand then."

Harry held out his hand to the little girl pressed to his thigh, and she wove her fingers into his.

Maddie was frowning when he looked at her.

"What?"

"'Tis nothing." She wouldn't meet his eyes.

"Clearly it's something, as you just frowned."

"I like to frown. It relaxes my facial muscles."

Harry laughed.

"Oh, very well. It is petty of me, but sometimes I miss being the only one she turns to." The words were a furious hiss. "And that sounded shallow. I'm sorry."

"Not terrible at all and completely understandable. It will

always be you she turns to when she's sad, happy, or in need of something. We are only a temporary distraction."

Her eyes met his, and suddenly they were alone, and everything and everyone else faded away. Her intriguing eyes were locked on his. Eyes that told him she felt whatever this was between them.

"Harry."

She'd just said his name, nothing more, and he wanted her.

"I don't know what to say to you," she whispered.

"What do you want to say?"

"I don't know."

It wasn't a conversation that made any sense, and yet he understood exactly what she was trying to say.

"You look lovely," he whispered. "Beautiful, even," he added, sounding like a fool. "Maddie, this—"

"I know." She cut off his words.

"What do you know?"

"That France is your home, and your life is there, not here with us."

He didn't know what to say to that, because her words were the truth.

"You really do look lovely," he said, because he had nothing else.

She looked down at her dress. "It's the most beautiful thing I have ever owned, along with all the others that were ordered for me. I told Max it was too much, but he refuses to listen, as does Rory. They spoil me."

She was nervous, her words spilling one on top of the other, and clearly uncomfortable with what they'd just discussed.

"I'm sure you deserve to be spoiled."

"No more than anyone."

"All right, now we will go inside, and remember my words," Dev said.

"As if we could forget," Somer muttered. "They are etched in my head."

"I heard that!"

Harry nodded for Maddie to go ahead of him, pushing aside the conversation he'd just had with her. Strange how the prospect of returning to France did not please him like it normally did.

"Keep up, Harry."

"No need to nudge me, Cam, I am moving."

"Cam is silly," Daisy whispered in his ear. "But I like him."

"Me too, but don't tell him I said that, all right?" She nodded.

"Oh, your Grace, Lord Sinclair... and all your families." The man who greeted them as they reached the entrance looked a little pale to Harry's eyes as he took in their large group. He had a faded black top hat with a gold band, and his jacket had small black patches sewn into the elbows.

"Mr. Rolland, how wonderful to see you still here," James said.

"Thank you, your Grace. Is the entire family here?" His smile was forced.

"We are," Somer said. "The younger members wish to partake of the delights we enjoyed, sir. I believe today there is to be a mermaid and a merman? It has been some time since we've seen them."

Mr. Rolland muttered something that to Harry sounded like "God save us all," then nodded, his eyes going to Beth, who was pulling Meredith's hair.

"We have a donation for you." Dev stepped forward and handed the man some notes. "It's our hope that after today it is not to rebuild your circus."

While their party laughed at the joke, Mr. Rolland appeared to choke on air.

"I—ah, I have the front row free, if you wish to take it, your Grace?"

"Indeed, we are grateful," James said. "Behave," he said to his son, Simon, who was poking his tongue out to someone.

Harry couldn't help it; he laughed. He'd never been around families like these. It was also likely to be an experience he never had again, which left a heavy feeling inside his chest.

"Right, let's take our places," Wolf said.

Harry started explaining to Daisy what he was seeing. "There are large clouds above the circular stage we are standing on." She listened; head tilted slightly.

Adults stood with a child or two before them. This, according to Cam, would ensure that when they felt the need to do something they shouldn't, they could stop them.

"Good Lord, what on earth is Lord Raynor doing here?" Wolf said, looking at a man who was directly across from where they stood.

"I saw him outside," Dev added. "He's here because his wife wanted to come. The man dotes on her. Can you see her? She wasn't with him when we talked."

"I would like that." Lilly sighed.

"To be doted on?"

She nodded at Dev.

"No, you wouldn't, you'd be bored in days."

"Perhaps we should just test that theory for two or three days a week to start with?"

"I haven't seen him about much this season," James said.

Harry ignored the conversation, as he had no knowledge of the peer they discussed and likely never would. He focused instead on the sweet woman standing at his side.

She was close enough to him now that their arms

brushed. He was conflicted; there was no getting around that fact. She touched something that had never before been touched deep inside him.

But your life is in France.

Strange how that was the thought that stuck in his head. No longer did his father's words, *never trust a Sinclair,* feature in his thinking.

CHAPTER 28

Maddie had never been anywhere like this before. She was surely too old to feel excitement, and yet it was there inside her. Moving a little closer to Harry, she tried to see around the edge of the stage before her.

"What's wrong?"

"Nothing. I just wanted to see better."

"Shall we change places then?"

"No, this is fine, thank you."

"Have you ever seen anything like this before, Maddie?"

"No. This is my first time."

"For me also."

"But surely you've been to the theater and plays?" she asked.

"Yes, but this is something entirely different. Would you like to go to the theatre?"

"Rory and Max have promised to take me when I am ready."

"Why are you not ready?"

Maddie wasn't sure how to answer that.

"Embrace the new experiences, Maddie. I promise you will not regret it."

It was all very well for him; he'd likely had this life for some time now. He owned the ship she'd come across the channel in, and as such he was likely a very wealthy man. With wealth came the privilege of doing as you wished. Living in a nice home with lots of food, and yes, going to the theatre.

"I am unused to this life. My brothers understand that."

"The only way to get used to it is by participating in it," he said in a reasonable voice that for some reason irritated her. Outside, they'd shared a moment. It had been raw and real. The look they'd shared had told her he felt something, just as she did. But when she'd said his life was in France, he had not disagreed. But then, what had she expected?

"I am participating in it. I have new clothes and go to places with my family. I live with servants and have a full belly—"

"I'm sorry you did not have a full belly before, Maddie."

"That is not the point."

"What is the point then?"

"I will do these things in my own time," she snapped.

"Excellent. And your clothes are lovely, as are you, but my point is that you won't adjust to these new things until you embrace them."

Maddie clamped her lips shut.

"Oh, come now, is debating a subject something you are also unused to? Did your late husband not argue with you?"

"We were not like that."

"That being?"

"Stop asking me questions, Harry, when I'm sure you have no wish to answer any that I would pose to you."

That shut him up.

He held Daisy as if she was made of the finest glass. The

little girl had her arms around his neck and was listening to the noise and voices around them.

In the three days she'd been with them, Maddie had come to love Daisy, as had Fleur and the others of their families. They had discussed what was best for her, and a kernel of an idea had taken root inside Maddie's head that she needed to think more about before she gave voice to it.

She'd also told Max she was ready to move into her new home. As such, they had been getting it furnished and ready for their occupation. Maddie felt ridiculously excited about the prospect of having a home again.

Mr. Rolland appeared suddenly above them on a raised platform. Arms raised, he began to tell them in a loud booming voice what they were about to see.

"Please brace yourselves, as the platform you are currently standing upon is about to start moving!"

"'Tis starting, Mama!"

"How exciting," she said to Fleur as beneath them the floor shuddered.

"Prepare to be dazzled by Mr. Rolland's performers!"

Slowly the lights went out around them and then a man and woman rose up through swirling mists.

"Behold the mermaid and merman from the far reaches of Atlantis!"

"I'm not sure mermaids or mermen come from Atlantis," Isabella said.

"Because they were half god, half man, do you mean?" Cam asked.

"Perhaps their society had grown to include mermaids and mermen," Hannah said.

"They could have swum from the Greek Islands, which is where Atlantis is," Mathew added.

"I think it more likely these two are from somewhere closer, like Clapham," Harry whispered.

Maddie giggled.

"That's a nice sound." He sent her a smile.

"What I don't understand," Hannah said, "is how they use the chamber pot?"

"Thank you, daughter, that will do. Just watch the show," Dev said. Around them, the adults muffled their laughter.

"Have you seen mermaids, Harry?" Isabella asked him.

"Of course. Seamen often see them. We just have to be careful, as their beauty can lure us down into the water. Many men have vanished, never to be seen again."

Round-eyed, the children looked back at the mermaid splashing about in water.

"Can Daisy come down here? I will tell her what is happening," Luke said.

Maddie watched as Harry spoke to the girl and then lowered her to her feet. She was soon surrounded by children. Fleur held her hand while Luke started talking to her.

"How has she been?" Harry whispered the words in Maddie's ear.

"She is doing so well. Bran is helping. He is constantly by her side and leads her everywhere."

"There is a school for blind children, Maddie. I will make enquiries for Daisy."

"I'm not sure that is best for her."

"I want her somewhere that she will be looked after but also taught to cope. This school has an excellent reputation, and she will be protected against those that would prey on her vulnerabilities."

"I understand that, Harry, and want that too."

"If only you could see what I see." He leaned closer, the words brushing her check.

"What do you see?"

"I have no wish to spoil your fun." He looked at her, and Maddie wondered if this feeling was far more than liking someone. She'd never felt as if her stomach was actually turning in circles before, and her heart about to leap from her chest.

"Ah, Maddie, what am I to do with you." Harry touched her hand, his fingers encasing hers.

"What do you want to do?"

"I wish I knew." He kissed her softly. "But we will never know, as nothing can come of this."

Maddie turned away and for the remainder of the show focused on the antics of the performers. She'd wanted to ask him why nothing could come of this but had held her tongue.

The problem was that with this slow blossoming of happiness inside her, she was beginning to believe she could now have more. She wanted what her family had, love and children, and one day perhaps that would be—just not with the man at her side, even if Sinclairs married Ravens.

She felt his eyes on her face, but Maddie never looked his way as the show continued. The children laughed and gasped, and she let thoughts come and go, but perhaps the one that really took hold inside her head was that maybe she really was worthy of being loved.

When you lived your life with so much anger and hate, you tended not to see the light, and yet now she was starting to. She would never just settle for friendship from any man again.

Her family had taught her that. Taught her that she was more than she'd ever thought herself to be. Not worthless, but worthy.

When the show finished and the mermaid and merman were once again gone, the children clapped loudly.

"Right, children, take the hand of an adult, and no pushing. We will leave in an orderly manner, and perhaps there will be somewhere we can stop for a treat on the way home." James's voice carried to all of them.

"He wears authority well, like Dev," Harry said.

"It's still hard to believe I have a duke for a brother."

"And you are worthy of him; never forget that." He turned away before she could say anything, but his words left a warmth inside her chest.

I am worthy.

They formed a chain. Harry had Daisy's hand, as did Fleur, and Maddie held her daughter's other hand.

"My doll, Mama! I dropped it."

"I told you not to bring it, Fleur. Where did you have it?"

"Up my dress, Mama. But it fell out."

"I will retrieve it. Go with the others, and I'll follow," she said, leaving with Harry's laughter following her.

Her daughter took Miss Pretty Face, as Fleur had called her new doll, everywhere, and it was constantly being misplaced.

Retrieving the doll took a matter of seconds, and soon she was heading back the way she'd just come. The hand that grabbed her came from behind, and then suddenly she was being lifted and carried. Her screams were muffled by another hand as whoever carried her dragged her behind a curtain.

Maddie fought, kicking and trying to escape, but the man who held her was bigger and so much stronger. Her back was pinned to his chest with one arm. She tried to sink her teeth into the soft flesh of his palm, but he pulled away, and then something was forced into her mouth. Her hands were wrenched behind her back and bound.

"This time you won't escape. Your family will not help you now."

She knew that voice. Dear Lord, she had not killed him. Shock gripped Maddie. She'd been so sure he was dead when she left her house. Suddenly she was back there in her small room in France with the feel of his body pressing hers down into the mattress. Fear gave her strength. She had fought him once; she would do so again. Lifting a leg she struck out at him, and connected with his shin. The grunt of pain was satisfying.

"Bitch!"

She fought as he lifted her, throwing her over his shoulder, and then he was running. His feet thudded on the hard wooden floor.

"Through there. Where's my money?"

Maddie heard the clink of coins, and then there was darkness. Not like the inside of the theater, where she could still see. Something had been thrown over her.

She heard a door close, and then they were climbing into something. The roll of wheels told her it was a carriage.

Desperate now, Maddie kicked and fought, but it was no good; he held her down, tying a blindfold over her eyes.

Fight this panic, Maddie.

"There is no escaping now, my sweet Madeline. Now you will be mine, and we have a great deal of fun ahead of us. I have quite a bit of retribution to extract from you for the lump you gave me from that stone, my dear. I shall enjoy the experience hugely."

She lay on the floor with his feet on top of her. Fear and rage battled for supremacy inside Maddie. The latter won. She would not let this man take what she had only just found. Happiness was now her right, so she would fight with everything she had, and when the right moment presented itself, she would find her way back to her family, no matter what it took.

CHAPTER 29

Harry watched the door they'd just exited for Maddie to appear. He was tense and had no idea why. The children were chattering, and adults trying to herd them to the carriages. He continued to wait for her. Something wasn't right.

"I'll go and see what's delaying Maddie."

"It's only been a few minutes," Cam said.

"Something feels off."

"It's likely your belly from all the sweets you consumed."

"Hardly. You ate far more than I." Harry checked on Daisy, who was seated with Luke, Fleur, and Rory and looked happy, then headed back inside Mr. Rolland's place of business.

"I'll be back soon."

It was empty save for the staff milling about cleaning and tidying away things.

"I am looking for a lady." Harry gave a brief description of Maddie. "Have you seen her?" He approached a young boy.

"Sorry, everyone has left, sir."

"I was watching the door she should have walked

through, and she didn't, so clearly she is still in here somewhere." Harry's tension was climbing. "Where is the other exit?"

The boy pointed to his right. Harry hurried that way. Switching his vision, he searched for Maddie. She was not in the building.

"Something has happened to Maddie!" he yelled, knowing it was likely Eden or Warwick would hear. Harry walked into the rooms at the rear of the building and found the mermaid, merman, and one other man.

"I am looking for a woman, Mrs. Caron. She was inside, but did not leave by the front door. Have you seen her?"

They all shook their heads.

"Where is the rear entrance?"

He ran in the direction they pointed and found Fleur's doll on the floor. Picking it up, he continued to the door and opened it. There was no sign of Maddie. He looked but could not see her anywhere on the road. Had she doubled back and was now with the others?

Please let her be with the others.

"What's happened?" Dev arrived with Cam and James.

"It's Maddie. She came back in for Fleur's doll, and when she didn't appear, I looked for her. I have checked, but her color is not inside this building. I found the doll near this door."

"Can I help, Your Grace, Lord Sinclair?" Mr. Rolland appeared.

"A woman who came with us has gone missing. She came back inside for something and did not return," Dev said.

"I assure you, there is no one in here, my lord, but my staff."

"I'll check that she has not returned and is with the others." Dev ran back the way he'd just come.

Harry brushed by Mr. Rolland and headed to where he'd seen the staff gathered.

"Do any of you know where Mrs. Caron is?"

"There's been no woman in here," the mermaid said.

"Let me rephrase that question." James stepped forward. "A woman, who is my sister, was here. Now she's not, and I believe she has been taken with nefarious intentions. If one of you know something, I suggest you tell me now."

No one spoke.

"I'll beat it out of them," Harry snarled.

"We don't know if they are involved as yet, so no one is beating anyone." Cam placed a hand on Harry's shoulder.

"She is not outside." Dev returned.

"Then she has to have left by the rear door where I found Fleur's doll. But who with and why?" Harry said, looking at the three staff before him. The mermaid had been part of the stage performance. The merman was young and looked nervous. Again, he'd been part of the performance, so Harry doubted he was involved in this.

He would guess the eldest was in his sixties, and he had no expression on his face. Being someone who could control his emotions so that no one realized what was inside your head, he recognized it in another.

"How many staff work here, Mr. Rolland?" Dev asked.

"Just those who stand before you, and Sam, who is cleaning. If you know anything," he said to his staff, "I implore you to speak. These are the people who burned down this building."

"In our defense, that wasn't really our fault. Someone was trying to kill me," James said, standing next to Harry. He too was looking at the nervous staff.

Harry stepped closer to the older man, sure that he was the one who knew something. "Tell me what I want to know or I'll beat it out of you."

"Well now, there's no need for that," Mr. Rolland blustered.

"If I get to five, you'll be sorry." Harry started counting, his eyes on the man and no doubt now a vibrant green. He got to three.

"The man said he wanted a way out that wasn't through the front door!"

"No, Jonas!" Mr. Rolland was horrified.

"I was putting the props away, and he approached. He carried her over his shoulder. He paid me more than you do in a month to help him get out the rear door."

"You let him walk out of here with a woman you knew he was taking against her will, and did nothing to help her?"

"I needed the money!" The man wasn't impassive now.

He wanted to hurt him, inflict pain on him because of what he'd done to Maddie. Instead, Harry controlled his rage and blocked out the image of Maddie helpless. He had to find her; nothing else mattered.

"If she is harmed in any way, I will come back for you, and believe me when I say I know how to make to someone suffer."

The man lost all the color in his face.

"Give us his description," James demanded.

"Sh-shorter than you," he pointed to Harry, "and he has brown or black hair. I don't know, the light wasn't good when he approached me, and he wore a hat."

"Dress?"

"L-like yours, and spoke as he does," the man nodded to Dev.

They ran from the theater and found the others waiting.

"I can see by your faces you have not found her," Emily said. "Eden and Wolf have gone on horseback to search for her."

"Take the children back, Em. James, Harry, Dev, and I will

search now and meet up with Eden and Wolf." Cam hugged his wife hard.

"Warwick, you locate Max, Rory, and Nicholas. Then find Mr. Brown and Mr. Spriggot. Tell them what has happened, and when that's done, start searching," Dev added. "Keep the news of Maddie's disappearance from the others. Make up a story for Fleur about her mother having to go shopping for something."

"Give her this," Harry thrust the doll at Warwick.

Warwick took it, expression grave, and then he and the rest of the family left.

Cam mounted behind Dev, and they began to thread their way through the crowded streets in search of Eden and Wolf.

Harry struggled to clear visions of Maddie struggling in the hands of whoever had taken her. He tried to shut out what could even now be happening to her and focus.

"Harry, search right, and I'll search left," Dev said.

He let his eyes move methodically through buildings and shops, searching, trying to find any clue as to where Maddie could have been taken.

"This must have to do with what happened to put her in jail," James said.

"That's my way of thinking, but what we don't know is why someone wants Maddie. Has trouble followed her from France? Or is it something to do with her family connections?" Dev added.

"Wolf and Eden are there." Harry pointed ahead, and soon they were galloping to catch up with them. They drew alongside minutes later.

"Have you found anything?"

"I spoke with a man who owns that shop there." Wolf pointed to a building. "He was outside when a carriage came through not long ago at speed. As this is usually a busy thoroughfare, it's rare to see such a thing. It turned down Turnham Road, which is there." Wolf pointed ahead.

They didn't hesitate, and in seconds were heading in that direction.

"She could be anywhere," Harry said, feeling desperation grab hold of his throat. He needed to find Maddie; every second she was gone, his fears grew.

"Dismount and form a link. We will use our senses, and this will heighten them."

Harry knew what they could do; after all, they'd healed him, but he'd never been a part of it until now. He did as Dev directed him and soon found his hand in Eden's. Cam then wrapped his fingers around Harry's wrist. The jolt of awareness that rippled through him was more intense than what he'd felt when just a single member of his family touched him. This was as if every sense in his body had fired to life.

"Focus," Dev said.

Harry closed his eyes, and when he opened them, the world around him was filled with color. He discarded the ones he knew and looked for Maddie.

"I smell her scent, she has passed through here," Cam said.

"I don't hear anything that would indicate she's here," Eden said. "But that doesn't mean she isn't."

"I don't see her colors," Dev added.

They mounted and rode, slowly, along the street. The fact that Cam had caught Maddie's scent in the air told Harry they were going in the right direction.

"There." Harry pointed to a narrow building. Painted white, it stood out among the gray ones on either side. "She's in there!"

"Don't charge in." Dev grabbed Harry's arm as he prepared to dismount. "We need to see what we're dealing with."

"She could be hurting."

"Is her color weak?"

"No."

"Dismount, and Eden will listen."

Harry usually did as he wanted, when he wanted, and he wanted action now. Instead, he did as the others were and stood in the road outside the building.

"I don't hear Maddie, but there is a woman talking about something disconcerting," Eden said.

"Tell us exactly what is being said, sister," Dev moved to her side.

"'The master has brought another in. We've prepared her so she's ready for the fun.' And another woman is saying, 'It won't be fun for anyone but him.'"

"How many are inside?" James said.

"Five," Wolf replied.

"What is this place?" Cam asked. "I've never been here before, and as vices were my particular specialty, I'm sure I should have."

"I don't know," James said, "but we're about to find out."

Hold on, Maddie, I'm coming.

CHAPTER 30

The journey had not been a long one, and soon Maddie was being lifted from the carriage, thrown over a shoulder, and on the move once more. They'd climbed stairs, and then she'd been lowered onto something soft, which had to be a bed. The thought was a chilling one.

"Get her prepared, and force something down her throat if she won't comply. I don't want her fighting until I am ready."

She'd hadn't killed him. She wasn't a murderer. He wouldn't touch Maddie that way again. She'd fight with everything thing she had, just like that night in the cottage.

The door closed. A hand pulled the blindfold from her eyes. She found two women before her.

"Don't bother fighting us. We've had plenty of experience with girls like you. You'd be best to just go along and get it over with."

"Why are you doing this? How can you live with yourself, knowing what that man is capable of, what he'd do to me!"

They wore a uniform Maddie would expect a maid to wear, both large, with sturdy builds. She could not fight them both, so she let her shoulders slump and the tears of frustration fall. If they thought she was defeated, she may have a better chance of escape.

"Don't carry on; we've no time for it. You're not going to die, and some even enjoy it."

"You'll pay alongside him when my family arrives," Maddie said.

She was pulled from the bed and her hands untied.

"No one will find you. A man's outside the door if you try to leave, so you won't escape."

They stripped her clothes from her body, and she let the anger inside her build. She would show no shame before these women. Maddie had fought her entire life for survival. She'd been cowed plenty of times too; her mother had seen to that. Rory had saved her from some of the beatings and slept beside her so none of her mother's "friends" harmed her. He'd then seen her married to Jacques and living in supposed safety.

This was just another thing she had to fight her way free of.

They forced her into her bath and scrubbed her with sweet-smelling soap. Maddie submitted to it all and uttered not one word. Only when she'd been dressed in a night rail that was sheer and showed off her body did they leave.

Hurrying to the window, she found it had boards halfway up. She dragged one of the two chairs closer so she could look down and saw the drop was too far to jump even if she got the boards free.

Knowing her time was limited and that he'd come back to the room soon, she searched for anything she could use as a weapon. They would come for her, her family. Harry would not stop; neither would her brothers or sisters. She had people that cared for her now. They'd find her with their senses, and Maddie must stay safe until then.

She was not alone.

The room held very little. A huge bed draped in satin sheets and thick fur coverings. There were mirrors everywhere, even on the roof. The bed had leather cuffs on the head and foot boards, which made Maddie shudder at how helpless she would be if he got her into those. A sofa, two chairs, and a small desk were the only other furniture. Rifling through the desk, she found nothing.

That man will not take me against my will.

Picking up the hairbrush that the woman had left behind, Maddie studied it. Could it be a weapon? One of them had said she'd bring back a tray soon. Could she use this to subdue her? *Then what?* Was the end sharp enough to fool her it was knife?

Voices outside told her someone was returning. Hurrying to pick up the gag they'd used on her, she moved to press her back to the wall beside the door. Maddie gripped the bristles hard and hoped she could carry this through. She had to do this for Fleur and, yes, Daisy. The little girl had come to mean so much to her in the few days she'd been in their lives.

The key turned in the lock. She watched the door swing open. One of the women entered, and the door shut behind her. Maddie moved up behind her, pressing the handle into the woman's back.

"Move or make a noise and I will force this blade into you," she whispered. "Walk to the bed and lower the tray to the floor."

With her heart thudding, she walked at the woman's back. They tray was lowered.

"Force this into your mouth." Maddie handed her the gag. The woman hesitated, so she pressed the brush harder. She whimpered and stuffed the material into her mouth.

"Take off your clothes."

"He'll kill me," she whispered.

"So will I."

She stumbled out of her uniform and soon stood in a chemise only.

"Now lie facedown on the bed."

The woman climbed onto the mattress and did as she was told. Maddie secured her arm in the cuffs, then hurried around the bed to do the same with the other one. She then cuffed the woman's ankles.

Maddie hurried to pull on the woman's clothes, and took the hat from her head and tugged it on. The clothes were big but would have to work. She now had to get by the guard on the door. Taking a deep breath, she put the side of her hand in her mouth and bit down hard enough to make a mark. She then screamed and kicked the tray across the room. Running to the door, she threw it open.

"She bit me!" Maddie didn't look at the man who stood beside the door, just ran along the hall as fast as she could until she found some stairs. Once there, clutching her hand, she hurried down.

"She bit me!" she cried again as she met another woman, and continued to run, head down, hand pressed to her chest. Along another hall, then another set of stairs.

She reached a spacious entryway with sofas and yet more mirrors. The front door was in sight when she heard his voice.

"Stop!"

Maddie kept running, but he was gaining on her. She had the door handle in her hand when he gripped her shoulders.

"I said stop!" He wrenched her round, and there was the man who had sent her fleeing from France.

"Let me go!" She fought against him, but his strength was more than hers. He gripped her hard, pulling her into his chest.

"I paid for you, Madeline. You've caused me far too much

trouble to ever let you go. We're going to have a great deal of fun, you and I, especially now I know how adventurous you are. I'm sure your mother taught you some tricks; she certainly knows how to please a man."

"I'm not my mother!" She fought him as he dragged her back across the floor.

"Fight all you want, you will not escape me, my sweet. You belong to me for as long as I want you."

"You don't own me!"

They both turned as the door burst open and in ran Harry. Maddie nearly sobbed with relief; instead, what she did was make a fist as his hold on her relaxed and punch him hard in his groin like Rory had once taught her. He groaned and released her.

"Harry!"

He caught her in a fierce hug, then forced her behind him to where Eden stood.

"'Tis all right now, Maddie, we have you." She let the duchess wrap an arm around her. "We shall now watch while Harry takes Lord Raynor apart on your behalf."

Lord Raynor, as she now knew he was called, was attempting to flee up the stairs. Harry leapt the first four and grabbed him, he then threw the peer back down.

"That's got to hurt," Cam said, jumping to one side as Lord Raynor crashed into the tiles.

"I'm gutting that bastard!" Harry followed, grabbing the man by the lapels and hauling him upright. He punched him hard, sending the peer stumbling across the floor into the wall.

"That will do, Harry." Wolf attempted to grab him, but Harry shook him off and reached for Raynor again.

"You really can't kill him, Harry." Dev and James waded in with Wolf's help and pulled hm off the man.

"Let me shoot him!"

"No, we can't allow that," Cam said, taking off his necktie as he approached the now groaning Raynor, who had fallen to his knees. "He needs to stand trial and be totally humiliated and then incarcerated. We must to do this right, Harry." He bound the man's hands.

"I want to kill him." Harry snarled like a raging beast as he struggled for release.

"Not happening," Dev said, gripping his arms. "Maddie needs you, Harry, and you are scaring her."

She wanted to deny that. She wasn't scared anymore and wanted the man who had caused her so much suffering to feel as she had, but Dev was right. It would not be good for Harry to kill a man on her behalf.

"I'm all right, Eden." She eased out of her arms, moving to where Harry stood, still restrained. She touched his cheek.

"Harry, enough now."

Harry shook his cousins off, and suddenly she was looking into his brilliant green eyes. The eyes of a man she now knew she cared for deeply.

"Are you all right?" His hands shook as they touched her face. "Did he... did he hurt you?"

She shook her head. Now the fight had gone out of her, she was shaking.

"Tell me the truth." His eyes searched her face.

"I am unharmed, Harry, I promise."

"Thank God." He held her as if she would shatter. "I was so scared, Maddie."

"I thought I would never see you... any of you again."

"It's all right now." He kissed the top of her head. "You're safe."

"What I want to know," she heard James say, "was why he went after my sister specifically, because something tells me it wasn't random."

Dear Lord, she would have to tell them.

"Tell me what I want to know, Raynor."

Maddie eased out of Harry's arms and moved to James's side.

"He asked you a question!" Harry stepped round her and grabbed the peer's shirt.

"You have nothing on me!" Raynor gasped.

Maddie looked down at the man, took in the bruised and bloodied face, and wondered how this one man could have caused her so much terror.

"We will interview everyone in this house, throw vast amounts of money about, and get every dirty, underhand thing you have ever done within these walls, Raynor, so never doubt the lengths we will go to ensure you are locked away," James said. "No one touches a member of my family and gets away with it."

James's words made her feel warmer.

"Release him, Harry. All the blood is rushing to his head," Cam said.

Harry dropped him hard enough that Raynor's head clunked on the floor.

"I-I have had dealings with him before," Maddie said slowly. "My mother sent him to me when I forced her from my house. He paid her to have a night with me."

"You lie!" Raynor glared at Maddie. Harry put his foot on the man's chest to hold him down

"Speak to her with anything other than respect again, and I'll kill you, and no one will be able to stop me."

"I don't lie. You came to my house!" Anger was slowly replacing the fear. "You tried to take advantage of me when my daughter slept nearby!"

She told them everything then. Why she'd run, and the belief that she'd killed him with the rock she'd always had beside her bed. Jacques had put it there one day when he went away for the night. Telling her it was for protection should anyone try to enter the house.

"Let me kill him," Harry growled.

"While I have no issue with his death, I would hate the fallout from that, Harry," James said. "Things could get messy. So we will let him suffer the humiliation of a public trial."

"If Raynor came to her cottage in the dark how did he know what Maddie looked like?" Cam asked.

Maddie hadn't thought of that.

"Answer the question," Harry reached for the peer again.

"Her mother!" Raynor tried to evade him. "The village near where they lived. I met her there, and she pointed her daughter out to me. Offered her to me."

Maddie wasn't sure why her mother's perfidy still had the power to hurt her, and yet it did.

Raynor was taken away in his carriage by Wolf. To where, Maddie had no idea. All she knew was now she really was safe. No longer did the shadow hang over her that she'd killed someone.

When they left the property, Harry took her arm and led her to his horse. He lifted her onto its back and climbed on behind. She felt the eyes of the others on them, but no one said anything, simply mounted, and they were soon riding back through the streets of London.

"So much has happened, and yet the hour is still early," Maddie said. People walked about the streets, and the sun was still high.

"Are you sure he did not hurt you, Maddie?" Harry's voice sounded tight, as if he was in some kind of pain. She rested her hand on the one he had around her waist.

"I am, and thank you for finding me, Harry. All of you." She looked at James and Eden, who rode beside them. "I am so relieved it is over."

"You are family. We will always protect you," James said, and to him it was that simple. "But in future you should not keep something like what happened in France a secret, Maddie."

"I promise not to do so. It's my hope I never have to worry about something like that, as I hope to never see my mother again."

"You won't." Harry's tone was clipped.

She rode the rest of the way in silence, but could still feel the tension in the man behind her.

Maddie was elated that any danger to her was now past. She really could live her life here now and be happy. There would really be only one dark cloud on her horizon, and she doubted there was little she could do to change that.

What she felt for the man at her back was now startlingly clear. When he'd entered that building she'd felt hope, and no one had ever given her that. Hope and something more powerful. Love.

"Are you all right, Harry?" The hand around her waist tightened.

"I am."

He did not add anything, and Maddie knew he did not want to talk, so she enjoyed the feeling of being held by him, because there was every chance she would not experience it again.

Harry's life was in France, Maddie's was now here; he'd made that clear.

When they reached Max's house, she found Rose and Emily in the hallway. They both hugged her hard.

"Come, you will feel better when you remove that hideous uniform," Rose said. She was taken from Harry and led upstairs to change.

She told them what had happened and what had happened in France. For the first time in her life she wanted to share her story, and especially with these two women who were her sisters.

"Thank you," Maddie said when she was once again in her own clothes.

"For what?"

"For accepting me, for persisting with me. I really do love having sisters, it's just taken me time to understand that."

"We were the same," Emily said. "And we love having you also. Now, the tea should have arrived, and that will help settle you."

She felt settled by just being here with her family now. Yes, what had happened had been terrifying, but she'd fought back, and her family and Harry had come for her, as she now knew they always would.

"Dev and Cam have gone to find the others and tell them you are safe," James said when they found him in the nursery.

"Mama!" Fleur ran at her, and Bran led Daisy over.

She held her girls close.

"Where is Harry?" Maddie looked around the room but saw no sign of him.

"He had to go, something about a meeting," James said. "Which I didn't believe for a minute."

"He's scared," Rose added. "Scared of what he feels for you, Maddie."

"Why?"

"Because from the day he was old enough to understand, his father made him promise not to trust a Sinclair. Never to reconnect with his family," James said. "The man is battling with that."

"He cares for you, Maddie," Emily said. "My fear is he'll sail away from us before he realizes just how much."

"But I am not a Sinclair."

"You are one and the same because you live here with us,"

Emily said. "You will need to make him see reason, sister, if that is what you want."

What did she want? A life with Harry? Maddie thought that perhaps that was exactly what she wanted. But how was she to make the man she loved realize he wanted the same thing?

CHAPTER 31

Harry sat at his desk, preparing things for departure. His grandmother was due to arrive shortly with her entourage and get settled in her cabin before they sailed on the next tide.

Picking up the letter Wolf had sent him, he read it once more.

Lord Raynor will be charged and is at present being held until a trial is set. Maddie is well and recovered and would like to see you, as would Fleur, Daisy, and the rest of us. We shall be extremely displeased if you leave London without at least saying goodbye.

Yours,

Wolf (your cousin, in case that slipped your mind.)

Harry read the words once more. Maddie was well, what did that mean? Had she been unwell in the four days since Raynor had abducted her?

He'd woken in a cold sweat last night thinking of her in his hands. How was it possible her own mother had sold her to that evil bastard? His father hadn't been the best, but still, Harry had been cared for.

He loathed Maddie's mother, even if she had given the

world the beautiful and sweet Madeline Caron. How she must have suffered at her hands. He hated that she'd known any pain.

He missed her. It was like an ache in the bones, and he hated it. No one had made him feel that way. She'd slip into his head constantly, and he'd wondered what she was doing. Were Daisy and Fleur all right? How was the investigative agency going? They'd all slipped past his guard and become part of him, and he had absolutely no idea what to do about that.

Harry looked at the note again. Was Maddie sick? Should he go and see her one last time? The pain in his chest at the thought told him no.

Looking down once more, he attempted to read the ledger before him. He couldn't allow thoughts of Maddie to stop him from doing what must be done before they left England.

"Enter," Harry muttered as a knock sounded on his door.

The door opened and closed, but he kept his eyes on the ledger before him, finishing his tally of the numbers before looking at whichever crew member had entered.

"What do…" His words fell away as his eyes met Maddie's. "What are you doing here?"

She wore pale lemon today, the dress soft and feminine. A rose satin ribbon was tied beneath her lovely breasts, and the ends fell down the fall of the skirt. It was simple in style yet anything but on her. Her bonnet was straw and also had rose ribbons. Just looking at her made him ache for something he could never have. He saw no sign of the suffering she had endured at the hands of Raynor.

"I came to talk to you about Daisy."

"Alone?" He got to his feet. "That was reckless."

"I have a maid with me. She is waiting in Max's carriage. I wanted to see you alone."

"You should not have walked onto this boat without an escort, Maddie. Surely your brothers have no notion of where you are."

"No, I told them I was going shopping."

"Which you aren't?"

"I will be, after I have talked to you."

"Alone?"

"With the maid."

"She is not enough protection." He waved to the seat across from his desk.

"I am no longer in danger, Harry." She sat.

"And are you fully recovered, Maddie?" Harry did the same.

"I am, and knowing that man can no longer harm me or any women is a relief."

"He won't touch you again." Harry hadn't meant to growl but it came out that way.

"I know. My brothers will ensure that does not happen."

Her brothers, not him. Harry had no claim to her, so he should not mind hearing her words. He did.

"Your cabin is nice, Harry."

He looked around the room that had been his home whenever he'd been at sea. His bed was wide, simply because he was a big man. He had a small table, and his desk. A shelf where he stored his ledgers and books. His clothes were in a trunk.

"Thank you. Can I get you anything?"

"No, thank you. Will you leave soon?"

"Yes." *Tell her you're leaving today.*

"Do you not wish to stay and spend more time with your family?"

She wasn't looking at him, her eyes over his shoulder.

"My life is not here, it is in France." His words sounded hollow even to his own ears.

"And yet you have only your grandmother there, so in fact more of your family is here."

"I run my business from France and live there. I have friends there that are important to me."

"Can you not live in both places?"

Harry saw the hope in her eyes and squashed it.

"No. Now what did you want to discuss about Daisy, Maddie? I have had my man here in London send word to that school. He will contact you directly with the details."

She looked at her hands briefly. When her eyes met his again, the emotion was gone.

"I don't want to send her away to a school. I want to keep her with me and Fleur." She said the words quickly. "Let me explain, please."

Harry closed his mouth on the instant refusal.

"She and Fleur are inseparable, and I have come to love Daisy also. I know it has only been a short time, and I also know that if she is not to live with me, the family are already making plans to keep her with us. But I want her to be part of our lives in the house Max has given us, which I moved into yesterday."

"He gave you a house. I suppose it's on the same street?"

Her smile was small. Maddie wasn't really one for large gestures.

"Of course, and next door to where Rory and Kate will live. It's all a bit odd, and yet that's who these families are, don't you think, Harry?"

"Definitely odd."

She had changed in so many ways since that day he'd found her sitting alone with Fleur clutched to her chest, and not just in appearance. Small changes that had softened her. She smiled more and talked instead of sitting silently in the background. There was a confidence in her now too. Still shy, and yes, vulnerable, but she'd found strength nestled in the protective arms of her family. Raynor had not broken that; he'd not sent her back to the woman who had arrived in London.

"Have you talked to Daisy about it?"

"No. I wanted to discuss it with you first, and then I will speak with the others."

Why did the fact that she'd come to him first make him ridiculously pleased?

"Why me?"

"You saved her, Harry. There will always be a bond between you and Daisy, and I know you have been searching for a place for her to live and feel a responsibility to her. You don't need to any longer. She will stay with us."

Harry got to his feet and walked to the porthole. They would leave today. He should tell her that, and yet was strangely loath to do so. They would not see each other again for many months, that was if he chose to come back to London and visit with them.

He would miss them.

Then why not make a life here?

He rebelled at the thought. When you were told from the age of five not to seek out your family, you listened. It was ingrained in him he couldn't change that. And yet he'd spent time with them and knew they were good people.

Harry had never needed or wanted anyone else in his life until now.

"Do you not think I will be a good mother to Daisy, Harry?"

She'd followed him and stood just behind his right shoulder.

"Of course you will be a good mother for her." He made himself turn.

"You cannot have her here with you, Harry. It would be

dangerous for a girl with sight, but for one without it would be doubly so. Surely you see that?"

"I had not even considered that."

"Well, then?" She waited, hands clasped before her.

"Well, indeed." He touched her cheek. It was folly. He should simply give her his blessing and let her walk away from him. The hell of it was, he didn't seem able to.

"Maddie." Harry sighed, cupping her cheek. "How is it you disturb me so much?"

"I don't know." To his surprise, she turned her lips into his palm. "But you disturb me very much also."

That soft kiss was his undoing. The feel of her lips on his palm had his body simmering in seconds. He stepped closer until they touched, then kissed her, pouring all the longing and confusion that was his life into that moment.

He didn't want to scare her with the need inside him. It was just a kiss and nothing more, but when she wrapped her arms around his neck, he thought there was every possibility that he would shatter, his body was so hard.

"I am a widow, Harry."

"But an innocent, for all that." He kissed her neck, inhaling the soft scent that was hers alone. "I can't hurt you, Maddie."

"You could never hurt me, Harry."

He could, because he could take her. Here and now, and then sail away. But Harry wouldn't. He respected her and their families too much to do that.

She stepped out of his arms and removed her bonnet.

"What are you doing?"

"Undressing."

"No, Maddie, we cannot do that." His words had absolutely no strength in them. In fact, his knees had gone weak.

"Do you know, Harry, that no man has touched me with reverence other than you."

"Your husband—"

"Was a good man, but there was no passion. Will you show me passion, Harry, just once?"

"You ask too much of me, Maddie." His words were hoarse.

"Oh." She looked away, grabbing her bonnet. "I had thought—"

"I want you," he said as she turned away. "Never doubt that, but I can offer you no more than this."

She turned back to face him. "And yet I have asked for no more." Maddie made it to the door before he stopped her.

Placing a hand over her head, he reached around her and turned the key in the lock. Sliding his hand down her arm, he removed her bonnet and hurled it onto his desk.

"I only have so much restraint where you are concerned."

The buttons of her dress marched in a row down her back. He stroked her neck, then lower to where the buttons started. Leaning forward, he kissed the smooth, pale skin and felt her shiver.

"I won't let you back out now," he whispered in her ear. "Do you understand that, Maddie?"

Her nod was a small jerk of her head.

Harry started on her buttons, opening them slowly, then placing his lips on the skin he'd uncovered.

Will you show me passion, Harry.

He wondered if she knew just what those words had unleashed inside him. His need for this woman had been steadily growing, hence the reason he'd tried to keep his distance. But she'd come to him and wanted him to show her passion.

When he reached the last button, he slid his hands inside the now gaping dress and round the front of her stomach, stroking her through the fine lawn of her chemise.

"I am not—"

"You are perfect." He pressed a kiss to her back. "I want you, Maddie, very much."

He pulled her back against his front. Let her feel him.

"Feel what you do to me."

Her hand touched his thigh, fingers stroking him through his breeches, and he felt it everywhere. He pushed her dress from her shoulders, and as it fell to her ankles, Maddie stepped out of it, then turned to face him.

"You are beautiful."

She shook her head.

"Yes, you are."

"I don't need those words, Harry." Gripping the hem of her chemise, she pulled it up and over her body, naked now but for her stockings. "I want you to show me passion."

He stood back to look at her long, slender limbs and let his gaze move up past the thatch of dark hair between her thighs to the pale skin of her belly. Then higher to the soft swell of her pale breasts.

Maddie moved to cover herself, one hand on her stomach. Harry eased it aside. Dropping to his knees before her, he traced the soft lines that Fleur had left there.

"These make you more beautiful to me." He leaned in and kissed her skin before rising. She had tears rolling down her cheeks.

"Why are you crying?"

"You make me beautiful," she whispered. "Don't stop, Harry."

Their kisses grew more heated as she responded. He stroked the line of her back and trailed his fingers over her ribs.

Maddie undid the buttons of his shirt and pushed it from his body, and the feel of her hands on his skin were exquisite.

His hands were in her hair now, releasing the pins so finally he could see what he'd longed for. It fell in a thick brown wave to her waist. He sifted his fingers through it, settling it around her shoulders.

"Kiss me, Harry."

It was no hardship to feel her pressed to his chest. He was, quite simply, on fire.

He picked her up and carried her to his bed, lowering her onto the covers. Harry removed his boots and the rest of his clothes. Maddie's eyes followed his hands, watching his every move. When he was done, he braced a knee beside her thighs and heard the breath hiss from her lips.

"What?"

"I don't think I can do that." She wasn't looking at him now.

"Lie on your back with me on top?" He looked down at her, trying to work out what she wasn't telling him.

She nodded.

"Who hurt you?" The anger was swift and fierce.

"No one. It's just that he did that, and I don't want to remember that with you."

"He. Raynor?"

She nodded.

"But he didn't—"

"No!"

Pushing aside the anger, Harry lifted her into his arms. He sat on the bed, holding her.

"We don't have to do this, Maddie. I don't want to frighten you."

"I'm sorry, I should have thought more about this before we started." She looked upset. "Maybe we can do that?"

"There are other ways, Maddie."

"Really?"

"Really. I don't want to frighten you, but I don't have to be on top of you for us to make love."

"You don't frighten me, Harry, and I want this here with you. Please make love to me."

He'd never, not even in his head, called it making love. That thought should have had him running from the cabin. Instead, he set about making this beautiful woman understand that passion was not something to fear, but to cherish.

CHAPTER 32

Maddie did not want to think about any man but Harry. Not Jacques, who had lain with her in the dark, simply asking her to raise her skirts, or Lord Raynor who had grasped her breasts. She wanted to think only of Harry and how wonderful his hands and mouth made her feel.

This was passion, and she wanted more.

Doing what she was with Harry would push aside all the darkness from Raynor and leave her with memories of what could be.

Maddie kissed him, and he let her take the lead. Let her explore his lovely mouth and run her fingers through his hair. She touched the cords of muscle on his shoulders and arms.

"You are a beautiful man, Harry."

"Thank you, but I don't think men are meant to be beautiful, my sweet."

"You are." She kissed his chest, and the breath left him in a rush. Maddie then kissed wherever she could reach.

She felt the tension inside him, but he did not stop her.

His hands stroked her arms and back, but he did no more than that until she kissed his lips once more. Then he touched her breasts.

It was glorious. Heat spiked through her body, and she felt an ache start between her thighs.

"You have beautiful breasts, Maddie."

"I doubt they are," she felt a need to say. "I fed my child from them."

Her chin was lifted, and their eyes met. His were so green now, bright and fierce.

"I could write poems just on your breasts alone, madam, so do not argue with me."

"Do you write poetry?"

"No, but if I did, I would do so about your breasts."

Her laugh turned to a sigh as he licked the slope of one. He then covered every inch with kisses before swiping his tongue across her nipple and making her shudder.

"Do you feel the passion, Maddie?"

"Oh, yes."

"It has only just begun."

He tormented her with caresses and kisses, and Maddie was soon moaning with a need she'd never felt before. It built steadily inside her, and this too, she knew, was passion.

She was lifted and repositioned to straddle his thighs, now exposed to him.

"If you are frightened, tell me, Maddie."

"I will," she whispered as he pushed her hair over a shoulder. The kiss he placed on her neck had heat spiking through her as his hands moved lower to caress her thighs, his thumbs moving closer to that place that ached.

"Just feel, Maddie." He touched her.

"I do… it is wonderful, Harry."

Maddie wanted to be brave. Wanted to touch Harry as he

touched her. She stroked his ribs before moving lower and stroking the hardness of his need.

"Ah, Maddie," he sighed.

She wrapped her hand around him and stroked the length, and Harry moaned softly.

Then it was Maddie's turn to moan as he touched the bead between her thighs. He pushed his fingers inside her, and she felt all that wonderful tension climb.

"Harry."

"I have you, as you have me, Maddie."

Removing his hands, he eased hers from his body, then pulled her closer until she felt him probing at her entrance.

"Take me inside you now, Maddie." He lay on the bed, then lifted her and lowered her onto his hard length.

Bracing herself on her knees, she slid slowly down, feeling the muscles stretching to accommodate him until he was buried to the hilt.

"Christ, you feel good." He pulled her down and kissed her. Desperate for more, Maddie took it all. "Now ride me."

She'd only ever done it in the dark with Jacques, but looking down into the wicked green eyes, she thought that perhaps this was so much more than anything she'd experienced with her late husband.

This really was passion.

Maddie rose and lowered, and his breathing grew rapid, as did hers. This was her doing; she was in control, not him. She did it again, and then again, each time moving faster. His hands cupped her breasts as the tension climbed.

"Let go for me, Maddie!"

"Yes," Maddie breathed and then she felt it, the wonderful wave of pleasure that swept through her.

Harry drove up as she came down and then pulled out on a long, shuddering moan. She fell onto the bed face-first beside him, breathless, replete, her limbs weak. His hand skimmed her spine, then she felt a kiss on her head.

He moved, and she rolled to her side to watch him walk to the basin of water. He had a lovely body. Smooth skin covered muscles that rippled as he walked.

"Thank you."

He looked over his shoulder, and the smile that had been there fell away. "Don't thank me."

"You gave me what I asked for, Harry. Passion. You also protected me."

"I wanted that as much as you, Maddie." He returned to stand over her, handing her a cloth. "I don't need thanks for that. How was I protecting you?"

"By pulling out."

"I did. Neither of us need the complication of a child."

His eyes were no longer bright, but guarded. Suddenly the man who had shown so much emotion just minutes before was gone. Shut away behind the cool facade. Had this meant anything to him other than bedding a woman?

She'd come here hoping she could make him understand what he now meant to her and admit that he too felt something. Her family certainly believed that was the case. But looking at his face, closed and frowning, it seemed they were both wrong.

"You had better leave, Madeline, before someone comes looking for you."

"You want me to leave?"

"It would be best." He wouldn't look at her, and she realized then that he would not be staying in England, and she'd be foolish to believe he would. Harry did not feel for her as she did him. She'd asked him to show her passion, he had, and now it was time for her to leave.

"Yes, well, thank you again." Maddie made herself get off

the bed, keeping her eyes from his. She would not show him how much his words hurt her. She had spent a lifetime wanting to be loved, and she was worthy of that. If Harry could not give it to her, then one day someone would. Maddie now knew her worth. She did not have to settle as she once would have.

She began to dress. "I must thank you also, Harry, for showing me what can be between a man and woman." The wonderful connection they'd just shared was shattered at her feet. She needed to remain in control and get out of there before she did something she regretted, like telling him what lay in her heart.

"Not just any man and woman," he said softly.

"Do you have my pins?"

He handed her the pins silently, and Maddie bundled her hair up, jabbing them in hard enough to make her wince.

"Would you do my buttons up, please?" Maddie presented him her back and refused to react as his hands touched the skin above the neckline of her dress.

"When do you leave?" She made herself ask the question. Needed to know what day he would sail away from her, this man who had slipped inside her when she wasn't looking. Maddie had always believed she was not a woman who would experience this kind of fierce emotion; Harry had changed that for her from the start.

"Soon." He picked up her bonnet, holding it out to her.

"Thank you." She took it and stepped away from him to pull it on. Maddie tied the ribbons.

"Stop thanking me."

"Of course, sorry. If I don't see you again, have a good life, Harry. I will look after Daisy now, so you have no need to worry about her."

"About Daisy." He grabbed her hand as she turned to leave. "I want to help you support her in some way."

Her heart thudded. Did that mean he wasn't going? Did it mean if he did, he would come back and see her?

"Money, or tutors, anything you think would make things easier for her. Even though I will not be in her life, I feel some responsibility."

She shook the hand free.

"I renounce you of all responsibility for her care now. Daisy is mine, and I have no need of your money, thank you. I have brothers and sisters who will help me financially."

"Why have my words offended you?"

He didn't make a move to come closer, just stood watching her.

"They didn't."

"They have. I can hear it in your voice."

"We just made love!" Dear God, she'd yelled. Maddie never yelled or lost control.

"I know that. It was lovely."

Lovely! Get out of here now.

"It was lovely," Maddie said slowly, "and then you acted like I was... like I was just... oh God."

"Just what?"

"Any woman who you made love to, and of course I was. Silly me." She found a laugh. "Of course you have done that with many women, and I am just another."

"I did not offer more, Maddie. You said you wanted me to show you passion, and I did."

He was so calm, and inside she was crumbling.

"I did not ask you for more, I asked you for passion, and yes, you gave me that, but clearly, unlike you, I had not believed a person could then put it to one side, as if it was just a... a new glove!"

"You are not a new glove," he gritted out.

"It's all right. I'm just not used to this kind of thing. I'm sure in time I will be."

"What the hell does that mean?" He wasn't looking calm now.

"It means that now I know what happens when I take my next lover."

"You will not take another lover!"

"Of course I will," Maddie lied. She was not a woman to take lovers, but she'd wanted to shock him. "After all, you are leaving and have no plans to return. I cannot simply live my life alone."

"You will not take a lover!"

"Why? You don't want me, and I've realized that I'm worthy of more, Harry. Once I did not believe that—"

"You are not unworthy."

"I know that now, just as I know I deserve what my family have. To be loved and live my life with a man who wants me."

"Maddie." He moved closer. "Let me explain."

"There is nothing to explain. You don't want us... your family or me, and there is nothing I can do to change that." She turned away and reached the door. Something stopped her; perhaps the fact that she'd lived her life hiding in the shadows and had no wish to do so any longer.

"I love you, Harry Sinclair, but I did not tell you that to make you stay. I deserve more from life, and that includes having my love returned. Therefore, my love for you will not stop me living my life and in time will fade. I no longer have to settle for safety or a roof over my head. Now I have choices, and I intend to take them. Be happy, Harry."

She wrenched open the door, then slammed it behind her.

"Maddie!"

Ignoring Harry's roar, she ran along the deck, soon reaching the gangway.

"Mrs. Caron?"

"Oh, hello, Barney. I'm sorry, I must leave. But thank you for everything you've done for me!"

"Well then, goodbye, and I wish you well. We are sailing on today, so may God bless and watch over you and your little girl," he called as she sprinted passed him.

Tonight? He hadn't even had the courage to tell her that. *Fiend.* Reaching the bottom, Maddie ran to the carriage. The coachman saw her coming and opened the door. She turned before stepping inside and saw Harry standing on the deck. He hadn't followed her. He stood as she'd first seen him. Fierce like a warrior, watching her with those vibrant green eyes.

The difference now was that she knew him. Conflicted and yet determined to live his life true to his father's wishes. Maddie and his family were not enough to change that.

"Goodbye, Harry," she mouthed, knowing he would read her lips. Maddie climbed into the carriage. She would not cry, having learned long ago tears simply made your eyes red and your throat sore. Lifting her chin, she looked out the window and willed herself not to relive every moment of what she had just experienced with Harry. Later she'd think about that, and in the years to come.

She'd asked him for passion, and he'd given it to her and so much more. He'd replaced the ugly memories of what a man and woman could share.

Her heart ached for the love he did not or could not return, but that too would pass. Now she would look forward to the life she would live with her girls. A life filled with excitement and expectation. A life without Harry.

CHAPTER 33

Harry had stood at the railing and watched Maddie drive away from him. He'd told himself it was the right thing to let her do. What he couldn't work out was why.

I love you, Harry Sinclair.

Maddie loved him, and as he went through the process of getting ready to sail, he thought about what it had cost her to say those words. The woman who had not known love in her life. For her to come to his ship and offer him what she had, had taken courage. Her family had given her that. With security and love, she'd found confidence.

Why could Harry not rise above his childhood? His father had made him promise to never seek out his family, and he'd always stayed true to that. *Why?*

Doubts began to bombard him from all sides. Doubts and fears that in walking away from his family and Maddie, he was losing his chance at happiness.

The Sinclairs and Ravens had asked nothing from him, and yet he'd continually pushed them away.

He went through the motions of speaking to his crew and

ensuring he'd logged all the details he needed to as the thoughts continued to roll around inside his head.

If he'd never met them, none of this would have been an issue. He wouldn't want to have Cam tease him again, or Dev treat him like a younger sibling. He wouldn't have his cousins call him Uncle, or Fleur demand a story as she wrapped her arms around his neck.

And Daisy, the sweet little girl he'd saved. He'd walked away from her too without even a word of goodbye.

You are a callous bastard.

For so long it had been just him and Grandmère, but now there were others who cared about him.

Harry tried to push aside thoughts of Maddie. He didn't think about how soft her skin felt or what he'd experienced when he was inside her, as close as a man could be with a woman.

I love you, Harry Sinclair, but I did not tell you that to make you stay. I deserve more from life, and that includes having my love returned.

She did deserve to be loved. Why could it not be by him?

Be happy, Harry.

He'd always thought he was happy, and then she'd stepped into his life and turned everything around.

"Hell." He lowered his head to the desk and banged it. Why was this so hard?

"Why is it you must bang your head like that when things do not go as you planned, grandson? Even as a boy you did it. I find I like it less now."

He watched his grandmother walk to the chair opposite him and fold herself into it.

"I am busy, Grandmère. Perhaps you should go to your cabin, and I will come to you once we have left London."

Ignoring him, she settled herself and the skirts under which he knew she had many layers of petticoats and other things ladies these days rarely wore, but his grandmother still insisted upon.

Maddie had worn a chemise made of the finest lawn against her silken skin, and her stockings had small rosebuds embroidered on them.

"It means that now I know what happens when I take my next lover." She'd spoken the words before she left his cabin and driven a nail through his chest while doing so.

The thought of another man touching her made him want to strike at something.

"Why is it you are desperate to leave them, grandson?"

"Pardon?" Harry folded his hands one on top of the other on his desk and took every emotion but polite enquiry from his face. His grandmother could sense weakness; it would not do to let her see he was unsettled.

"I know you better than anyone, Harry. You came to me as a babe, and I have watched you grow. I watched that man poison your mind against your kin. Watched a bitter man try to ruin you. He loved my daughter, I never doubted that, but with her gone, there was only hatred."

"He was a good man." Harry did not like to talk about his father. The man had been cold and unapproachable, but he had provided for his only son. Harry had told himself he'd needed no more.

"I never said he wasn't," she snapped. "But he was bitter, and I heard him many times telling you never to trust a Sinclair. Forcing you to make a promise to obey his wishes. So much so, that now you are running away from where you belong. Running from love and the chance of a family. Why, grandson?"

"My home is in France."

"Is it? Which home is this?" She stomped her cane on the floor twice. "The one I live in? Because you are rarely there. Or perhaps this boat filled with men who drink and curse."

"I drink and curse, Grandmère."

"Do not interrupt me!"

"Your pardon."

"Or do you speak of those rooms you own that are empty of love and laughter? They are your people, boy. Don't run from them or her with the little girls. The one with no sight who sees so much, and the other ray of sunlight."

"Maddie," he rasped. "Her name is Maddie, not *her*!"

"What do you care? You are leaving them alone, to be preyed upon by strangers."

"She has family to protect her." What strangers? Surely no one would get near Maddie and the girls now? But then, she had just moved out of her brother's house. Why had they allowed her to do that? Surely she was better under Max's roof?

"Family that have their own to care for. No, that woman is alone with those little girls. Some man will realize what she presents and take advantage of her."

Everything inside him rebelled at that, but he kept the anger from his face.

"Think with you heart, grandson. Do you want to live your life alone without love? Without them, your family?"

"Love?" was all he could manage to get out around the lump in his throat.

"I spoke with her. Madeline Caron. I saw the girls as they talked of you. They all love you; it was there in Madeline's words and the look in her eyes, and then that Cambridge Sinclair confirmed my thoughts."

"What did he say?"

"That you were meant to be here with your people. Here with Madeline, the woman you love."

Harry looked at the only person who had really cared for him. Fierce and strong, she had been his savior many times, keeping him on the right path, not allowing him to be what he could so easily have been.

Their eyes met, and it was as he looked at her that he realized.

"Christ," he whispered. "What am I doing?" Suddenly the blindfold he'd been wearing was ripped away. He didn't want to leave them. Not his family. Sinclairs, Ravens, Huntingtons, or the rest of them. They were a part of him now, and he never wanted to let them go.

"Hell, I am a fool, Grandmère."

"You will not blaspheme in my company!"

"Your pardon."

"You are also not leaving London. I will, however, as I have several events planned. But I shall return in three weeks and expect you to be nestled in the bosom of your family with the woman you love, grandson. Do not disappoint me. I want those grandbabies as my own, and then many more, if you please."

"I love you, Grandmère."

"As you should." She rose, hugged him, then stomped from the cabin.

Now he'd let himself feel, it landed on him with a vengeance. His heart felt exposed and raw, and his eyes stung. He loved them and could not leave.

For so long, he'd convinced himself his life would be lived a certain way and had fought to stand by those beliefs. His grandmother had shaken those foundations, and now he knew differently.

His father had been wrong. Sinclairs could be trusted, and they'd been showing him exactly that since he arrived in London. Finally he believed it.

Leaving his cabin, Harry found his friend on the lower deck.

"I am staying here for a while, Faris. I shall return soon, but until then I will run the business from here."

"I wondered when you would see reason. Your grandmother spoke to you, I presume?"

"Does everyone but me know I should be staying in London?" Harry felt light inside, like the vise that had been clamped around his heart was released. He wanted to laugh; he wanted to find Maddie and hug his girls. God, he even wanted to hug his family... all of them!

"I thought we'd established I am far more intelligent than you," Farris said, looking smug. "Go now, and pack. I shall return in three weeks with more cargo and pay you a call."

"Thank you, friend. I will need a new business partner to oversee things in France. Would you be interested?"

He was likely getting ahead of himself. He had to speak to Maddie, but she had said she loved him. He would need a place to live and somewhere to run his business. There were so many things to contemplate, and yet he wanted this.

Farris held out his hand, and Harry shook it. "I would be honored."

"You know this business better than me anyway. I will be waiting when you return—"

"With your bride?"

"Is there anyone who doesn't know about Maddie too?"

"I believe Barney is oblivious. Now go, and I will see you at the end of the month. I will miss you, my friend."

"And I you." Harry gripped his friend's hand.

He packed and loaded everything into a hackney. It was now laden with books, belongings, and things from his cabin. He only hoped his reception would be a warm one.

The trip seemed to take an inordinately long time, and by the time he'd arrived outside Dev's house, the sun was setting.

Asking the driver to wait, he knocked on the front door, and the butler answered.

"Please have my things brought inside, Tatters, and then find a room to store them in."

"Of course, Mr. Sinclair. I will see to it at once."

"Is the family from home? It seems quiet in here."

"They are, Mr. Sinclair."

"Very well. I will speak to them upon my return. Good day, Tatters."

He ran to Max's house, as he had no idea which house on the street was now Maddie's.

"Good day, George," he said when the butler opened the door. "Is Mrs. Caron here?"

"She and the family are not at home, sir."

Harry wanted to gnash his teeth. Now his head and, yes, heart had finally cleared, he want to tell Maddie what was inside him.

"Is she with the other family members?"

"As to that, Mr. Sinclair, I am unsure."

And just like that, he was tense. Every muscle clenched. He'd thought what was running through him was simply the release of the tight rein he'd had on his emotions; now he knew differently. Something wasn't right.

Harry was soon running to James's house, where he pounded his fist on the front door.

"Where are the family, Buttles?" Harry asked when the door opened.

"Only the children and Misses Dorset, Somerset, and Kate Sinclair are in the nursery, Mr. Sinclair. The duke and duchess are from home."

Something was very wrong... very wrong. Harry could feel it now he was thinking clearly.

"I will speak to Dorrie, Somer, and Kate." One of them would know what was going on. Running up the stairs, he heard someone reading a story as he approached the nursery. Opening the door, he found a man seated on a chair and the children on the floor around him listening as he read from the book in his hand. The three older Sinclairs were seated behind the children.

He found Fleur, and Daisy next to her. In fact, all the children were here, even the older ones. What was going on? Dorrie saw him and pressed a finger to her lips, telling him she wanted him to stay silent. She then hurried to greet him, waving him out the door.

"What's going on?" Harry said once the door had closed.

"Come, we will move away from the nursery, as yet we're not entirely sure which of the next generation are gifted with what."

He followed her down the stairs to a small parlor.

"Dorrie, tell me what has happened?"

"Rose and Emily went to meet Maddie and do some shopping. None of them have returned." Her pretty face was pale, and Harry could tell she was close to tears.

He did something then that until that moment had never come easy to him. Harry hugged his cousin. She collapsed against him.

"They were due to return hours ago, and then when the tension started, we all knew something was not right. Wolf and Cam are desperate, as are the others. Kate, Somer, and I are with the children keeping them calm. We have told them their parents have gone to the theater."

"Where are the others?"

"Looking. They're out there riding about trying to find them. I'm so scared, Harry. How is it three women can have gone missing?"

"I don't know, but I need to go now and help search, Dorrie." His head was spinning. Maddie was missing, as were Rose and Emily. Why?

"I need a horse," Harry said.

"Buttles will get you one." Dorrie grabbed Harry's hand, and they ran to find the butler.

He rode away from the street his family all lived on a short while later and had no idea in what direction he should head. It would be dark soon, and they must find the women before then. He had to find Maddie and tell her what was in his heart. She'd left him believing he didn't love her, and the thought of her out there somewhere in danger, still believing that, was not to be borne.

She was his now, and he would not stop until he found her.

CHAPTER 34

They'd been waiting in her house. Emily and Rose were placing flowers in vases when she arrived. They'd taken one look at Maddie's face and bid her to put her bonnet back on, as they were going out to take tea and eat cream cakes to celebrate her new home.

She'd argued that Daisy and Fleur needed her. Emily had said they were at the park with their cousins and happy.

She'd relented, and they'd soon been traveling to a tea shop.

Numb over what had taken place, and still telling herself she was strong enough to withstand a broken heart, she'd attempted to chat with her sisters and failed miserably.

Heartache, it seemed, was an extremely painful thing.

The tea shop was not large, and they found a table in the rear. Once seated, Emily ordered tea and the promised cream cakes.

"Now, why do you look sad?"

"How can I be sad when I have so much?" Maddie replied to Rose's question.

"Your eyes are sad, and that smile would frighten anyone."

"I am not like you and smile all the time."

"But lately you have smiled more. Now how about you stop trying to fob us off and tell us where you went and why it made you sad," Rose said.

Emily patted Maddie's hand, and this, she realized, was what it would have been like to have sisters growing up.

"I-I really don't want to talk about it." She could feel the tears choking her.

"Too bad," Rose said. "You are unhappy, we are your sisters and love you, so we will simply keep annoying you until you tell us what we want to hear. It's how sisters work."

"It really is," Emily said. "I was like you, reserved, and—"

"And shut tighter than that box Wolf keeps under his bed he thinks I can't open."

Emily giggled.

"I went to see Harry."

"And?" Rose poured the tea that had just arrived.

"And we talked."

"I hope you kissed him too," Emily shocked Maddie by saying. "Harry looks like he would kiss well, don't you think, Rose?"

"Oh, definitely, and he is a Sinclair. We know they kiss well."

"He did kiss me, and it was wonderful."

"But?"

"But he is leaving today, and I will n-never see him again." Maddie sucked in a large breath.

"And you love him." Rose took her hand.

"Oh Lord, I really do," Maddie wailed. She'd never wailed in her life before.

"And did you tell him?" Emily asked.

"I did, but he does not return that love."

She sat there drinking tea and eating cakes and thought that if her heart wasn't shattered into a million pieces, she'd have loved this moment with her sisters. They made her laugh and told her Harry would come to his senses soon, as they had seen how he looked at Maddie.

"He loves you. I know he does," Emily said when they left the tea shop. Maddie didn't reply. She knew that Harry may care for her, but he'd never act on that.

Stubborn fool.

"Where is the carriage?" Rose looked about her.

"Here it comes," Emily said as it rolled toward them. "Does Max have a new driver?"

"I don't know," Maddie said, wondering if Harry's ship had sailed yet.

"I don't recognize either of those two." Rose was looking at both men up in the driver's seat. One leapt down as the carriage stopped, and with a bow, opened the door.

"Why are the curtains closed?" Maddie asked.

"I've never seen you before," Emily said. "How long have you been with Mr. and Mrs. Huntington?"

"Get in the carriage please, ladies." The man held a pistol, and it was aimed at Rose. "No noise, just step up and inside now or I will shoot."

They did as he said, because if he fired at this close range, he'd kill whoever he aimed at. Another man waited for them inside. He quickly gagged them, then bound them hand and foot. Soon the carriage was rolling away from the tea shop with Maddie and her sisters inside.

...

Maddie wasn't sure how long they traveled for, but the trip was not a short one. Rose and Emily leaned against her, which gave her strength. She was not in this, whatever it was, alone.

When the carriage stopped, their feet were untied and they were blindfolded.

"Step outside. Someone will lead you. Any attempt to escape, and I will not hesitate to shoot."

They did as they were told. Stumbling in the darkness, not knowing where they were, or what was about to happen.

"You are stepping down now."

She followed the directions given and listened for Emily's and Rose's footsteps behind her. Finally they stopped, and their blindfolds and gags were removed.

"You'll be sorry you did this!" Rose spat.

The men who had led them said nothing, simply motioned for them to sit on the floor and bound their feet again.

"They will come, and you will be sorry!" Her Scottish accent was thick as she yelled at the men.

"You can't simply kidnap three women. We are the sisters of a duke," Maddie said as the men left the room.

"Oh, I know who you all are, especially you, daughter."

"Dear God!" Maddie looked at the woman who walked into the room.

"After all, I slept with your father when I worked in his castle. He gave me a nice little house until I was of no further use to him. And isn't that just like a man. Turns away when he no longer has a need for you."

"Why have you done this?" Maddie cried.

Estelle Huntington was still a beautiful woman, at least on the outside. She'd had her children young and somehow managed to maintain her youthful veneer. It was just the inside that was poisonous.

She had thick brown hair showing no signs of gray and a heart-shaped face, but her cold brown eyes were always calculating what she could get out of any situation.

"Why not? Your brothers have money, and I want my share." Her smile was as cold as the rest of her.

"They'll come, and you'll be sorry," Maddie said. She

wouldn't show fear in front of this woman again. She'd spent her life doing that. She wouldn't allow that scared girl who'd only wanted her mother's love to surface. She had love now and was stronger for it.

"No one will find you here like they did that fool Raynor. I told him to forget you, but he wouldn't."

"Why are you in London?" Maddie would never call this woman Mother again.

"When I found Raynor bloodied on your floor, I tended him. I was quite impressed with your strength, Madeline. I had no idea you had that in you. You were always such a pathetic child."

"Don't speak about her like that," Emily growled in a voice Maddie had never heard before.

"He vowed revenge," Estelle said, ignoring Emily's words. "I said I thought I knew where you had gone, and he decided to take me with him to London to see my children."

"Why? We all know you've never had a maternal moment in your lifetime. After all, I gave you a room, and you betrayed me by taking that man's money and letting him abuse me."

"It's true, I feel nothing for any of you." She shrugged. "But I needed the money, and he supplied it, and that was after I first gave him what he really wanted. You were just a little sport for Lord Raynor, and then when you left, he was determined to have you and revenge for what you did. I'd read the letters Rory sent you, so I had your address. Raynor had you followed everywhere after we arrived until the opportunity came for him to grab you. Unfinished business, he said. Well, it finished him off." She laughed. "Of course, now I have this, there is no need for me to worry further."

"I don't understand?"

"He replaced the madam who ran this place with me.

Now he's gone, and this dirty secret is mine, as no one knows of the double life he lived."

"Why take us if you have this?"

"I doubt she's sane," Rose said. "Don't argue with her. They will find us soon, and then she will get what she deserves."

"No one will find you!"

"Oh, they will," Emily said. "Our family is very resourceful. They can find anyone. I would be extremely worried, were I you. I won't call you Mrs. Huntington, as that is Essie's name."

"Maybe we could call her whore, or harlot?" Rose suggested.

"Trollop?" Emily added.

Maddie watched her mother's face turn red.

"Shut up!"

"The truth is rarely pleasant," Maddie said. "I favor trollop." She'd never stood up to her mother before. The love of her family had given her the strength to do so, even if she was at the woman's mercy. She would cower to her no more.

"Shut your mouth or I will make you pay, daughter!" Estelle stormed closer.

"You can't hurt me anymore. I have family now. I don't want or need anything from you."

The shock in her mother's eyes was wonderful.

"They will find us, never fear. And when they do, Max and Rory will make you pay," Maddie said.

Estelle laughed once again in control. "How will they find you? This place has no connection to Raynor's brothel in London. Look around you, daughter, you're in the cellar. Can you not imagine what it's used for?"

"Hell is about to rain down on you, trollop, and were I not very aware of what a bitch you were, I'd almost feel sorry for you," Rose said calmly.

If her sisters were showing no fear, then neither would she.

"They won't find you. This is hidden, and only a select few come by invitation and pay highly for the services of my girls. Of course, some will pay for me only, as I can service their needs better than any woman."

"You're a whore, Mother, let's not wrap it up in anything different. You'd do anything to achieve your own ends. It's amazing you haven't contracted some type of disease."

"She does have those pock marks," Rose said.

"And her skin seems awfully lined," Emily added.

Maddie forced out a laugh, which infuriated Estelle.

The hand that shot out was so fast she never saw it coming, but she felt it, the sting of pain accompanying that slap.

"Don't touch her!" Emily cried.

"It's all right, Em, I am used to this particular brand of punishment from her. It's how she subdued her children most of our childhood. You are the epitome of evil. A cold, emotionless woman who never does anything without gain to yourself. I will never understand how you raised three children who could not be more different as day to night than you, but know this, never will you control me again." Maddie kept her eyes steady on the woman before her. They shared blood but nothing more.

"I gave you food and a bed!"

"Barely, and both were usually supplied by my brothers. I have nothing inside me for you but pity."

Estelle retreated to the door, clearly unused to this behavior from her daughter. "Don't try and leave. I have men here who would kill you should I ask it of them. One is even now on his way to the duke's house with a note for enough money to set me up somewhere far away from this cold, dreary place when I tire of it."

"We all know how you control your men, don't we, Estelle." Maddie's words followed her out the door. It was then slammed and locked.

"Oh, Maddie, I am so sorry it is your mother doing this," Emily said.

"No, it's I who's so sorry. This would not have happened were it not for me."

"It's all right, Maddie, they will find us," Rose soothed.

"The only blame lays at that woman's feet," Emily added. "They will arrive and then she will really know fear."

"Loath as I am to admit it, your mother is still a beautiful woman. It's those eyes though, cold and evil," Rose said. "I'm sorry she raised you but so pleased you are now with us. People love you, Maddie."

That made her sniff back the tears.

"The carriage trip took a while, so my guess is we are just outside London," Emily added.

"We shall wriggle a bit and put out backs to each other, then maybe I can loosen your knots, Em," Rose said.

"How can you both be so calm?" Maddie asked.

"They will find us because of who they are," Rose said. "They are stronger together, and I have to believe that soon this will be over. I cannot allow there to be any other option."

"We must be strong together," Emily said.

"I like having sisters," Maddie said. "I'm sorry if it has taken me a while to understand that."

"Considering we were introduced to the woman who raised you, it's amazing you three Huntingtons are as sane as you are. I think Medusa would suit her better than trollop," Rose said, making Maddie giggle.

"Now, as it appears we have time, please tell us more details about what happened in Harry's cabin. I want to be entertained, as it may be a while before we are rescued," Rose said.

"I can't believe neither of you is weeping or scared." Maddie changed the subject.

"My fears are for what our husbands and family are going through. Wolf and Cam will be like men possessed when they realize something has happened to us. I hate what they are feeling," Emily said. "But we have been through worse, and this too will pass. They will ensure that happens; we must just wait for them to find us. Now answer Rose's question, Maddie."

"I— We made love," she whispered. "And while you may think less of me for that, it was the most wonderful thing I have ever experienced. I love him so much that I have a pain inside me I doubt will ever go away."

"We don't think less of you," Rose said. "Making love with the man you feel strongly for is a wonderful thing."

"Agreed," Emily added. "And it's also likely the pain, in part, is from the three cream cakes you ate."

They laughed then, the sound loud enough to reach those outside and to show they were not afraid.

"He will not leave, Maddie. Harry loves you, I am sure of it," Rose said gently. "Have faith, sister."

"I will try." And she would, but right at that moment, Maddie doubted she'd ever see Harry again.

CHAPTER 35

*H*arry returned to the duke's house two hours later, after searching wherever he could and coming up with nothing. He had seen no sign of anyone, and the desperation inside him was now clawing at his throat.

Why could he not find his family when he was supposedly connected to them? Why could he not find Maddie?

"Harry!" James saw him as he entered the house. Everyone was gathered there in the entrance.

"Where have you been? I've looked everywhere for someone, anyone!" Harry exploded. "Have you found them?"

"We were out looking also," James said calmly... too calmly, in Harry's opinion.

"I didn't see you."

"If you are accusing us of something, just come out and say it!" Wolf roared at Harry. He looked drawn, his face pale.

"Christ." Harry rubbed a hand over his face. "I'm sorry. Have you any news on them?"

"As they are not here with us and my heart feels like it's been ripped from my chest, then no," Wolf gritted out.

"How is it you know they are missing?" Eden asked him.

"I called by earlier, and Dorrie told me. I have been out looking ever since."

Harry noticed Cam fared little better. The man who was always smiling and ready to tease any of his family was nowhere in sight. His face was drawn, eyes desperate.

"God's blood, I can't stand this. The thought of Rose hurting and me unable to reach her is sending me slowly mad."

"We will find her, brother." Alice gripped Wolf's hands. "You must believe that."

"It's torture," Cam rasped. "Em gets scared easily, even though she tries not to let anyone see it. I vowed to always be there when she needs me. I have failed her."

"No, brother." Eden wrapped her arms around Cam. "You could never fail her, and this was beyond your control."

"We will find them." Dev gripped the shoulders of the two men. "I promise they will be unharmed until we do."

"Why are you here, Harry? I went to ask for your help and found your ship gone." Nicholas said.

"I decided to stay in London."

"Why?" Dev asked him.

"I was not ready to leave." Harry didn't know what to add to that, so he didn't.

"And I'll ask again. Why?"

"Isn't the fact I'm here enough? Haven't you been at me since I arrived to acknowledge you all as my blood? My family, my people?"

"Yes, all of that is true," Dev said steadily in the face of Harry's clear agitation. "But I feel there is more."

"God's blood." The air whistled from his lungs. "I love her, all right! Maddie. I want a life with her and the girls."

"Do you now?" Rory's eyes narrowed as he moved closer to Harry. "We'll just see about that when she is back with us."

"We certainly will," Max added, looking the same.

"I will marry her if she'll have me," Harry growled. "And neither of you will stop that from happening."

"There will be time for that." Nicholas nudged Harry back and away from the Huntington brothers.

"A note has arrived, your Grace." The butler handed it to James, which put a halt to the conversation.

Tearing it open, James read the words out loud.

"Come to the village of Dumpledon alone at dawn tomorrow, Duke. There is a church. Walk down the path to the rear, then through the graveyard. If you wish to see your women again, bring the sum stated and jewelry. If you do not do as I say, they will never be seen again."

"Get the money," Cam snarled. "Whatever it takes."

"Dumpledon is about an hour's ride from here," Dev said. "They must be held somewhere nearby."

A knock behind them had Buttles running to answer it.

"I wish to speak with the Duke of Raven at once."

"That's Mr. Spriggot's voice," Max said, moving to open the door wider.

"Mr. Huntington, I have something I would like to discuss with the duke," Mr. Spriggot said, stepping inside as James appeared. With him was the large figure of Mr. Brown.

"A dire situation has arisen, Mr. Spriggot. If you can shed any light on it, we would be extremely grateful. Speak freely in front of all of us, please."

The investigator frowned, his eyes going around those gathered in the front entrance.

"If you'll excuse me for asking, your Grace, but could you elaborate on the dire situation?"

"Mrs. Rose Sinclair, Mrs. Emily Sinclair, and Mrs. Madeline Caron have been kidnapped. We have just received a ransom note," James said.

Harry hated standing here doing nothing while Maddie was out there somewhere in danger. He also knew that there was little point in running about with no direction, even if the delay chafed at him.

"If you will allow me, I will explain why Mr. Brown and I have called."

"Go ahead," James said.

The two men were now faced with a wall of Sinclairs and Ravens.

"When you asked me to look into Lord Raynor's activities, I did so. Most was as it should be, except of course the house your sister was found in. That was hidden from his family, but it's my understanding had been running for some time."

"What has this to do with my wife!"

"Cam, calm down and let the man speak," James said.

Mr. Spriggot did not look overly upset by Cam's outburst, perhaps because he'd had dealings with him before. Harry thought about grabbing the man by his collars and shaking the story out of him.

He wanted Maddie back, and he wanted her now!

"It was when I visited the staff at the first brothel that I came across Madam Fabron. She was not a happy woman, and upon further questioning, I found out why. Lord Raynor had another establishment where she was the madam. It seems he returned from France with a woman, and he set her up as the new madam and dismissed Madam Fabron after promising her that would never happen."

"A woman scorned, Mr. Spriggot?" Eden asked.

"Indeed, your Grace. She sang like a canary, if you'll pardon my analogy."

Eden waved his words aside.

"But what use is this information to us?" Wolf demanded.

"I believe the woman called herself Mademoiselle Estelle Huntington."

"Dear God!" The words came from Rory.

"I'll kill her this time," Max snarled.

"Who is she?" Harry demanded.

"Our mother, and a coldhearted bitch!" Rory said.

"Considering what you have just told me and the arrest of Lord Raynor, I wonder if it is possible that Mademoiselle Huntington had the three women kidnapped for monetary gain? Of course I could be incorrect—"

"You're not," Max said. "She's more than capable and has no love for her children. She'd do this if she had the means and the end result is a monetary gain for her."

"Where is the other brothel?" Harry demanded.

"I believe it is situated near the village of Dumpledon, sir. To gain entry, you must say the words, 'Graze on my lips; and if those hills be dry / Stray lower, where the pleasant fountains lie.'"

"You are not actually telling me that to gain entrance to a brothel we must quote Shakespeare?" Dev looked disgusted.

"I am simply passing on what Madam Fabron said, my lord."

"Stop talking, let's go!" Wolf roared.

They grabbed every weapon they had and were soon mounted up. They rode out as one, grim-faced and determined to do what it took to get Maddie, Rose, and Emily back.

"It hurts, this love." Cam rode beside Harry. "Be ready for that, cousin."

"I have no wish to back away. Maddie is vital to me now, as are Fleur and Daisy."

"When I have my wife back, I shall have plenty to say on that matter and your previous reluctance. I want the details as to what changed your mind, Harry. However, we will do so in a quiet place where a Huntington brother will not overhear and want to pummel you."

They rode in silence, a cloud of anxiety hanging over

them. Mr. Brown had accompanied them, and as Dev had said, the more eyes and fists the better.

"The property cannot be seen from the road, but Madam Fabron told me there are two large oak trees that appear to be... ah, well, in a suggestive pose. This was to Lord Raynor an omen that he should buy the property," Mr. Brown said.

When finally they came upon the trees, Harry had to agree that they did appear to be in a suggestive pose.

"I'll have something to say about that too when I have my wife back," Cam said.

They walked in after tethering their horses. Warwick was to listen, and those with sight to see if their women were near.

The drive wasn't long, the trees thick. Lord Raynor had chosen well; no one would look here if they did not know the house existed. Dark stone walls were thick with ivy, and the foundations no doubt sunken into the ground for many years. Harry doubted the original inhabitants planned for it to become a brothel.

"They are here," Dev said. "I see their colors. All three are well and look like they are in some part of the house that is below what we can see."

Harry checked, as he knew Wolf did also. Maddie's color was strong, as were the others.

"Max, Rory, Harry, and Mr. Brown, take the rear. Try and gain entry, as we do not want your mother to see you if she is inside. We will get in through the front door using the words Mr. Brown gave us."

Harry ran around to the rear and found a door. Pistol in hand, he opened it and slipped inside, finding himself in a hallway. Moving along the wall with the others on his heels, Harry checked rooms for people using his vision, but so far they had come across no one.

Reaching another door, Harry changed his vision, and

found Maddie was no longer below him. Opening it, he found stairs.

Lamplight lit the way, and with each step his tension climbed. She was close now; he could feel her. Saw her colors and knew soon she'd be in his arms. Someone would pay, but right now he just wanted to see Maddie.

At the bottom, they found more doors with small barred windows set in them. Grabbing a lamp, he raised it to look in the first and found a bed but no occupants. The second was the same. It was the third that held what he was looking for. The three women slept, all leaning on each other, as yet unaware who stood outside their cell.

"Maddie," he called through the bars, and she jerked awake.

"Harry?"

"Quiet now."

"Cam?"

"Wolf?"

"They are here, but upstairs keeping everyone busy. For now we must get you out. Stay silent, you are safe now."

"If you'll allow me." Mr. Brown stepped forward and began to pick the lock.

"A handy sort of fellow," Rory said.

When the door opened, Harry ran inside and dropped to his knees before her. "Christ, Maddie, are you all right?"

"Yes… but I don't understand why you are here, Harry? Your ship—"

"—has sailed without me."

Pulling out his knife, he cut her ties while Max and Rory freed Rose and Emily. Harry pulled Maddie to her feet and held her. His arms were squeezing her, but he didn't seem able to stop.

"No!"

Harry pushed Maddie behind him as a woman appeared

in the doorway with a gun in one hand. The mother, he thought. The similarities were there.

"Well, well, well, how lovely to see you again, Estelle, and under such pleasant circumstances," Max said.

"You can't take them!" she cried. "I want the money."

"I don't think so. In fact, I think what you'll be wanting soon is a nice quiet little cell where you'll live out the rest of your days in hell. Exactly where you put your children for years," Rory said.

"Lower the gun, Mrs. Huntington." Harry stepped away from Maddie and the others, drawing her fire. He had no wish for it to go off and the woman he loved to be hurt.

"Stop moving or I'll shoot you!" The gun wobbled in her hands.

"It is over, Estelle. Drop your gun." Max moved to the left, and her hand turned toward him. Harry took the shot, and the gun fell from her fingers.

"You shot me!" She clutched her hand.

"You should have aimed for her heart, Harry, and rid us of her for good." Maddie reached his side. She unwound his necktie and stomped to where her mother leaned on the wall, weeping.

The sound of feet heralded Cam, Wolf, Dev, and Nicholas arriving. The husbands running to their women.

Harry moved closer to Maddie, as did her brothers, and watched as she bound her mother's hand tight.

"Why are you doing that? She doesn't deserve your kindness," Max said.

"I will never be like her," Maddie said when it was done. "Never. And this proves it."

"I will take her now," Mr. Brown said. He grabbed Estelle's arm and walked her away, and Maddie felt nothing but relief.

"It's over," Max rasped, grabbing his siblings into a hug.

"She will trouble us no more."

Maddie cried then, and Harry stood silently at her back, wanting to hold her. Needing to tell her what was in his heart. But he could wait, as she'd waited for him to come to his senses.

As it turned out, he got no chance to speak with her. A carriage was borrowed, and the three weary women traveled back to London in that.

When they arrived at Max's house, he was there to help her step from the carriage.

"Will you allow me a few minutes, please, Maddie?"

"I want to see Fleur and Daisy, then go home." She refused to look at him.

Surely she hadn't fallen out of love with him in a matter of hours? Following her inside as his stomach clenched, he wondered what he should do now.

"Take her into that room," James whispered in his ear. "And don't take no for an answer. There is a key inside; turn it so her brothers don't bother you. Go now while they are occupied."

He stepped to her side, wrapped his fingers around her wrist, and tugged her sideways.

"Harry, what are you doing?"

"I want to talk to you." He nudged her through the door, then turned the key in the lock.

"I need to see Fleur and Daisy."

"They can wait a few more minutes; this cannot."

Her hair was loose, her dress dirty, and his heart felt full of love. How had he been foolish enough to believe he could walk away from this woman? He would have lived half a life without her.

"Step aside, Harry. I should wash, and I am hungry." She looked everywhere but at him.

"Why won't you look at me?"

She did, and he saw the devastation.

"Maddie." He stepped closer, but she backed away from him.

"Pl-please let me leave."

"I will never let you leave me. I love you."

"No!"

"Yes." He felt like he was missing something. Why did she not believe him? Why was she behaving this way when on the ship she'd been so different? "I didn't think I knew how to love, Maddie, until you came along. I believed I knew what I wanted, the path I'd set for my life. You taught me different."

"Harry—"

"Let me speak, please, sweetheart."

She folded her arms as if to protect herself. As if he would hurt her.

"My father was a fair man, but a cold, unloving one. He taught me to hate any Sinclair that carried my blood and made me promise to never form a bond with any of them."

"It was wrong of him to put that on you, Harry. You have to know that?"

"I think I started to believe it when I first met them, my family. They were open, loving, and accepted me when I had done nothing to prove my worth."

"You are worthy." Her eyes were fierce as she defended him.

"Thank you, and I promise to always try to be for you and our girls."

"No."

Harry closed the gap between them, grabbing her arms, forcing her to face him.

"You love me, I know you do." *Please God, let it be true.* Harry wasn't sure he could live with any other result.

"I can't!"

"Why can't you love me, Maddie?"

"You saw her, that woman, my mother. She is my blood!"

"Yes." He had no idea where she was going with this.

"I am part of her!"

And then he understood. Like Harry, she bore the scars her childhood had left behind.

"As I am not my father, you are not your mother, my sweet. You are kind and loving. I think it is I who is unworthy of you."

"You are worthy of anyone." She looked at him, and the fear he saw in her eyes burned deep in his chest for the pain she'd suffered.

"Where has the fire gone that you showed me on my ship, Maddie? The confidence that has blossomed inside you?"

"She does this to me," she whispered. "She makes me weak."

"Don't let her—and you could never be weak."

She raised her chin and looked at him.

"Much better. I love you, Madeline Caron. For me, there will be no one else. It is you I want a life with. You I want to build our family around. You have made me see what love is and have hope for a life I'd only ever dreamed of. Please tell me you still love me."

Her eyes narrowed, and she looked like her brothers in that moment.

"My love is not a fickle thing, Harry Sinclair. I have never given it to a man before, and I did not do so easily with you. I love you and always will."

"Excellent—"

His words were interrupted by a fist thumping on the door.

"Are you in there, Maddie, with Harry?" The door handle rattled as Max tried to gain entry.

"As I was saying"—Harry pulled her closer—"I love you

with all that I am, Maddie. You are the other half of me. If you left me, I would sail the seas a broken man."

Her lips tilted.

"Are you laughing at me, woman?"

"That was very dramatic, Harry."

"Maddie," he whispered. "Tell me you love me. Tell me you will be my wife."

"It scares me how much I love you, Harry. Scares me because of where I came from and the life I was forced to live for so long."

"Happiness scares you?"

"Yes."

"As it does me, but if we navigate it together, it will be easier. My grandmother made me realize what a fool I was being by refusing to acknowledge what lay in my heart. It was like suddenly the sky had cleared and there it was, the truth of what I felt, laid bare before me."

"But your home is in France."

"My home is wherever you are. I have nothing without you."

He pulled her closer until they were just inches apart.

"You hurt me after we made love, Harry. I do not give myself easily to others, but with you I took a chance, and you turned away."

"Because I am a fool."

Her smile was small.

"But you are the fool I love."

"Say you'll marry me."

"I will, Harry. I wish it with all my heart."

There was nothing else to be said after that. Harry gathered his love close, and for long minutes no words were needed.

Finally they both had found peace and a place to lay their hearts.

CHAPTER 36

Harry sat with Fleur on his left and Daisy on his right in the little church on Raven Mountain. His grandmother, who was extremely happy with Raven Castle and her connection with the duke and duchess, sat beside Daisy.

Heloise Paquet wore a crown Eden had insisted she don for the wedding, which sat in her upswept hair and gave her a royal air, according to James. His family were more than happy to pander to his grandmother's delusions of grandeur.

"Your flowers are lovely, Daisy. They make you look like a princess."

"Thank you, Grandmère." Daisy leaned into her grandmother, who she loved as Fleur did.

Harry had told Maddie last night that Heloise had softened. When he was a child, she'd rapped his knuckles for any small transgression. Fleur and Daisy seemed able to do what they wished around her. Maddie had told him that was because her life was no longer a struggle, and she did not have to work from sunup to sundown, which Harry had not even considered, much to his shame.

"Does Bran look nice too, Grandmère?"

"He looks noble," she said, patting the dog's head where he sat pressed between her and Daisy.

The groom was standing with his brothers, James and Max, and looking pale. All wore black jackets and waistcoats with a silver stripe that Fleur liked. Tall and impressive, they were men he now counted as friends.

It always amazed him that when the actual day came to exchange vows, the groom and bride were often nervous, even when they'd given and received their love freely already. Surely this was just a formality.

"Uncle Rory's hand is shaking, Harry."

"I can see that, Fleur. I think he's excited about marrying your aunt Kate."

"I'm going to marry Luke. He said so." Fleur swung her legs back and forth, kicking the pew in front. The woman turned to look at them.

"Don't kick the seat, sweetheart."

"You're that Harry Sinclair. I can tell by your face." The woman had a craggy face and lips that almost folded inside her mouth.

"That's a very nice hat," Fleur said in her sweet little voice.

In fact, it was a hideous creation. Mustard in color, with huge red and green flowers pinned all over it and a tuft of what looked to be straw on the top.

"I particularly like the nest of birds on the crown." Fleur was excellent at flattering people. It was a rare talent, Harry had told Maddie yesterday, that would ensure she did well in life, even if there was no truth in her words. The woman's hat truly was hideous.

Harry shot a look at his grandmother and was pleased to see she was chatting with Nicholas, who had taken the seat beside her. She was likely to comment on the woman's hat, and it would not be flattering.

"Harry is going to be my papa. And this is Daisy, she is my sister. And wedged down beside her is Bran. He is my sister's eyes. And it is my uncle Rory who is marrying my aunty Kate today."

The woman looked at Daisy and Bran, and her lips pulled out from her face and curved upward into a smile.

"Well now, I know Bran. I met him when your uncle Rory was here. He stacked my firewood for me, you know. I'm Mrs. Radcliff."

He'd heard mention of Mrs. Radcliff. According to Dev, she knew the entire history of every occupant that lived in Crunston Cliff and was a formidable woman.

"God's blood, Sybil Dally, if I see you and your man kissing on the main street again, I'll be showering you both in a bucket of water. It's no place for such carrying on!"

Harry turned to see a woman scurry into the seat across from them, red-faced.

"And you, Lenny Tattler. Have the sense to tidy yourself up before you court that sweet Milly Reid. Woman will run a mile if she gets a whiff of your scent!"

Lenny Tattler shot Mrs. Radcliff a look that suggested he'd like to fire back a volley of insults. Instead he dropped into the nearest seat too, which happened to be occupied. The woman squawked. Lenny was thrown sideways and landed luckily in a spare seat beside her.

Harry turned back to face Mrs. Radcliff. She was smiling, looking very happy with herself.

"Well now, I believe the bride has arrived." She faced the front again.

"Is she as fierce as she sounds?" Daisy whispered.

"More so." Harry placed and arm around his girls. *His girls.* In the two weeks he'd been in their lives, his love for both of them had grown, as it had for their mother.

Harry was living with Dev and chaffed that Maddie and

the girls lived in that house without him. They had not set a date, but it would be soon, he vowed.

With happiness and the knowledge she was safe and loved, Maddie had blossomed. She laughed freely, teased, and had a wicked sense of humor. Harry fell deeper under her spell every day.

Harry had told Max and Rory he would buy his family their own house. He knew he would end up living exactly where Maddie was already, but he would insist on paying for it, no matter the battle he would face to do so. A man had his pride.

He loved this big, odd, and wonderful family he'd fallen into.

Turning as the music started, he saw her, his beautiful, brave girl. And she took his breath away.

She wore pale blue, and it floated around her body as she walked. In her hair was a wreath of flowers. He felt that fierce tug of emotion he always associated with her now, the need that reached all corners of his body.

His love. His life.

"Mama looks beautiful." Fleur sighed.

As she reached his side, she smiled at Fleur and then him. That special smile that spoke of her love. Her eyes passed to Daisy. Harry leaned down to tell her how beautiful her mother looked, and she smiled. He loved coaxing these from her. Like Maddie and Fleur, Daisy had not had much reason to smile in her life. He would be ensuring that changed.

The service was lovely, but as he could only see Maddie and she him, they spent the entire time gazing at each other. When it was over, he ushered the girls out of the church. They instantly went to where the other children gathered, Daisy's hand in Bran's fur as he led her where she wanted to go.

Harry moved to Maddie's side, back slightly from the newly wedded couple, watching with a smile on her face.

"They look in love," he said, placing a hand around her waist. Harry had noticed that too about his family: they touched those they loved often and cared nothing about who saw. He'd embraced that.

"That was lovely, wasn't it, Harry?" She leaned into him.

"I don't remember any of it. All I could see was you."

She turned to face him, her hand taking his.

"Let's do this soon, Harry."

"Now? I'm sure we could get the minister to marry us too. I have the license." He was only half joking.

"Really?"

"Really. I love you, sweetheart. I don't want to live another day apart."

Her eyes shot left and right, and Harry had no idea who she was looking for.

"Could we?"

"If you don't want to wait, I'm sure we could. But if you want to have the dress and everything else, then I will wait."

"Oh."

"Oh?"

"Oh, yes, please."

"Are you sure, Maddie?"

"I love you, and I don't want the dress and all the rest. I just want you living in our house with the girls. I want our family complete, Harry."

"Christ, I love you." He kissed her. "Stay here, and let me see if I can arrange it."

"I want to help."

They spoke to Rory and Kate to make sure they did not mind sharing their wedding day. Both had been excited at the prospect. Max, James and Dev, were next. No one put up a protest.

"We are going to marry also, Grandmère," Harry took his grandmother to once side. I'm sorry if it is a rush, but we love each other and have no wish to wait."

"Excellent. I can wear my crown longer."

After that, the entire thing went off without a hitch.

He was soon standing at the altar with Wolf, Cam, and Dev, and in she came with Max, behind Fleur and Daisy, and of course Bran. Emily, Rose, and Samantha followed.

Everyone was happy about the impromptu second wedding. Elated, actually, and Harry had to say he was no different.

"It's the Sinclair and Raven way to be odd," Mrs. Radcliff declared.

Harry couldn't stop smiling.

"I do," he whispered, leaning in to take Maddie's lips.

"They're not meant to kiss yet!" Hannah squealed.

"Well, they weren't meant to be getting married either, so I think it's all right," her mother said.

"You may kiss the bride."

He pulled her closer and leaned in. "I love you, Mrs. Sinclair."

"Oh, and I love you, Mr. Sinclair."

THE END

COURTING DANGER

Thank you for reading GUARDING DANGER. I hope you enjoyed Harry and Maddie's story. Book 9 COURTING DANGER in the Sinclair and Raven series is available now!

If only he'd taken more care, she wouldn't be facing her destiny.

Somerset Sinclair vows not to follow in her elder siblings' footsteps. There will be no marriages or daring rescues of any man carrying Raven blood. Somer has a career, and nothing is about to thwart that.

Sinclair Investigative Services is flourishing.

. . .

Everything was going to plan until Professor Cole Alexander Gusford Charlton foolishly stood under a chimney pot. Now there's an arrogant, handsome man making her heart beat a little faster. A man of Raven blood whose life she saved, and who irritates her into irrational behavior.

Somer is determined to break the pact that bound her family to his. Her heart would remain intact, no matter how hard it was becoming to keep her distance from the professor.

Gus had one passion, his studies. A highly sought-after scholar, he had no room in his life for a woman as infuriatingly opinionated as Somerset Sinclair. She calls him stuffy and refuses to show him the respect he deserves.

Yes, she'd saved his life, but he'd thanked her for that. Now he must forget her and her strange family, and his life will return to normal.

The problem is she has an unusual occupation that throws her headlong into trouble and no one appears worried about that, except him.

When Somer's investigations turn deadly and the threat to her life real, Gus knows his dreams of an uneventful scholarly existence are in fact empty without her in them. He will do whatever it takes to keep her safe. But will Somer fight her destiny or realize that life would be empty without Gus at her side and in her heart.

. . .

From USA Today Bestseller Wendy Vella comes an exciting Regency series about legend, love and destiny, with a hint of magic.

DEVILLE BROTHERS SERIES

From USA Today bestselling author Wendy Vella comes a sizzling new series full of passion, scandals and intrigue. Tasked with protecting the King, the Deville brothers are part of a secret alliance forged centuries ago, but when it comes to affairs of the heart they are yet to be tamed.

Seduced By A Devil

Desperate for his help

Gabriel Deville, Earl of Raine, has never met a woman like Dimity Brown. Mysterious, alluring and utterly infuriating, she has no respect for him. In fact, the piano teacher treats him like he is the underling, not her. His beloved sister, however, calls her friend, and when Dimity disappears, he cannot refuse his sibling's urgent plea to find her.

. . .

Gabe's first shock is finding Dimity in a seedy tavern, dancing on the bar. The second is seeing the feisty young woman vulnerable and scared. He soon realizes that what he feels for her is a great deal deeper than anger and he will stop at nothing to keep her safe. Earning her trust and uncovering her secrets will be a challenge, but securing a place in her heart will be the biggest challenge of his lifetime.

Powerless to resist

Dimity had believed her life would never be anything more or less than it currently was, but then her father dies, and everything changes. She is thrown out of the only home she has ever known, and finds a letter in her father's things that turns her life completely on its head. Penniless, confused and desperate, she has nowhere to turn until Gabriel Deville steps back into her life.

Lord Raine is arrogant, ridiculously wealthy, and far too dangerously handsome. Despite the sparks that had always flown between them, their interactions had been coldly civil. When he insists she accept his help, Dimity takes it, certain she can resist him, and what is growing between them long enough to unravel the secrets of her past.

Can they overcome their differences and society dictates to forge a life together?

Books in the Deville Brothers Series

Seduced By A Devil
Rescued By A Devil
Protected By A Devil
Surrender To A Devil
Unmasked By A Devil

ABOUT THE AUTHOR

Wendy Vella is a bestselling author of historical romances such as the Langley Sisters and Sinclair and Raven series, with over two million copies of her books sold worldwide. Born and raised in a rural area in the North Island of New Zealand,
she shares her life with one adorable husband, two delightful adult children and their partners, four delicious grandchildren, and a pup who rules the house called Tilly.

Wendy also writes contemporary small town romances under the name Lani Blake

Printed in Great Britain
by Amazon